MY DEAR ANTONIO

A LOVE STORY

MY DEAR ANTONIO

A LOVE STORY

RYAN BYRNES

Walrus Publishing | Harrisonville, MO

Walrus Publishing
an imprint of Amphorae Publishing Group, LLC
Copyright © 2024 Ryan Byrnes
All rights reserved.

For information, contact info@amphoraepublishing.com

Manufactured in the United States of America
Cover Art: Adobe Stock
Cover Design by Kristina Blank Makansi
Interior layout by Kristina Blank Makansi

Amphorae Publishing Group, LLC
117 South Lexington St., Suite 100
Harrisonville, MO 64701

Library of Congress Control Number: 2023938090
ISBN: 9781940442495

I dedicate this book to the great grandparents I never knew—Anna DiNicola and Antonio Orlando—last of my family to call themselves Italian, first to call themselves American.

This is a dramatization of their lives.

HOME

"Where do we come from?" her granddaughter asks.

"We come from heaven above, and one day we will go back," Anna replies. She cannot be bothered to part from her sewing. On and on the needle goes, pulling the thread along.

"But what place do we come from? Before America, where did you call home?"

"Home?" Anna repeats, finally setting down her needle and thread. The word sounds foreign to her, as foreign as the countries she once lived in. She has called many places home and has lived in three countries. Yet never once had she felt at home. She is from everywhere and nowhere.

She weighs the question in her mind. How do you string together the threads of time gone by? How do you trace the landscape of your life when its peaks and valleys often seemed so haphazardly ordered? There are some purposes too grand for her to accept, that escape the imagination, so she sticks to what she knows.

What is home?

Her home is yearning to be somewhere else, the dream of other shores, abandoning the old and chasing the new. Her home is the ache of loss that can never heal, the thousand and one other paths she might have taken. Her home is the scorching sun on her back, the dust from the fields blistering her face. Her home is the smell of steaming couscous, of fiery chili paste, of sweet jasmine flowers. Her home is the chanted prayers of French and Arabic and Italian and Hebrew and Latin. She recalls the icy Atlantic, its inky waves shrouded in mist. She recalls the gold-carpeted shores of the Mediterranean, a red eye of sun fading on the horizon, throngs of flamingos flapping their rose feathers. Her home is the one place she will never belong.

"Are you listening?" Anna asks her granddaughter.

"I'm all ears."

"This is where we come from."

PART 1

DECEMBER 1912

1. BLUE SATIN

Anna's only crayon is worn to a blue splinter. She raises her sketches to the solitary lightbulb of her family's Brooklyn tenement, squinting in deep thought at the final iteration of her costume for this Christmas's *presepe vivente*.

Squeezing her eyes shut, Anna can already feel the feather-soft satin embrace of the Virgin Mary's robe cascading to her feet, its folds of robin's-egg-blue streaking in a train behind her like the tail of a comet, its borders unfurling a crawl of embroidered gold vines. Candlelight will cast a flickering holy sheen on the brocade until inking into midnight folds. She will even wrap herself in a veil, a cream veil of the finest lace embroidered with roses and gold thread of course.

During the Nativity play at next week's Christmas Eve Mass, the Sicilian families of Brooklyn will whisper *che bello* as they admire her costume, and for just one evening Anna will hold her head high like the Queen of Peace, known for her strength and not her weakness, her gifts and not her sickness. She wants nothing else. She sighs and cradles the crayon drawing beneath the lone bulb, happy to lose herself in rapt adoration until the electricity shuts off and the light flickers out.

The apartment door creaks open to signal that her sister Rosaria is the first of her family to return from work, disrupting Anna from her thoughts. Before Rosaria can close the door, a gust from the snowstorm sweeps through the apartment, flapping the corners of Anna's cardigan. They have a coal burning stove in the kitchen, and Anna prods the coals with a spoon to ward off numbness. In a flash, the gust of wind bleeds an hour's worth of warmth from the apartment. One breath of the freezing air, and Anna's throat dries into sandpaper. She coughs into her sleeve until she is hunched over.

"I'll make you honey tea to soothe that cough," Rosaria stamps the snow off her shoes, kissing Anna on the forehead. The melting snowflakes in Rosaria's coiled hair drip onto Anna's cheek.

"Oh Anna, those are impossible," Rosaria *tsks* at the sketches while she unwraps her scarf.

Her sister's pessimism lights a flame of anger within Anna. "But Father Elmo says that with faith, all things are possible," she huffs.

"Father Elmo doesn't sit at a sewing machine ten hours a day for fifteen cents an hour. This can't be done, *sorella*."

"Fifteen cents an hour? I worked on these designs for zero cents an hour," Anna protests, "just because I've been sick doesn't mean I can't—"

"This isn't about your asthma—it's about your costume. I mean, look at this drawing," Rosaria snatches the paper. "Embroidered roses? Gold thread? Anna, this costume would take months to finish, and that's not even considering the cost of the satin."

"What if you brought me satin scraps from the shirtwaist factory? Do you think your boss would let me use them?"

Rosaria shakes her head. "I'm sorry *amore*, but I don't want to draw attention to myself at work," Rosaria says. "They don't know I'm fourteen."

"What's wrong with being fourteen?"

"The legal working age is sixteen."

"Fine," Anna wrenches the drawing back from Rosaria. "I'll find the fabric myself."

By all rights, the costume of the Virgin Mary in this year's Nativity play belongs to Anna. She was the one who updated the countdown in her diary every month for a year until finally meeting the twelve-year age limit. She beat ten other girls in the audition, and she spent all day brainstorming costumes. Every year the costumes are exquisite, and Anna *will not* be the one to break the tradition. She doesn't think she can take the fake compliments should her costume turn out poorly. *Oh Anna, what a promising costume. Oh Anna, you are such a worker bee. Oh Anna, you've come so far since your illness.* In a perfect world, Anna imagines she would have rivers of blue satin—enough to sew a dress for every day of the week so she could give people something to talk about besides her asthma. But until then, a few yards would have to suffice.

Anna peers out the window where the wind hurls sheets of snow over the streets. Where normally she would see the swampy Dyker Park unfurling all the way to Fort Hamilton and the choppy waters of Gravesend Harbor, today she can barely make out the faint glimmer of car headlights. To think that people are driving in this whiteout—they must be stubborn or desperate or both, something Anna can sympathize with. She remembers the secondhand shop down the street and the rolls of fabric they put up for sale, all the fabric the big department stores in Manhattan rejected. Maybe she could find some materials for her costume there.

"Don't even think about going into that blizzard," Rosaria says while Anna stares out the window. "I could barely breathe out there with that wind, and you'd be in far worse shape."

Anna does not answer but squints into the white haze, remembering the little boy on their street who had asthma, who had contracted pneumonia from the cold, who is now residing in heaven. The people at church cried about it for weeks, and the parish raised enough money to place his coffin in a horse-drawn carriage and a five-person band to march in the procession. Anna sometimes has nightmares of the funeral.

"Listen to me," Rosaria says. "I was almost hit by a car on my way home from work. I couldn't see a thing out there."

Anna strides across the one-room apartment, opens the closet, and pulls on her rubber boots.

"I'll tell on you!" Rosaria raises her voice. "When Mamma comes home from work, I'll tell her what you did. She'll get the wooden spoon."

The vision of the blue satin draws Anna forward, and she wraps her scarf tightly about her mouth and nose for protection against the wind. She pulls the flaps of her hat down over her ears, then descends the stairwell of their apartment building to street level, where the snowdrifts are already piling two feet high against the facades. Anna takes her first step into the pearly vapor.

Her rubber boot sinks up to her ankle in the snow. A car suddenly squeals past her, and Anna can only see a faint outline of the vehicle before it disappears again in the whiteout. She trudges through the snow, leaving deep footprints behind her. The wind slaps her cheeks red and raw, and she marches past Signore Canino's cobbler shop, past the bakery where they make her favorite Saint Agatha cookies, past Signore Barabino's drug store where Mamma had once purchased a syringe and little vials of adrenalin solution for Anna's asthma attacks. Anna had watched Mamma empty out her coin purse to buy that syringe, an amount Anna fears she could never repay.

Finally, Anna arrives at the secondhand shop, and by this time her throat is dry and ragged. She tries to push away the creeping terror that she will have an attack, but her heart is racing, and she resolves to find the fabric as fast as possible.

Inside, she rifles through the rolls of fabrics, each of them stained, ragged, threadbare. *Twenty cents for one yard of fabric*, a sign says. The clerk, who has one leg and sits behind the desk, his crutches leaning against the wall, looks up from the newspaper he's reading and squints at her.

"How much satin can I get for twenty-five cents?" Anna asks.

"Not much," he laughs, and when Anna does not laugh back he scratches a calculation onto the back of an envelope and replies softly, "nine inches."

"I'm working on a costume for the Nativity play at my church," Anna slaps her crayon sketch on the clerk's desk. "Can you help me?"

The clerk studies her drawing.

"This much fabric would cost a day's wages. It just won't work," he shakes his head. "But if you want to improvise, I'd recommend you start with that over there."

The clerk points to the back shelf, where Anna finds a blue tablecloth encrusted with spatters of marinara sauce. *Twenty-five cents*, the tag reads. The tablecloth has no sheen, no shape, no features, a joke compared to the blue satin robe of her dreams. Surely, when she slips this on at church and performs the Nativity play, the Sicilian families would not even look twice at her. Her embarrassment ignites into anger as she considers how beautiful her costume could have been. But this is the only deal anyone has given her today, and Anna knows she would be foolish to refuse.

"Thanks for your generosity," she slams her quarter on the clerk's desk, fuming.

Anna trudges home, sloshing through the snow drifts on the sidewalk. The freezing air makes her nose run, and she coughs into her sleeve, each breath requiring all the strength of her diaphragm. By the time she has retraced her tracks back to the drug store, Anna feels the wind suddenly pick up. A stop sign sways like a metronome on the corner, counting down the seconds she has remaining. A sudden gust of wind unfurls her scarf and as she tries to re-wrap it, another gust whips it out of her hands. She gasps and turns to grab it as it flies away, disappearing in the flurries. Her mouth and nose are now exposed to the blizzard.

Already, Anna's throat is closing, and she knows what's coming. By the time she reaches her street, she breaks into a full sprint, yanks open the door, slams it shut, pushes herself up one flight of stairs, yanks open the apartment door, and slams it behind her. Her heart thumps faster than after a cup of espresso. She pants, trying to draw air into her lungs. Her panting turns into coughing, and soon she is gasping harder than she ever has before, bending over the kitchen sink as she hacks through her worst asthma attack yet.

"*Anna!*" Rosaria cries.

Running the faucet, Anna gulps water to clear her throat, but the tap water merely splashes against her throat, which is swollen shut and burning like a glowing coal. She spits it back into the basin. She can't swallow. She can't breathe. Her lungs flutter and strain with panic. There's no relief. She clutches at her throat. The apartment spins around her. She tries mouthing the words to Rosaria *get the syringe.*

Rosaria panics. "What are you trying to say? You want me to get your medicine?"

Anna knows that her sister is too hesitant. She must save herself. The cabinet hinge creaks as she flips it open, tearing out bags of pasta and jars of preserved vegetables, digging through until she finds the syringe and the glass vials of adrenalin solution gathering dust in the back of the cabinets. Her chest spasms. Her hands shake. She breaks the glass vials and draws out the liquid with the syringe, just like the druggist instructed. But where to jab it? Her hands shake as he tries to remember the druggist to for a spot near the collarbone. But what if she jabs the wrong spot and hurts herself? What if she dies like the little boy? Would the church would give her a parade of her own, and they would take her away on the black carriages with the band marching behind?

She jabs the needle and presses the syringe with her thumb, then throws it across the apartment. It stings. Immediately, she feels the adrenalin solution tingling in her shoulders, then working itself all the way to her toes. Her throat loosens, the inpouring of fresh air into her lungs like a breached dam is overwhelming. She pulls out a chair from the table, sits, closes her eyes and breathes, deep as she can. Outside, the blizzard howls.

A few minutes later, she surveys the aftermath of her struggle to stay alive. A torn sack of semolina flour and a shattered jar of pickled artichoke hearts are splattered across the tiles. She sits just a little while longer—until she feels calm again—and then grabs the broom and sweeps up the mess so Mamma won't be upset with her. Rosaria makes her green tea with honey and then tucks her under the covers of their shared bed.

As Anna's eyelids droop and her head bobs on the edge of sleep, she trains her sight on her blue tablecloth dangling from its hanger, billowing in the window-draft as if the spirit of the Virgin Mary has possessed it. She studies the meandering lines of stitches running along the cloth, the dark marinara stains of the costume Rosaria had said was impossible. But Anna knows in her soul, all things are possible.

2. UNTETHERED BOAT

With glazed eyes, Antonio watches Papà nail the board over the front window of their barber shop. *Thud, thud, thud.* The hammer strikes the nail three more times, sealing the window, entombing the family barber shop in darkness. The rickety sign that hangs over the door, *Barbiere Orlando*, creaks in the cold wind, washed in the bleeding light of the sinking Sicilian sun, finding its final use as an epitaph.

Antonio has no words. They have erased all evidence of his past and also of his future. He stands on the snow-dusted streets of Partinico with a hole in his chest, no longer Antonio Orlando but some newly formed, free-floating cloud, a boat untethered from its pier.

"Do you need a handkerchief?" Papà pats him once on the back and only once.

"No. Handkerchiefs are for criers," Antonio says, quickly raising his sleeve to dry the corner of his eye, wondering how much of his weakness Papà had seen.

"Come," Papà opens the door, "help your brothers clear out the shop. That's a good *figlio*."

Antonio swallows the lump in his throat and forces himself to walk inside the shop, where he helps his brothers, Salvatore and Pietro, wheel out the crates filled with reclining barber chairs and porcelain washbasins. Without the mirrors to reflect light, the shop feels smaller, like a dark cave closing in on him. He helps his brothers unhook the last of the family photographs from the wall, scrub down the doorpost where they have penciled in their heights for thirteen years, sweep away the ancient loose beard stubble that has rested in the corner for generations, stubble that probably belongs to some ancestor. By the time they are finished, the shop looks as if nobody has ever trimmed mustaches here, as if Antonio has not spent every Saturday morning of his life sitting in this room, watching his brothers shave beards, dreaming of the day he would be old enough to cut hair alongside them.

In one of the crates, Antonio finds a framed photograph in shades of sepia, and he sees himself as a baby in this very barber shop, dressed in a clean white baptismal gown with Mamma and Papà beaming on either side of him.

"Will this go with us to America, Papà?" Antonio raises the photograph. "As a keepsake?"

"I'm afraid not, Antonio," Papà shakes his head and squats down to Antonio's height. "We are only taking the things we can carry. These photographs will remain in Partinico."

"But I can carry it to America," Antonio hugs the photograph to his chest. "It's a small picture. I will make room for it on the boat. And then, when we are in America and open our new barber shop and I am old enough to cut hair with you, we can hang it over my workstation."

"What do you mean?" Papà tilts his head.

"When I go to America with you," Antonio repeats. "I will take the photograph with me."

"*Carissimo*, did Mamma not tell you?"

"Tell me what? Mamma tells me a thousand things. Which thing are you talking about?"

"You are not going to America with us, Antonio."

The statement slams into Antonio like a bullet. He swallows back a sob. "Then how will I help you start the new barber shop?" His voice sounds like a squeaky hinge. "How will you teach me to cut hair?"

"You will stay behind in Partinico with Mamma. Your brothers and I will work in America and send you money, but you are too young to come with us now."

The tears come now and although he's looking right at him, he can't see his papà "But, but, but—"

"You will be the man of the house while I am gone," Papà continues, raising his voice over Antonio's protests.

"But you can't just—"

"You will take care of your Mamma and listen to what she tells you."

"Papà—,"

"Would you do the honors, Antonio?" Papà presses a key into Antonio's hand. It is the key to the barber shop.

His lower lip quivering, Antonio takes one last blurry look at the family barber shop, now like a foreign place in its sanitized state. He walks outside and, with Papà and his brothers watching, turns the key one final time, locking the shop as he would a tomb.

After the barber shop is shuttered, Antonio climbs the stairs to the apartment where Mamma boils discarded lemon peels to flavor pasta because it's all they have in their cabinet. The pot sizzles, drawing rumbles from Antonio's stomach. He listens to his papà and brothers discuss the business of the day—shops closing, the mafia planting bombs in the piazza, the able-bodied men sailing to America for work. Antonio says, "Everything will improve in springtime." But they ignore him, carrying on their adult conversation.

After he goes to bed for a *riposo*, he wakes around two and walks into Papà's bedroom to find the bed covered in suitcases, the chairs draped in white barber coats and neatly laid out with scissors and razors and tins of shaving soap. Antonio snips the scissors and stares at his reflection in the window, imagining himself trimming an endless line of pencil mustaches. He even tries on Papà's white barber coat, dreaming of the day when it will fit. Mamma walks into the room, frowning when she sees Antonio wearing Papà's coat.

"Why is Papà leaving us?" Antonio asks Mamma. "Why doesn't he stay and help? It's like he doesn't even think of us."

"Your brothers and papà are going to America to earn money for the family," Mamma says. "This is why we will have enough to last the winter."

America. Antonio scoffs. Sicily may not be the wealthiest land, Antonio knows, but it is the land where he was born, where his entire family tree takes root, yet everyday he hears Papà rail against the barren state of the local olive groves, the almond groves, the lemon groves, where Antonio would climb trees with his brothers and laugh until their sides were sore. Papà must hate their home. He does not even have the decency to spend Christmas with them before leaving, and this is what foments Antonio's hurt, turning it into anger. From under his bed, Antonio digs out a comb carved from walnut that he'd meant to gift Papà for Christmas. Fuming, he runs outside of town, sprinting through the rows of olive trees, throwing the gift as hard as he can until it disappears in the snow. When the deed is done, Antonio stares down at his empty hands. Tears threaten again. Racked with guilt, he scrambles through the snow to try and find the comb again. But it's gone. Just like Papà and his brothers will soon be.

After breakfast the next morning, the anger comes back and Antonio tackles Salvatore, not in the playful way brothers usually wrestle, but he really tries to twist his arm and kick his knees out from under him. Of course, Antonio's punches bounce off the bigger, stronger Salvatore.

And then Mamma makes Antonio put on his Sunday best—a starched cap, a narrow black tie, a pinstripe shirt with sleeve garters, a jacket tailored by Mamma—and off they go to wave off Papà, Salvatore, Pietro at the Palermo harbor.

"Goodbye Papà," Antonio hugs him, pressing his face into his father's musty coat.

"Be good for Mamma," Papà croaks. "Say your prayers. Make the family proud."

Antonio watches them carry their suitcases up the gangplank to the deck of the ocean liner where the three smokestacks billow foul smoke and the ship-whistle peals so loud he must press his palms over his ears. The ship slowly chugs out from the harbor, churning up a beeline of white froth behind it, until it is a speck on the horizon.

The house is quiet for dinner that night with just Mamma at the table. Papà's words echo in his head, *you are the man of the house now*, and the thought makes Antonio feel exposed, vulnerable without the shield of his older brothers. How dare they shave off such a large piece of his world. After Papà, Salvatore was the bedrock of the family. Pietro was the businessman. And Antonio was the privileged darling. But with them all gone, Antonio must take the place of all three! The very idea of it was exhausting. The gaping silence at the dinner table makes him want to scream.

"If Salvatore was here right now, I would hit him!" Antonio shouts suddenly, slamming the table. "He and Papà are cowards!"

Before Antonio can blink, Mamma's hand whips out and slaps him across the face. "Papà loves you more than you could ever know," her voice cracks and her face turns a mottled red. "Go and get us some firewood."

Antonio sprints as hard as he can down the street, past the pillared ruins of the ancient Roman temple, up the hill where the road narrows into a trail thick with knee-high esparto grass and red sumac dancing in the brisk wind. Propelled by the thought that his brothers are happier without him, he climbs higher and higher until Partinico shrinks below him. Out of breath, he finally bends over, hands on his knees, panting. He cracks off dry branches from wild carob trees and throws them, screaming. Kicking at anything within reach. Pulling at his hair. Tears of frustration and anger and loss streaming down his cheeks. Later, when he is calm again, he stands at the top of the hill and surveys the countryside. The land is the color of straw, partitioned by roads and red-roofed villages, like the veins and organs of a living thing. And all sloping down to the Mediterranean where his papà and brothers are sailing away from him.

How dare they abandon him. Abandon the family business. After generations of work the barber shop is now left to rot, for weeds to spring up and for cobwebs to gather. This will not be the end, Antonio swears. Maybe Papà and Salvatore and Pietro have abandoned the shop, but Antonio will not. He does not know when, but one day he will wake up and those boards will be taken down from the window, the reclining chairs returned, the mirrors restored. On that day, he will wear Papà's white coat and snip hair, as he was born to do, and he swears before God and Saint Anthony that this will come to pass.

3. BROOKLYN CLAY

The morning after Anna's asthma attack, Mamma and Papà walk her to the drug store where Carmine Barabino had sold them the syringe and the bottles of adrenalin solution. Anna bundles herself with two cardigans, a wool coat, and two scarves because she is not taking any chances this time. She feels fragile, one sharp gust away from shattering like glass, just like the hundreds of little bottles of creams and salves that glitter behind Carmine Barabino's counter. Inside the warmth of the drug store, the air thrums with hurried Italian conversations, a chorus of sneezes and siffles, and the ringing bell over the door that announces their arrival.

"I have a problem, Carmine," Papà says.

"Signore and Signora DiNicola," the druggist leaves his customers when he sees the grave look on Mamma and Papà's faces. "Is this about your daughter?"

"She's not improving," Mamma says in a low tone perhaps so that Anna will not hear her, though she fails on this account. Anna leans in to listen, and their hushed tones make her afraid.

"Her attacks will ease when the warm weather rolls in," Carmine mutters, "but Brooklyn is always a difficult place for children with asthma. Factories pump smoke directly into our neighborhoods even on a good day."

"This is no way for a child to live," Papà whispers. "She is one breath away from another attack, and one attack away from pneumonia."

Again, Anna thinks of the funeral they held at church for the boy with pneumonia. She could be next. For a moment, she wonders if she has brought this on herself, that perhaps by coveting the blue satin of the Virgin Mary's robe Anna has condemned herself to punishment. But just as quickly, she dismisses the thought. If anything, the Virgin Mary would help her to become the girl she was made to be—not one to be pitied, but to be admired.

"There is one thing you can do to reduce her symptoms," Carmine says.

"What?" Mamma and Papà ask, voices hushed.

"Move Anna to a mild climate. Cut her loose from this polluted city. She needs fresh air, a wide, warm country where the harbors aren't full of ice. Do you have any family back in Sicily who might take her in?"

"Sicily?" Mamma shakes her head. "That's no place for a child. Anna wouldn't last a year in the old country."

"What about your sister Rosa?" Papà asks. "Does she still live on that farm in Tunisia?"

"But how can we trust Rosa?" Mamma says. "You know the harm she did to us. What if it happens again? What would you say then, Michael?"

"Where's Tunisia?" Anna pipes up, and the adults fall silent when they realize she is listening to their conversation.

"Nowhere you should concern yourself with," Mamma finally says. "I won't give you away to Rosa, not if I can help it."

"We should give Anna a say in the matter," Papà says, causing Mamma to protest. Papà bends down to Anna's eye level. "You don't have to decide right away, Anna," Papà says. "Take a few days to mull it over, but if you want to leave Brooklyn and go live on a lovely farm where the weather is always warm, it might make you feel better. If this is what you want, we will make all the arrangements for you. You won't have to worry about a thing."

Anna imagines saying goodbye to Mamma and Papà, not knowing when she would see them again. And she tries to imagine a place where it is always warm. "I don't know, Papà," is all she can say.

That weekend, Papà takes Anna by the hand, and they ride the trolley to a half-finished suburb down on the Brooklyn shoreline. Here, the piers stretch along the water while the Brooklyn Bridge and the Manhattan skyscrapers shrink behind them. The outlines of half-finished houses rise from the snowy shoreline, and Anna inhales the sea breeze that is piercing cold and stinking with fish. They stop at a plot of land tucked between two wooden houses, where Papà has piled enough bricks and cement to lay a foundation, and his friends from church are hard at work digging and singing Sicilian folk songs. Anna watches Papà take up his pickaxe alongside them. He has five thick callouses on each of his palms and permanent wrinkles radiating from the corners of his eyes from long years of squinting, planning, and worrying. Although he is fifty-one, he still brings down his pickaxe as strong as any young man.

"I'm going to build a house for you on this spot, *amore*. Picture it. If there's a blizzard outside, all you have to do is turn a dial to warm yourself. We will have sockets for electricity. We will even have two flush toilets. Two."

He pulls out his notebook and shows her a sketch of the toilet, a porcelain bowl with a wood seat piped to a water tank bolted in the ceiling. Of course, if she traveled to the farm in Tunisia, she would never see the finished house.

"How would I manage in Tunisia, Papà? I only speak English and Italian. How will I make friends? What if Zia Rosa is cruel? I could just stay home and find another way to deal with the asthma. Maybe I will grow out of it, and so going to Tunisia will be pointless."

Papà sets down his pickaxe and frowns. "Sit down," he motions to a stack of brown bricks. "Do you know how I first came to America? I stepped off the boat and they gave me two dollars to dig under the East River, so I said yes, I am here to work. I laid granite slabs beneath the East River for the Brooklyn Bridge, six months at a time, for six years, and every day I thought of you. Finally, I received my citizenship papers, and I saved enough money to bring you and your sisters to America." He stares out toward the shoreline.

"Piccolina, if I could survive in America without even knowing the language, then you will do just fine moving to Tunisia. You will learn. And when you return from

Tunisia, we will have a new house waiting for you." He gestures to the pyramid of bricks. "You must always keep this thought close to you, that the work of life is never finished. You might build one foundation, but then you will be forced to build another, and another, and it only ends when you go to meet the Good Lord. Anna Maria DiNicola, you must choose for yourself. Would you rather stay in Brooklyn and get sick again or seek a better life elsewhere?"

Anna can see the outline of the Brooklyn Bridge in the distance, where the steamboats chug, dropping off single-file lines of Italians clamoring for a spot in the New World. She imagines what it might mean for her to leave, for a lone ship to chug in the opposite direction, against the flow of the migrations, back to the Old World.

"Those who dig in their heels dig their graves. What will you choose, Anna? Will you bury yourself because you are afraid of change, or will you dig a new foundation?"

Anna stands up, grabs the pickaxe from her father, and drives it into the Brooklyn clay.

On the eve of her final day in America, Anna poses in front of the mirror, mixing and matching different garments purchased on discount at the second-hand store. Finally, she settles on a combination of men's work trousers, an emerald scarf, and a scarlet hat from the Kentucky Derby that is thirty years out of style. She also unrolls tinfoil from the kitchen and wraps her shoes until they are shining like silver.

"Someone's been having fun," Mamma stands in the doorway, entertained at Anna's outfit. "Why the tinfoil shoes?"

"I want them to look like Dorothy's silver slippers," Anna says. "From *The Wonderful Wizard of Oz*. If I'm going on an adventure to a faraway land, it's only fitting I dress like an adventurer, to keep me brave. And if I ever want to come back home, I only have to click my heels and say, 'There's no place like home.'"

"You're the bravest girl I know," Mamma's voice cracks, and she pulls Anna close, kissing her forehead. "That's what I'll miss the most about you."

Mamma quickly disappears into the bathroom, wiping her eyes, while Anna admires her outfit in the mirror.

4. SULFUR

Antonio watches Mamma toss the last of their semolina flour with eggs and the few remaining drops of olive oil, carefully running her knife down the fleshy dough to cut spaghetti strands. She boils the spaghetti, pours it into a basin, then takes Antonio by the hand to the Salvia's farmhouse.

Antonio used to go to school with Giuseppe Salvia, and he never thought the Salvias struggled with money. Like all the other lemon farmers, the Salvias strap two wooden barrels onto a mule and walk many miles to a well. Like all the other lemon farmers, they go to bed early because they do not have enough kerosene to keep their lamps burning. They are no different from the rest of his neighbors.

"Why are all the houses empty, Mamma?" Antonio asks.

"The lemon farmers do not own their homes, *figlio*," Mamma explains. "They take loans from the bank and from the Black Hand mafia. If they don't produce enough lemons, they fall into debt, and their house is taken away."

"Where do they go?"

Mamma has no answer to that.

They arrive at the Salvia's house, which has still not recovered from last year's earthquake—a spider web of cracks run between the chimney and the wall, loosening the bricks. Antonio can see through the crack into their kitchen. Their lemon trees are brown in the wintertime and their boughs droop. Antonio remembers last year's harvest, when instead of weighty, canary-yellow fruits, the Salvia's trees could barely drop a few wrinkled, green spheres that rolled around like pebbles in his palms. Signora Salvia answers the door, and upon seeing the pot of spaghetti she falls to her knees, traces a cross on her torso, and kisses Mamma's dirty shoes. Antonio squirms at the sight. He has never seen an adult lose their composure in such a way. The only thing that hurts him more than the Salvia's hunger is their loss of dignity.

"Please stop that," Mamma says to Signore Salvia, and they chat a few minutes before parting.

While they are walking home, Antonio notices Mamma wiping her eyes.

"It is enough to make a person cry, Antonio, the way most people are forced to live," Mamma says. "Every time I eat, I feel the eyes of the hungry on me."

He does not know what to say or what has driven her to confide in a thirteen-year-old.

"We must support the Salvias as best we can through their debt to the Black Hand," Mamma says, "because our family might be next."

"Mamma, where did Giuseppe go?" Antonio finally asks.

Mamma turns her head away in an effort to hide her face, swallowing.

"The Salvias cannot pay their debts to the bank or to the Black Hand," she says. "They were forced to sell Giuseppe. He is going to work in the sulfur mines near Caltanissetta now."

Antonio knows the reputation of the sulfur mines. Once, while taking the train to Agrigento to visit a cousin, he saw a sulfur mine out his window. The sight still haunts his nightmares. The caves billow acrid volcanic smoke, and the little boys, the *carusi*, climb out carrying the yellow stones that cut into their backs. Some of the *carusi* do not have shoes, and some are naked. The boys are burdened with the debts of their parents, so far behind they can never pay it off, and they are forced to work in the mines their whole lives, whipped if they ever try to escape. Their work is so difficult that the *carusi* are stunted in their growth; even the men are short like children, with disfigured backs from years of carrying stones. And the smell—Antonio cannot erase the smell from his memory. It is like a distillation of the manure from the *cinisara* cows. At church that Sunday, when Father Lunetto delivers a homily describing the horrors of hell, Antonio imagines the boys in the sulfur mines.

Slowly, Antonio realizes that his family is no different from the Salvias. Just like the wilting lemon trees, his family's barber shop is fruitless. At the end of every month, Signore Sciortino and his bodyguard knock on their door, and Antonio watches Mamma put on a fake smile and pour out her coin purse for them, and when they leave, she locks the door and calls him a no-good *liccanu la sarda*—a sardine-licker—in the old Sicilian language. In his visits, Signore Sciortino glances at Antonio, and he knows the man is sizing him up like cattle, imagining if he would make a good worker in the sulfur mines.

The nightly routine sees Mamma lock all the doors and push the family wardrobe in front of the door for good measure. They sleep together in Mamma's bed, the innermost room that protects from the gunshots. Antonio never gets used to it, a splitting gunshot cracking through the silence, shocking him awake, setting his heart racing.

He cannot fall back asleep after that, not fully at least. Not knowing in what part of town the gunshot originated, he can only imagine the possibilities of who might have been injured and whose family failed to pay their debt to the Black Hand this time. Antonio knows that if his family continues to decline, they will fall into debt, just like every other family on the block, and he knows all too well that once a family falls into debt, the Black Hand strips them like ravens.

One night, Antonio feels a wave of pressure wash through the house. His ears pop, and a *boom* rattles his bones. The next morning, he ventures outside to find a crowd forming down the street, where the windows are blown out and facades are streaked with soot.

When Antonio tells Mamma that the Black Hand planted a bomb last night, she makes new rules—he is not allowed to wander the neighborhood anymore, he must walk straight home from the market following Corso dei Mille, he cannot talk with anyone outside the family.

Antonio is out of school now and has no job, so during the day he watches his aunts carry in baskets of fava beans and fennel fronds, setting them on the table. While his aunts discuss the news of the day, they open the pods and empty the individual beans into a bowl.

"Help us with the beans, Antonio," Zia Concetta pulls up a seat for him. "Come join the women."

A few laugh, and he knows they are teasing him, but Antonio joins anyway. Another aunt bounces little Saverio on her lap.

"Any news from America?" Zia Concetta asks Mamma.

"Giuseppe is saving up for a house in America," Mamma says. "Once he becomes a citizen, he will bring the rest of us to America as well. Thank God. But I mean to send Antonio first. The Black Hand have their eye on him, and we cannot keep him here much longer."

Antonio looks up from his beans, heart plunging, stomach twisting.

"Am I really going to America?" he asks, recalling how tall the weeds have sprung around their barber shop.

"Tickets are difficult to come by these days," Zia Concetta explains. "They are very selective about who they take. It was nearly impossible to send my boys. You are all but required to be a man of working age, know English, have a trade, have a family already there willing to sponsor you. And they can deny your papers at any moment, for any reason."

"But we do not have time for all that," Mamma says, and then lowers her voice to a whisper. "The Black Hand is watching us."

Zia Concetta says nothing, perhaps out of fear. Soon, the bean pods are empty and piled high.

That evening, Antonio is drawing crucifixes in the dirt with a carob branch when Mamma hurries down the street, pulling him inside, slamming the door behind her.

"Pack your bags, Antonio," she says, short of breath.

"Don't make me go to America." He pictures himself on the boat, watching the green hills of Sicily disappear under the horizon. No matter how horrifying Sicily can be, he knows of no land more special to him, the land where his papà and his papà's papà have grown their barber shop. To abandon it all, to let the weeds spring up and the cobwebs gather, would be a sin.

"You're not going to America. I'd have to pay a bribe for that," Mamma says. "It would take too long to arrange, anyway. We need to get you out of Sicily now, *cucciolo*—the Black Hand are coming for you. Your godfather in Tunisia has written to me and says he will take you instead."

Antonio's dreams of working with his father wilt. He only sees his godfather on weddings, funerals, and baptisms. But his godfather does send him postcards from Tunisia on his birthdays, and Antonio has saved them all, sepia photographs of bustling markets lined with eucalyptus trees. Tunisia. A world away.

Mamma stuffs his bags with the things she says he will need—a few vests and shirts and caps, a pantheon of saint cards relatives gave him for his First Communion, a brown paper bag of almond cookies. Mamma folds a ticket into his coat pocket for the ferry-ride.

"Mamma? Mamma?" Antonio reaches out for her, but she pulls away, further and further. He is light-headed. His legs wobble.

"Think of me when you see Tunisia," her voice cracks. She flattens his cowlick with the palm of her hand. "*Amore.*"

5. CROOK OF MY ARM

Anna drags her suitcase behind her, and it smacks against every wood board on the pier.

"Hurry. Boarding closes soon," Mamma motions for her to follow quickly.

On both sides, hulking ocean liners loom over them, each with their slanted red towers spewing smoke over the East River. The lines of Sicilians funnel down the walkways and step onto the pier, mouths falling open as they crane their necks to view the Brooklyn Bridge and the spires of Manhattan—the Singer Building and the Woolworth Building, where construction workers operate cranes and balance on steel I-beams fifty stories up. The newly arrived children, dimples and all, point out the towers to their parents as if they'd disappear. Anna supposes that she would be impressed too, seeing Manhattan for the first time. She'd never realized how lucky she was to live in such a city, with its water tanks providing running water twenty floors up, its electrical wires making nightfall a thing of the past, its telephones ringing out voices in real time from across the ocean.

The Sicilian families hurry up the pier with their passports and luggage, aiming for the soaring towers while Anna and Mamma hurry in the opposite direction. The newly-arrived immigrants watch them board the ships bound for the Old World, their brows knit in confusion. The American Dream is all Anna has ever known. She understands the immigrants are escaping famine and poverty. But Anna has a new dream. She is ready for a change. She now embraces the Tunisian Dream, full of turquoise beaches, hundreds of flamingos strutting in the water, dishes of baklava shining with honey. The thought of it is novel to her. For the immigrants, that life is weary and weathered, but to Anna, it draws her into the future. For Anna, the Old World is made new.

"That was us thirteen years ago," Mamma points to a mother wearing three wool jackets to shield against the cold, carrying a baby, flanked by teenage daughters who in turn look after toddlers. "I wish them well."

Anna watches the newly arrived Sicilian family take their first steps off the walkway. The mother pulls her daughters close, frightened at the crowds. They gradually gain their footing, more confident this time, and make a way for themselves down the pier. Anna watches the family until they are a speck on Wall Street, until they disappear amongst the sidewalk pedestrians.

When the ship vibrates with the thundering engine, Anna squishes her face into the porthole to watch in awe as the Statue of Liberty grows and then shrinks in the mist behind them, and soon America is not even a grey line on the horizon. While Mama fusses around the room, Anna unpacks the *The Wonderful Wizard of Oz* from her suitcase. She curls up in bed, eyes racing across the pages, and imagines that her boat is magical like Dorothy's tornado, transporting her to a fairy-tale kingdom, and to see her sisters again she only has to click her heels and whisper *there's no place like home*. If only it were that easy.

Her temples throb, and soon her head pulses so hard that she closes her eyes while the ship rocks her, making the bedsprings creak and groan. She jumps out of bed and vomits last night's lemon cod into the toilet.

Mama opens the porthole so Anna can inhale the cold sea breeze. Soon, her headache eases, but her stomach lurches and she vomits into the toilet, imagining it draining into the ocean, disappearing in the beeline of foam churned up in the tossing waves trailing all the way back to America.

"This is going to be a long ten days for you," Mamma says, holding back Anna's hair while she grips the toilet rim.

"It's not my first time on a boat," Anna says. "I got used to it before. I can get used to it again."

"Oh, *gattina*," Mamma says softly. "You were six months old back then. You burped milk on me more times than I can count. Back then, we did not have as much money, so we were crowded into the lower deck. We slept in a metal room where I could not even stretch out my arms, with six bunks for strangers and one sink. The crew treated us like criminals. Every waking moment was spent rushing back and forth between you and Anastasia and Rosaria. If you see photographs of me from that time, you will see dark bags under my eyes."

Mamma smiles.

"You ate your first solid food on that ship—polenta. I spooned it in your mouth and watched it dribble down your chin. You started to crawl around that time, and you would explore up and down the hallway. I would hold you in the crook of my arm, and you would kick your feet against me, almost like you were already ready to stand up and get a start on life."

Mamma trails off into silence. She sits on the edge of the bed and strokes Anna's hair, pressing the same loop of curly black hair around her ear. Anna knows that Mamma's mind is not with the thirteen-year-old Anna, but rather the six-month-old Anna, and Mamma's lower lip trembles once and only once. The thought of Mamma breaking down makes Anna feel like she did last summer when thieves robbed them in the alley, and so Anna lays there and lets Mamma cup a hand to her cheek and reminisce until she drifts on the edge of sleep.

"Mamma," Anna suddenly raises her head. "Anastasia told me about the *Titanic* sinking, and I—"

"Do not worry," Mamma cuts her off. "Pray to Saint Christopher, and he will keep us safe. I will also keep you safe while I still have the chance, before I leave you with Zia Rosa."

Mamma scoffs after talking about Zia Rosa, as if the idea of Zia Rosa caring for someone is a joke.

"Why don't you like Zia Rosa?"

Mamma grits her teeth.

"That woman does not deserve to be called Zia. I am ashamed to even call her my sister. She wronged our family when you were a baby in Sicily. She did a vicious, evil thing that only Jesus would forgive."

"What did she do?"

Mamma says nothing and busies herself braiding Anna's hair.

"Mamma, you fought Papà so hard when he talked about Zia Rosa, and I wondered—"

"Nothing to wonder, *amore*."

"Do you think Zia Rosa will take care of me if I get sick?"

"It does not matter what I think," Mamma says with enough contempt to show Anna that it *does* matter what she thinks.

Mamma breaks eye contact and stares at the life preservers on the opposite wall.

"Mamma, will Zia Rosa take care of me?" Anna repeats.

Mamma finally returns to the present.

"Not as well as me, Anna. Not as well as me."

6. FOR COURAGE

The ferry from Palermo to Tunis shudders to slow its progress, and Antonio presses his palms over his ears as the horn blast cuts through the air, announcing their approach to Tunis harbor. Kerosine lamps rock from the ceiling. He squirms through the crowds to ask for his luggage, coughing at the putrid plume of smoke spouting from the smokestack. He grew up watching the simple wooden sailing boats, little hollow crescents bobbing in the water, casting nets for tuna and sardines near Castellemarre del Golfo. Those types of ships have been sufficient for thousands of years, even back to the Romans. He does not approve of the thundering pistons, the rusting metal, the choking exhaust of the ferry.

Leaning on the rails of the deck, Antonio watches Tunis break over the Mediterranean. He first sees a thin yellow line on the horizon, shimmering with mirage, and the sun catches in the sea, fiery white like a shard of glass, where distant bumps of olive-green hills grow. He makes out the curve of the coastline on both sides, unfurling its arms to embrace the ferry, gradually narrowing until they reach a canal where the French flag and the Tunisian flag flap from a steep rampart. The boat squeezes through the canal before entering the harbor, and finally Antonio can see the city proper stretching along the shore—blocky, white-washed houses with flat roofs, soaring domes, spiking spires. Blurs of turquoise speckle the cityscape—turquoise shutters, turquoise doors, turquoise awnings. Antonio sniffs, and the smell of the salty Mediterranean gives way to something new, some combination of meat, bread, smoke, and sweat—the smell of city life.

Antonio follows the line of passengers down to the Tunis docks, averting eye contact. He is constantly aware of the treasures in his left shoe, where he keeps the final gifts from Mamma—his passport, a few lire, and a scrap of paper with the address of Zio Pietro's barber shop: *Rue Pierre de Coubertin, no. 4.* When his shoes reach solid pavement, he still feels the world continue to rock. His stomach roils in protest. At thirteen he is not yet tall enough to peer over his fellow travelers' shoulders, and the noise of the crowd is disorienting. Are people glaring at him? Wondering why he is here alone? Are they looking down at him in judgement?

He stops a moment, staring at the travelers briskly trotting the port, amazed at the catalogue of hair styles showcased before him—walrus mustaches, mutton chops, comb-overs, and coiled hair that bounces in kinky tufts on each shoulder. If justice existed, he would have a special corner of heaven reserved just for him to stand tall with a pair of scissors, perfectly sculpting each of these styles.

A rough hand shoves Antonio aside as two French-speaking men in crisp cream suits hurry past, carrying folded sun-umbrellas and silver pocket watches. Another family pushes past with two little boys wearing little cylindrical caps that don't quite cover their heads, the mother entirely draped in a white cloth, wearing a conical gold head covering tied with red ribbons.

Antonio's clueless wandering draws their glares, but he does not know where to go, who to show his passport to. Feeling the rising flutter of panic in his chest, he lugs his suitcase to the nearest crowded bench and takes a seat next to strangers, gathering his breath. His legs tremble as if operating a foot pedal.

"Are you lost?" a girl asks.

Antonio turns to see the girl sitting beside him on the bench. She is wearing men's trousers, a green paisley scarf, and a maroon, feathered hat, wide-brimmed enough to droop over her forehead like overgrown bangs. Antonio has never seen a child dress in such a colorful way, more colorful than the frescos at the church of Maria Santissima Annunziata. Perhaps she is from the circus.

"I know where I'm going," Antonio tells her, though he does not have a map and cannot name even one of the buildings in this city.

He notices the black coils of hair over her olive skin. A fellow Sicilian? He would guess she is Sicilian if not for her accent.

"My name is Antonio Orlando," he says. "What's yours?"

"Anna. Anna DiNicola."

"A Sicilian name. Did you come here on the ferry too?"

"I'm from New York," she says. "I came on an ocean liner."

"So, you are American?"

Antonio has never heard of people returning from America. He has only ever seen folk move to America, with no more stomach for the world they left behind. He studies her like a rare creature, wondering what makes her American. Is it her face? Her accent? Her clothing?

"Sometimes I am American," she shrugs. "Sometimes I am Sicilian. I don't really know."

"Well, I say you're Sicilian," Antonio declares. "Like me."

She smiles and adjusts her hat.

"Are you frightened?" she asks.

Antonio does not answer but looks down at the ground, clearing his throat several times.

"Take this for courage," the girl says, and she presses something into his hand when her mamma isn't looking. A pewter medallion.

The medallion catches gold in the Mediterranean sun, and Antonio sees the token is engraved with the image of the Virgin Mary, the folds of her robes enclosing the baby Christ. A sacred spark shivers his spine, and that is how he knows the blessing is working. He smiles.

"Thank you," he says to the girl, before she stands up with her mamma and disappears into the crowd.

PART 2

JANUARY 1913

7. BLOOD ORANGE

Anna follows Mamma across the port, though she has not adjusted to solid land yet. The world spins around her, and after days of seasickness and vomiting, she just wants to curl up in a soft bed and sip soup. The winter here only requires a cardigan, like early autumn in Brooklyn, so she is at least grateful for the temperature.

For the entire voyage, her imagination ran wild about the wonders of Tunisia. She imagines it as an exotic kingdom like the Land of Oz, with sparkling emerald cities and yellow-brick roads and magical castles. However, when she arrives, she sees many of the same sights from Brooklyn.

The port opens to a central boulevard wide as a running track with electrified trams, a greenspace, a fountain, a cathedral. The streets split into neat square blocks strung with electric lines, and all the signs are written in French. She sees wealthy couples wearing expensive jewelry, homeless people on the corner asking for money, soldiers marching with bayonets. Where are the flamingos?

At the end of the pier, a veiled woman stands fixed among the bustling streams of travelers.

"Angelina? Anna?" the woman says.

Mamma shakes the woman's hand and does not smile. The woman rests her hands on her hips, sleeves girded. This is not the greeting Anna would expect after her mother and aunt spent all these years apart.

"Anna, say ciao to Zia Rosa."

Zia Rosa struggles to squat at Anna's eye level. The woman is tan from her years under the Tunisian sun. She adjusts the shawl embroidered with flowers around her head, hinting at coils of dark hair beneath. Anna kisses her on both cheeks.

Zia Rosa suddenly reaches out and holds Anna's face in her hands, studying her. Her tremoring hands are speckled with age spots; veins show under her wedding ring. She wears a dress down to her shoes, a beaded necklace of coral, and an even smaller gold necklace with a cross.

"I remember when you were baptized back in Sicily," Zia Rosa says. "You were a such happy bambina. I miss the sound of children laughing in my home, you know. An empty nest is such a bore."

"I'm sure it must be terribly difficult to have the whole house to yourself," Mamma raises her voice. "Far more difficult than raising five children."

Zia Rosa breaks eye contact.

"Let me take you back to our estate in Ariana," Zia Rosa says. "My servants have food waiting for you."

Zia Rosa's house reminds Anna of a wedding cake. The stacked complexes of rooms are washed with white lime, outlining a tile courtyard that is cool under the shade of the orange trees. As Anna passes through the turquoise carriage doors, she feels like a new person. Behind the keyhole-shaped arches bordering the courtyard, she spots a few servants hard at work, shouting instructions to each other in Arabic.

"*Che bello!*" Anna says, her cheeks sore from smiling.

"Rosa—you have an entire plantation here," Mamma says, fuming. "Were you sitting on a fortune all this time, living off the sweat of servants?"

"It's not polite to discuss finances," Rose smiles weakly.

Mamma clenches her fist, her knuckles white against olive skin.

Anna looks across the courtyard and spots a low table— only as high as her ankles—set with platters of food. She spots bowls of oranges, a mountain of yellow grains with carrots and parsnip and lamb uncurling ribbons of savory aroma. They sit on the floor, on a pile of sheepskin blankets and pillows—Anna, Mamma, Zia Rosa, and one spot that sits empty.

"Your Zio Leonardo won't be joining us today," Zia Rosa says. "He is busy managing the farm right now."

They each bow their heads in prayer and hold hands before eating. Zia Rosa leads them.

"Bless us o Lord and the food we receive. Let food not lack anywhere in the world, especially to children."

At the mention of children, Mamma crushes Anna's fingers in her grip, finally releasing them when the prayer ends. Whenever Mamma is in a bad mood, Anna feels a tightness in her chest, like she has done something wrong. Anna wonders if she is using bad manners at the table. Is that why Mamma is angry?

Anna does not know when to start eating because she does not have a plate; none of them have plates. She watches Zia Rosa wash her hands in a dish of water, gather up the yellow grains and carrots and lamb in her hand, and bring them to her mouth.

"You eat couscous with your hands," Zia Rosa explains. "I've fallen into the practice after my years here."

"Okay," Anna dips her hand into the warm heap of food, breaking every rule Mamma has ever taught her about table manners.

"Try one of these oranges, Anna," Zia Rosa rolls the fruit toward her. "We grew them in our courtyard."

Anna digs her fingernail in to tear the peel off, gasping when she finds the inside bright red. It tastes sour, like grapefruit, and the citrus smell lingers on her hands.

"It's a blood orange," Zia Rosa explains. "A local variety."

"Now for some business talk," Mamma says, emptying a purse on the table. "This is Anna's syringe, and these bottles contain her adrenalin solution. They expire every six months, so you will have to buy new ones at the local druggist. Do you have a druggist in mind? Do you have a trustworthy physician in case Anna has an asthma attack?"

"It's not polite to discuss business at the table," Zia Rosa says.

Mamma's mouth drops open.

While Anna continues to shovel couscous with her hands, a woman wearing a white cloth from head-to-toe walks up to their table and sets down a plate of that flat bread, saying nothing.

Mamma gently smacks Anna on the cheek.

"Say thank you to the cook, Anna. I didn't raise you to be an entitled princess waited on by servants," Mamma says, then mutters, "unlike your zia."

"Thank you," Anna says to the cook. She finishes eating her bread and tears off a new hunk.

"I know you don't like to discuss money, but I will not hold my tongue," Mamma says. "I would like to send you a monthly check."

Zia Rosa raises her eyebrows.

"What for?" Zia Rosa asks.

"For the things Anna can't do without—her medicine and her education," Mamma says.

"I think I can manage the expense."

"Rosa, I'd like to play a role in Anna's childhood, even if it's from across the ocean. I would feel better if I could send a check."

"We have plenty of funds," Zia Rosa says. "After all, she is family."

"You know nothing of family," Mamma growls and stands up from the table.

Mamma does not see the servant standing behind her with the bottle of wine, and the two of them collide, shattering the bottle on the tile. The white wine spatters over the tiles. Mamma leaves the table, slamming the turquoise door behind her.

"*Khamsa wa khmis aalik*," Zia Rosa tells the servant.

Anna chases after Mamma. She has never seen such an outburst from her mother before and is not sure if she should be following or just leave Mamma with her personal space.

"Mamma, don't be upset."

She catches up to her at the edge of the farm, near an outhouse that feeds into a manure-scented lagoon, roaring with ducks and flamingos. The land is spotted with prickly bushes and tufts of grass.

"Mamma, I don't know what I did, but I'm sorry. Can we be in good spirits since you are leaving soon?"

"You are not at fault, *carissima figlia*," Mamma says, kissing her. "You are managing perfectly. I'm the one at fault because I cannot stand to be without you, Anna. I worked so hard to take care of you, to bring you to America, to build a better life for you. But now I must return you to the Old World and leave you here with my sister, God forgive me. You will never know how much our family used to suffer on account of Zia Rosa." She reaches out and pulls Anna close. "I…I am sorry I'm unable to take care of you."

Anna knows her mother will be leaving, but she cannot imagine what might happen after that. She suddenly sees the rest of her life stretch out before her, unfurling into the unknown, into utter darkness. When Mamma steps on that ship for America, she will not be returning. Anna will be on her own with Zia Rosa and Zio Leonardo, and this will be her life now. She feels like she did on the beach at Coney Island, when she clung onto Mamma because she did not know how to swim, and Mamma peeled her off and let go of her hand. A lump in Anna's throat swells, and she worries it will trigger an asthma attack.

Anna has never seen Mamma's tears before. She's never seen any adult cry and didn't know they could cry like children. She doesn't know what to say, so she clings onto Mamma for as long as she can, while the chance remains.

8: LEMON SODA

"Rue Pierre de Coubertin!" the tram driver calls as the tram clanks to a stop.

Antonio's heart races. He heaves his single suitcase down the steps, careful to step over the tram rails, and right there, painted in white letters across a glass storefront is *Barbier, Pietro Palazzolo*.

For a while, Antonio stands there with his bags, afraid to open the door after coming all this way. Antonio knows he is a burden to the adults in his life, who are always busy with much more important work, like keeping the family afloat. Surely Zio Pietro, at the height of his workday when the men are coming home from work with a few extra francs and a five o'clock shadow, would notice Antonio from the corner of his eye, say ciao, and apologize that he must return to his appointments. He would have Antonio sit on a stool in the corner and wait until the workday is over. Like an afterthought.

Obligation is the engine of life, his papà would always say. Antonio recalls the preaching of his father and of the priests in Partinico, stressing the importance of supporting the family, of holding beliefs and defending them well. Antonio inhales, puffs out his chest, and crosses the threshold, the tinkling doorbell announcing his entrance.

Zio Pietro's barber shop is an art gallery. Four mirrors and four chairs are exhibited along each wall, more than double the capacity of the shop back in Sicily. White and yellow tiles checkerboard the floor, and the walls are painted the color of the sea. An old man plays an accordion in the corner while a shoe-shiner operates a stall by the window. Employees clip away at a spectrum of mutton chops and pompadours and undercuts, perfuming the air with minty aftershave and pine pomade. One of the barbers pulls a lever, and his chair reclines for shaving. Antonio gasps. The washbasins are porcelain, and the water runs clear for the tap's turning. Antonio's brothers would write about indoor plumbing in their new homes, but he never imagined it could be as easy as turning a tap.

"Antonio!" Zio Pietro has a cloth draped over his shoulder, where he wipes shaving foam off a razor. He sets down his razor and unbuttons his white coat, leaving his customer with half a beard.

"Finish up for me, Michele," he calls to another worker. "And cancel the rest of my appointments today."

"What should I tell them?" the worker asks.

Zio Pietro breaks out into opera and sings, "Tell them my favorite nephew has arrived!" Then he slides open an insulated ice box against the wall and presses a cold bottle into Antonio's hand—a lemon soda.

Antonio stares at himself in the mirror and sips his lemon soda, and afterwards his hand is wet from the cold beads on the bottle. The drink relieves his pounding headache; he has not taken food or drink since leaving Palermo that morning, and the ship left him foggy-headed and sleepy. Zio Pietro easily sweeps up the suitcase that Antonio struggled to carry and guides him up the stairs to their apartment, which sits directly atop the barber shop.

"I'm sorry to be a burden," Antonio says while they are climbing the stairs. "The Black Hand gave Mamma a scare, and she said I had to leave right away, and—"

He pulls Antonio in for a bear hug. "My favorite nephew. You've gotten so big!" Zio Pietro always speaks in a high-pitched tone with Antonio, a habit he likely fell into after using the same tone since Antonio was a baby. He laughs off Antonio's concern with a wave of his hand.

"I will write your mamma to tell her you've arrived. You've become a world explorer today, haven't you? All the way from Palermo harbor on your own? Next thing, we will send you to the moon!"

Soon, Antonio slips off his shoes and falls into his cousins' bed, sinking into a mattress much softer than the one he shared with his brothers back home. Exhausted, he closes his eyes even though daylight streams through the window. Pride swells in his chest, and a smile touches his lips. At thirteen, he has crossed the Mediterranean without a scratch, all on his own. He falls asleep happy that he fulfilled his promise to Mamma.

9. CAN YOU DO A BOB?

The next morning Anna waves Mamma goodbye at the Tunis harbor, and when she returns to the estate with Zia Rosa, nobody speaks a word. Anna sinks into the divan in her new bedroom, her first bedroom not shared with a sister, and promptly decides she hates the isolation of privacy. She wants noise. She wants to hear her sisters call her name. She flops over on her belly, buries her face in her pillow, and cries.

Later, when her tears have run dry, she allows herself to examine her room. The lime-washed walls are crowded with pottery shelves. Her window shutters are painted blue as a robin's egg and carved with a honeycomb of stars, causing sunlight to cut a bright set of stars onto her floor. Below her feet, the floor tiles shine with a grid of emerald flower motifs, even fancier than the Ritz Carlton Hotel back in New York. She studies her bed, which is set into an alcove in the wall and partitioned with red and gold-embroidered curtains.

A knock on her door startles her. "You must be Anna." A man stands in her doorway wearing a sheepskin vest and a red flannel sash around his waist. He is half-bald. "I am your Zio Leonardo. I was thinking you would be interested in helping with the sheep."

He is trying to lure me from my bedroom, Anna thinks. She knows she could sit and be sad all day, but she does not want to live as a hermit. *Those who dig their heels in the sand end up burying themselves*, she hears Papà saying. To deal with what the Lord has allotted her, she must peel off her sadness, put it to rest, and live while she still can. After all, the wonders of Tunisia beckon to her. What might she see today? A golden beach? A new food? Flamingos? Anna gives her uncle a nod and soon she is walking with him beyond the gate, across the flat, lush expanse stubbled with stiff tufts of grass, and into his barn.

She watches Zio Leonardo gather his lia sheep one by one and work the shear until a mountain of wool accumulates at their feet and the sheep shake themselves off, bald.

"I wish I could shear my hair off like the sheep," Anna says. "My long hair is unbearable in this heat."

Anna pulls on her hair—thick, coiled, dark, and falling past her shoulder blades. The long hair was fine for Brooklyn, but in Tunis it is already unbearable.

"You want a haircut?" Zio Leonardo asks. "I know the perfect barber."

On Saturday, when Zio Leonardo plays the accordion at the barber shop on Rue Pierre de Coubertin, he invites Anna to accompany him. They walk down the dusty country road and thread the needle through the medieval gates of Tunis, picking through the crowded markets where the air is spiced with harissa and briefly cooled under the shadow of a domed mosque. They follow the ancient streets until the narrow winding ways are diced into a modern grid, criss-crossed with wires and lit by electric lightbulbs. The bell rings behind them as they enter a little barber shop on the corner. The shop doesn't have any customers this early in the morning, just the barber and a boy sweeping near the back.

"Look who it is!" the barber raises his arms and sings in a deep opera voice.

"Pietro!"

The two men grip each other's arms and kiss each other on their cheeks.

"This is my niece, Anna," Zio Leonardo says. "Anna, this is Pietro Palazzolo."

"It's nice to meet you," Anna says, shaking his hand. "I'm here for a haircut."

"I'll give you one for free because your uncle is such a friend to me," Pietro says. "What haircut do you like, Signorina?"

"Can you do a bob?"

"Very adventurous," Pietro says with a big smile. "I will do my best. Up." He pats the seat of a barber chair for Anna to climb into.

Pietro drapes a barber's cape around her shoulders and buttons it at the neck. He reaches for a bottle with a rubber bladder and squeezes, spraying enough water to make her hair shine but not so much to make it drip. He pumps the pedal a few times, raising the chair off the ground to his eye level.

Anna turns to the window as the clamor of thundering crashes reaches the shop.

"*Oye!*" Zio Leonardo cries out, setting down his accordion and rushing outside to where a wooden cart with a broken wheel has tipped over sending dozens of barrels rolling down the street behind it. In the middle of the street, a man is lying on the cobblestones, clutching his leg.

Pietro quickly sets down his scissors. "I should help too," he tells Anna. Then he whistles at the teenage boy sweeping in the back of the shop. "Antonio! Watch the shop while I am gone."

Anna gasps as the boy turns and walks toward her. She recognizes his finely combed hair slicked with pomade and expertly parted. *It's the boy from the harbor.* He fidgets with the broom, but when he meets her gaze, she knows he recognizes her too.

With that, Pietro disappears outside, leaving Anna in the raised chair with the cape buttoned on and her hair still wet, waiting until she can continue her haircut.

She watches Antonio brush his broom back and forth over the same tiles which are already clean. He keeps his head down to avoid her gaze.

"How are you adjusting to Tunisia?" Anna asks. "Is it very different from Sicily? I know it's different from New York, especially the temperature. Some days it's so hot I just want to cut all my hair off. That's why I came here."

Antonio looks around the shop at who she might be talking to. He points at himself and silently mouths the word *Me?*

"We're the only two in the shop. Of course, I'm talking to you. Can you do a bob?"

"I'm just an apprentice," he mumbles. "I've never actually cut hair before. You should wait for Zio Pietro to come back."

"But he could be out there for a while, and I'm sweating over here. You've spent an awful lot of time in barber shops, right? You should know how to do a bob."

"You might not like it—"

"Your uncle left you in charge of the shop when he left. That makes you the second in command, right?"

That stops Antonio. *Second in command.* Anna waits a few moments to let it sink in, and Antonio seems to stand a little taller. "I suppose I know enough," Antonio finally says. "I cut hair in my dreams, after all."

"Great," Anna smiles, settling in for her cut. "I believe in you."

She can hear him gulp loudly as he grasps Pietro's comb and holds it to her head. She instructs Antonio on how she wants her hair cut—to the nape of her neck in the back, covering her ears, a single curl over her left cheekbone.

"You mean like the girls in America?" Antonio frowns.

"Yes, I like the modern styles," Anna says. "Why are you making that face? Does it not earn your official seal of approval?"

"People will think you are a boy with a haircut like that. Why not a plain, honest haircut?"

"Honest? I'm asking for an original haircut that expresses my personal style. What could be more honest than that? And I see you're expressing yourself plenty with that slicked-back pompadour and that apricot-fuzz on your upper lip," Anna laughs, noticing that Antonio is not laughing back.

As a reparation, she tips him a French coin that Zio Leonardo gave her. Antonio snatches it and drops it into a slitted hatbox labelled in shaky handwriting: *Savings*.

"Is that yours? What are you saving for?" Anna asks.

"For when I return to Sicily," Antonio pats the box. "One day, I'm going to buy back my papà's barber shop, where I will work with him and my brothers. Like old times."

"It'll take you a hundred years to save the money at this rate," Anna says with a short laugh. Then she sees the fire in his eyes and the determination in the set of his jaw and adds, "I'm sorry. I didn't mean..."

"I do not know how long it will take," Antonio says, shaking the box while the coins jingle inside. "But it *will* happen."

"I'm sure you'll be able to do it," she says in a placating voice.

"I was born to work in that shop, just like my papà and his papà. You know what they say in the old Sicilian language—*ci dissi u surci a nuci, dammi tempu ca ti perciu*—the mouse said to the nut, give me time and I shall reach you."

"But Tunisia is a paradise. Are you really so eager to go back to Sicily? Why not focus on going forward, to the future?"

"There is no future here," is all Antonio says, pressing the spray bladder to wet her hair again.

She can tell Antonio is flustered. "Why do you say that? What's so wrong with Tunisia?"

"There's nothing here for me." He gathers her bangs, picks up the scissors, and gives a single *snip*.

"*Bedda matri.*" His eyes are wide as he looks at her forehead and the clump of hair in his hands. "I've made a mistake."

Anna looks in the mirror and sees all her bangs are gone, showing her entire forehead and hairline. She lets out a high yelp and slaps her hands over her face. The bells jangle like a dropped tambourine as the shop door slams open. Zio Pietro is standing there, his dark brow furrowed with rage.

"*Antonio!*" Zio Pietro roars, snatching the scissors away. "When did I say you were ready to cut the girl's hair?"

"I warned her!" Antonio sends an accusatory finger her way. "I told her I'm just an apprentice, but she made me feel like I could do it!"

Anna shrinks into her seat as she finds herself caught between the master and the apprentice. Very chivalrous of him to rat her out.

"Don't blame her for your own delusions of grandeur! You can't pick up this trade like a habit. It takes years. You never hold scissors to someone's head like that. Do you think you're the fourth Musketeer? You hold them like this, here." He holds the shears out for Antonio to see and then waves him away. Go, off with you. Back to work."

Antonio slinks back to his broom, head hanging, feeling stupid and sullen. Pietro manages to salvage the haircut into a bowl cut, and while Anna does not like how she looks, she enjoys feeling the air cool the back of her neck. It may not be ideal, but at least it is new.

Meanwhile, Antonio stands in the corner, sweeping hair trimmings, sullen. She flashes a bright smile and waves to let him know she forgives him, that she holds no grudges toward the poor boy over the botched haircut. After all, she feels guilty for encouraging him, and he certainly warned her. He never even looks at her. After her haircut, Anna walks up to him.

"This is for your future barber shop." She drops another one of Zio Leonardo's French coins into the hatbox.

His slumped shoulders straighten. He gives her a small smile. "You're not mad about the haircut?"

"I'll give you a pass on that one," Anna combs her fingers through her hair. "You're allowed to give me two more bad haircuts, but three strikes and you're out, like in baseball."

"Baseball? Is that a ballroom dance?"

"It's a sport they play back in Brooklyn."

Hmph. Antonio gives a soft snort, entertained.

She walks to the door and is about to leave the shop when she turns and calls back to the boy with the broom, "Remember, three strikes!"

10: JASMINE FLOWERS

For the next week, Antonio mans the brooms with his cousins Vincenzo and Pete, who are a few years older than him, and the slightly younger Giuseppina, who sweeps away the hair every time a customer leaves. He learns the names of all the regular patrons and asks them questions like, "How much pomade do you think Giolitti uses?" to show them he knows what pomade is and who the Prime Minister is.

"Do I have a politician or a boy for a nephew?" Zio Pietro says. "You are as rigid as biscotti, Antonio. Remember to laugh while you are young, because one day you will be tired and ugly like me."

Zio Pietro laughs at himself in the mirror.

"Cutting hair is a serious business," Antonio says, wiping the razors on a cloth to dry them. "People trust us with their hair. It's nothing to laugh about."

"Anna makes you laugh whenever she comes in," Zio Pietro teases, and Antonio turns away to conceal his blush.

"We should visit your mamma," Zio Pietro says to Giuseppina, who is sweeping away a nest of jet-dark curls.

"It's been too long," Giuseppina says, propping her broom against the wall. "Let's buy some flowers first."

Antonio follows them down the street, deep into the medieval section of Tunis, and he takes in all the delicate pillars supporting keyhole arches and domes. The houses are painted with white lime and the doors and shutters are washed with turquoise. Two musicians on the corner beat goblet-shaped drums with their palms while nearby an eggplant vendor shouts in Arabic.

The memory of the Black Hand planting bombs in Partinico is still fresh, and Antonio can feel the shockwave rattling his bones. Antonio follows his uncle closely, taking care to keep distance from strangers. Yet for some reason, Zio Pietro strolls around the neighborhood like a man of leisure.

A line of khaki-clad French soldiers march with bayonets down Rue de Paris. Other men walk past in swishing robes, their heads wrapped, sporting the most delicate grey beards which they showcase beneath the shades of the outdoor cafes, chatting while smoking shisha and playing backgammon. Zio Pietro says a few words to them in Arabic, and he introduces Antonio, who is suddenly utterly speechless.

He is terrified to see so many French police officers in the neighborhood. One police officer scouts each block. Back home in Sicily, the police were paid off by the Black Hand mafia. Judging by the size of the police force in Tunis, Antonio reasons that it would take an awfully wealthy mafia to pay them all off.

"The mafia of Tunis must dwarf the mafia of Sicily," Antonio says, crossing his arms in protection, staying close to Zio Pietro as they pass the French police officers.

"Don't worry about the police here," Zio Pietro waves him off, "it's not like Sicily. The French police aren't paid off by any mafia."

Zio Pietro smiles and waves at every person he passes on the street. He stops at a bakery and buys a box of little white marzipan donuts for Antonio and Giuseppina to share.

"If there's no mafia in Tunisia, then who bribes the police?" Antonio asks.

"Nobody," Zio Pietro says. "They are employed by the French government."

"But we aren't in France."

"Tunisia is a protectorate of France. Do you under-stand?"

They see a French police officer searching the pockets of a Tunisian man. They continue walking.

"I think I understand," Antonio says slowly. "The Black Hand pay off the police in Sicily and call themselves the protectors of Sicily. The French pay off the police in Tunisia, and so they call Tunisia a French protectorate. France is like the Black Hand."

Zio Pietro frowns and shakes his head at the boy, but Antonio feels like he understands the situation perfectly.

They purchase a bouquet of white jasmine flowers in the market from a girl with a tattoo on her chin, and then take a tram north of the city, where the land gives way to lush, green scrubland fringed by distant hills.

"Are your mamma and papà separated?" Antonio asks Giuseppina. Antonio does not approve of such things. In his entire life, he has only seen one instance of separated marriage, and that was when a local lawyer ran off to the riviera with a French woman, leaving behind a wife and three children to struggle. The scandal fed a years' worth of gossip.

Giuseppina's chin juts out. "So what? They're together in spirit."

"I just don't understand why someone would want to do that," Antonio says. "They vowed to be faithful to each other. They made a solemn vow before a priest. Why would they part ways?"

"You're awful!" Giuseppina turns to him. "My parents have shared the same soul since they were banished from Sicily, when the Duke treated them so horribly and sent them into exile."

"Why were they banished?"

"You'll have to find that out on your own," she crosses her arms. "Papà doesn't like us talking about it. And in case you were wondering, I don't care whether you approve of my parents or not."

Antonio shrugs. He does not mean to offend her. But he has principles, after all, and he must defend them. From the tram window, Antonio watches the farms roll by— neat rows of apricot trees and twisted olive trees which sit barren in the winter air. Antonio sometimes wishes he was a farmer, working the land. Papà always says that any job done properly, no matter how small, is noble, but working God's earth to produce fruit is the most noble. Finally, they arrive at a church near the coastline, and they step off the tram.

Antonio looks around, wondering if this is the right stop. He does not see any houses where a divorcee might be living, just a church, and the aisles of headstones behind it.

They walk through the cemetery gate, and the graves stretch out in neat rows like the trees of a lemon grove until they finally arrive at a humble white stone chiseled under the name *Maria Minore Palazzolo*.

Giuseppina carefully bends to her knees and sets down the bouquet of jasmine flowers. Zio Pietro and Giuseppina each trace a cross on their torsos; they stand and listen to the waves and the rustling palm leaves.

"It's been too long, Mamma," Giuseppina says, stroking the stone.

Antonio feels a rush of shame weigh on his chest. He makes the sign of the cross and prays with them fervently, giving Giuseppina all the time she needs.

When they return to the apartment, Antonio stays up past midnight under the electric lightbulbs, even though a kerosene lamp would do just fine. He takes out pencil and paper and starts writing.

My sincerest apologies, cousin Giuseppina. I misunderstood your words, and I have insulted the name of your mamma and shamed myself in the process. I will go to confession and tell the priest of my sins, and I will donate my allowance to the church as well. I hope this is enough.

When the morning dawns, Antonio purchases a second bouquet of white jasmine flowers from the souk, and he sets them with the card in front of Giuseppina's door. Then he descends the stairs to work.

11. VELVET

"Would you like to visit the market with me?" Zia Rosa asks, standing at Anna's bedroom door while Anna combs her bobbed hair.

Anna does not look up but hears the woman *tsk tsk*, and feels her cheeks burning with self-consciousness.

"I don't know why you like that style," Zia Rosa mutters. "You look like Joan of Arc after she joined the army."

"Joan of Arc would challenge you to a duel for saying that. Anyway, I like my hair bobbed. It's self-expression."

"Self-expression? I'll express you to the wig shop," Zia Rosa sneers. "When I was a girl in Sicily my only concern was to help my mamma put food on the table, and now children are concerned about *self-expression*. The frivolity."

Anna sits in her chair and picks up her embroidery work. She has sworn off regular communications with Zia Rosa, for the time being at least. Whenever she looks at the woman, she can only remember Mamma's parting words: *You will never know how much our family used to suffer on account of Zia Rosa.* And the fact Mamma could not even put to words what Zia Rosa had done leaves

Anna no other choice but to imagine all manner of dark sins. Perhaps Zia Rosa was a thief, and that is how she wound up in this mansion while the rest of the family moved to Brooklyn. Anna dismisses the thought. She does not think Zia Rosa would be capable of such a thing, not from her gentle manner.

Faced with silence, Zia Rosa eventually gives up and leaves. Anna tries and fails to embroider a simple green leaf on her embroidery hoop. Through her cracked-open door, Anna watches Zia Rosa lounging on the divan, her nose buried in an Italian romance novel. The servants bring her a bowl of salted almonds, and Zia Rosa, without looking, gathers the almonds in her fist and crunches away. Fatma, the servant, brings Anna bowls of almonds as well.

"No thank you, Fatma," Anna says. "I don't want to be served. I had enough people serving me back in Brooklyn with my asthma."

Fatma nods, and Anna dives back into her work, struggling to loop the green thread to form even the simplest leaf design.

"You like embroidery?" Zia Rosa asks, returning to her bedroom door.

Anna shrugs, not gracing Zia Rosa with the gift of her spoken word.

"Let me show you something," Zia Rosa says, motioning for her to follow.

Anna, crossing her arms over her chest to show she is still resolute, follows Zia Rosa down the hall, where she cracks open a dusty walnut chest.

"I used to be a seamstress, you know," Zia Rosa says, "when I worked for the Duchess in Sicily. I still keep my sewing supplies with me for emergencies, though my hands are very shaky these days."

"The Duchess?" Anna's curiosity overshadows her need to give Zia Rosa the silent treatment and to keep her at arm's length.

The chest hinges creak, and Anna gasps at the heaping folds of velvet and lace. She spots scissors, pins, needles, thimbles. Still, Anna keeps her guard up, not allowing herself to indulge Zia Rosa too much.

"Please talk to me more, Anna. I know you may not like me, but you're stuck with me, and the time would pass easier on speaking terms. Perhaps I could teach you about sewing."

"I know enough about sewing," Anna crosses her arms.

"Like what?"

"I know that you reap what you sew," Anna mumbles. "Like if you ignore your family for decades, don't expect them to want to spend time with you."

Zia Rosa sighs.

"You know all those dresses in your wardrobe?" Zia Rosa asks. "I made them in my younger days. They were originally for the Duchess. I could teach you how to make garments like that."

Anna had checked the wardrobe on her first day at the house, marveling at the intricate embroidery and pleating of the dresses. She is about to say yes, but then remembers she is stsill mad. Instead, she clenches her jaw and says nothing. Zia Rosa frowns and starts to close the chest.

"Tell me more about this Duchess," Anna says suddenly.

Zia Rosa's face sours. "I should not have mentioned her."

"I want to know."

"No. We won't speak of it again."

"Fine," Anna snaps. "Then I won't speak to you again."

12. WHAT OUR FAMILY IS LIKE

Antonio closes the door of the bedroom he shares with his cousins and tries his best to smooth out the crumpled sheets on his bed. Zio Pietro had given him a mismatched sandwich of brown and cream linen sheets, like the paper packages of filo dough they sell at the market, and no matter how tightly Antonio pulls the sheets under his mattress they are still scarred with wrinkles. He huffs and pulls at his hair, realizing his bed is no different from the three others crammed into the room—unkempt. He can't abide such a thing.

While Antonio rifles through the linen closet for some acceptable blankets, he knocks something loose and hears a heavy clank. Digging further, he arrives at the back of the closet, where tucked under the blankets is a bronze jewelry box, just big enough to require two hands to lift.

Antonio raises the box to the light beams streaming through cracks of the blue-shuttered windows. The bronze box crawls with swirling laurels, scenes of kings and queens, knights on horseback. A family crest of a winged lion adorns the top face. Surely this box would sell for hundreds of lire. Does Zio Pietro have that kind of money? Perhaps it belonged to the previous residents of the apartment? But this district of Tunis was built recently, and there could not have been many previous residents of this apartment.

With a simple click, the hinges swing open, revealing a roll of yellowed paper. The handwriting varies from mature, well-practiced cursive to childish chicken-scratch. They are letters. Antonio knits his brow as he wonders if it is improper for him to read such personal documents. Duke Vincenzo Grifeo II, they are all addressed, with dates stretching back six years.

Grifeo? Antonio drops his face into his palm as he searches his memories. He has heard that name before. The Grifeo family sometimes visited Papà's barber shop in Sicily—fading aristocrats with threadbare velvet jackets who lived in the crumbling castle outside Partinico.

"So, you like to snoop?" Giuseppina enters the room, carrying neatly folded linens in her arms.

Antonio follows his impulse to slam the box shut, and again he feels shame wash over him. What's more, Giuseppina lays down a set of linens on his bed, with no wrinkles to speak of. She must have pressed them for him just now, noticing his frustration over his current sheets. Her small kindness makes him feel even more guilty.

"Cousin Giuseppina, I swear I didn't know what this box was, I just found it in the closet."

Giuseppina's frown softens, perhaps because she hears his apologetic tone.

"I suppose you've done me a favor," Giuseppina shrugs and snatches the box. "You've taught me that I should find a better hiding place for it."

She is walking out the door when Antonio says, "Wait."

Giuseppina stops.

"I saw a name on those papers," Antonio says. "Duke Vincenzo Grifeo II. Who is he to you?"

"You're just going to judge me again, like you did with my mamma. You'll have to find out on your own."

"Giuseppina, please. What I said about your mamma was wrong. I can be tightly strung sometimes, I admit. But I promise I will keep my mouth shut and listen this time."

Giuseppina lingers by the door, her hand turning the doorknob halfway as if deciding whether to stay or go, until she finally closes the door for privacy and takes a seat on her bed, the springs squeaking.

"Duke Vincenzo Grifeo II is my grandfather," she says.

"That means your Mamma—"

"You promised you would keep your mouth shut."

"Yes, of course."

"Mamma was the daughter of the Duke. She grew up in a castle just outside Partinico. Her family needed her to marry a prince to continue the noble lineage, but during the famine she fell in love with my papà, a common barber. When the Duke heard this, he was so outraged that he disowned her, and my parents had to flee the country. So, they moved to Tunisia, and Mamma changed her maiden name to Minore, which was originally her father's nickname. They opened a barber shop, and then I was born. This jewelry box is one of the few things she brought with her."

Antonio finds himself straightening his posture when he realizes that he is in the presence of a Duke's granddaughter. Now, when he looks at cousin Giuseppina, he notices the quiet air of dignity that cloaks her, the way she holds her head high and summons respectability with a gravitational pull. Giuseppina opens the bronze jewelry box, cradling the stack of letters like she would a baby.

"Ever since I was seven years old, I've been writing these letters to the Duke. I don't know how or why, but he keeps sending my letters back with no reply. So, I hold onto them."

Antonio peers at the letters in Giuseppina's hands, and he catches a few lines from them.

Why did you make my Mamma leave Sicily?
Why don't you ever visit me?
Please tell me what our family is like.

Suddenly Giuseppina clicks the box shut. Her lip trembles, and she rises from the mattress to leave Antonio sitting alone with his neatly folded bed sheets, still warm from the iron.

"Thank you for the linens," he says.

She shuts the door without a reply.

13: WHITEWASHED WALLS

While Anna drifts on the edge of sleep that night, her imagination circles around Zia Rosa's offhand mention of the Duchess, and the awful ways it could connect to the deed Mamma could not bear to say.

In the morning, when Zio Leonardo is tending to the goats and Zia Rosa is reading, Anna pulls on her softest slippers and tiptoes up the stairs, cringing every time a wood board creaks. She saunters down the hallway like a cat stalking its prey, looking over her shoulder to make sure no servants are watching her. From here, she can look out the windows to the courtyard and the orange trees below. Anna has never seen Zia Rosa's bedroom before and only knows the door she and Zio Leonardo disappear behind around eight o'clock because they are aging and tire early. Anna imagines their bedroom to be lush with painted tiles and velvet pillows like their house, but her imagination fails when she turns the knob and slips inside.

Zia Rosa and Zio Leonardo's bedroom could be a closet. The bed does not have a canopy, just a straw mattress, and the only adornment on the whitewashed walls is a crucifix and a notecard-sized icon of Saint Francis. Anna feels cramped just standing there. With all her wealth, why would Zia Rosa choose to sleep here? It is half the size of Anna's room. Anna would never guess that Zia Rosa is the type to crave simplicity. While Anna is standing there, she closes her eyes and feels transported back to her family apartment in Sicily, feeling the proximity of the walls within arm's reach.

Anna takes her search to the bookshelf, filing through Zia Rosa's collection of romance novels. She finds a volume simply entitled *Sicily*, packed with sepia photographs of strangers. The men wear military uniforms adorned with medals, high collars, shoulder tassels, swords at their belts. Finally, Anna finds a photograph of an ancient woman draped in furs and jewels, and standing beside her, holding her arm to prop her up, is a younger Zia Rosa wearing a white maid's apron. Her face only has the earliest whisper of wrinkles radiating from her eyes, cheeks sunken, hair tied back in a scarf, and she sends her petrified gaze into the camera. *The Duchess and Her Heir*, a pencil scrawling reads in the corner, *1897.*

Her heir? But that means—

Anna looks at the walls, the ceiling, the floor under her feet. This was paid for with the Duchess's money. When Anna was a baby, when all the crops in Sicily were sizzled to a crisp and families were starving, Zia Rosa acquired enough inheritance money to escape with Zio Leonardo to Tunisia where she could start a new life for herself. Anna's family, on the other hand, caught in the crossfire of the mafia violence, with children to feed, crowded onto a dark immigrant ship and left for America. If Zia Rosa had come by this money during the famine, why didn't she donate any to Anna's family?

The shock dawns on Anna as the pieces of the mosaic fall into place. Mamma had been so upset to discover Zia Rosa's mansion and her servants, and now Anna understands why.

She slams the book shut and stuffs it into the bookshelf, her face hot. Anna stomps down the hallway and thunders down the stairs, too angry to even try for secrecy. Her aunt is lounging in the entry hall with her book.

"Why did you abandon us, Zia Rosa?"

"I'm sorry, my child," she mumbles, not looking up. "I had to leave church early because of my—,"

"I'm not talking about church. I know why Mamma was upset with you. You hoarded your money during the hard times in Sicily when your family needed you most."

Zia Rosa straights her posture as if Anna's words had delivered an electric shock.

"Anna, how did you…? There's no such—"

"I don't know why I'm even living here. I should just pack my bags and head back to Brooklyn. If I had known before—" She pivots on her foot and starts to stomp back to her bedroom.

"Wait!" Zia Rosa pleads. "You don't know the full picture."

Anna can hear the pain in her aunt's voice.

"You must understand. Those were hard, hard times. People starved. You can't judge me for leaving."

"You could have helped us before we left Sicily," Anna crosses her arms.

"But I did, my dear."

"My mamma doesn't see it that way."

"And I pray for her forgiveness every day. She and I have not spoken as much as sisters should, her being in America and me being in Tunisia. Carrying a relationship through the mail is a difficult thing. But don't think for a second that I abandoned you. I love you, Anna, as if you were my own child."

Zia Rosa reaches her arms for a hug, but Anna steps back, just out of reach. "What have you done for us?" she whispers.

"I don't know if I should say," Zia Rosa lowers her arms. "I don't want to make you feel indebted."

"It's better that you tell me."

"I don't want to change things between us."

Anna snorted. "And things are good between us? How can I trust you if I don't know you? No more secrets. I need to know."

"Yes, yes, you're right," Zia Rosa exhales before speaking clear and slow. "I was the one who bought your family's tickets to America."

Anna lets out a long breath like a boiling tea kettle with all the steam let out.

"When you were a baby, your family was trying to escape Sicily, but tickets were hard to come by, you see. America places quotas on the number of immigrants they allow, and the paperwork can be nearly impossible if you don't have good connections. So, I put in a word for the tickets. I spent just about everything I had at the time."

Anna feels sudden welling of wet emotion in her eyes, and her spine rushes with shivers like at church.

"I don't tell this to many people, my child, but I bought this estate with the dream it would one day be filled with laughing children, and now the emptiness has become a prison. I was so happy when you decided to come. I could teach you so many things, like sewing and French and Arabic. I could help you enjoy your time here."

Again, Zia Rosa reaches out for a hug, but Anna crosses her arms over her chest. Anna considers shaking her head and leaving Zia Rosa alone with her book and her salted almonds. She cannot forget the look of pain on Mamma's face. And yet Anna cannot bring herself to reject her aunt, with her pleading eyes and her years of loneliness.

Anna steps toward Zia Rosa and allows herself to be wrapped in warmth, to be pulled so close she can smell her aunt's pomegranate perfume and feel the cold touch of her jewelry. She hugs Zia Rosa in return, feeling an outpouring of tenderness she had not felt since saying goodbye to Mamma.

14. SHAVING SOAP

Around ten o'clock, when the morning rush dies down in their barber shop, Antonio squints at himself in the mirror to see a shadow on his upper lip that will not go away. A few days earlier, Anna had likened it to apricot fuzz, and he holds the memory in his thoughts, turning it over and observing all the facets like a jewel. He touches the ridge of skin between his nose and mouth, finding it feather-soft. Finally. He has waited his whole life for this day, and yet the budding mustache bends into a frown because Papà is not here to see it.

"Shaggy nephews are not good for business," Zio Pietro says. "You should shave that."

"When I have time," Antonio says.

Zio Pietro slides open a drawer and pulls out a razor that glints under the lightbulb.

"Here, Nino," and he reaches for Antonio's face.

"Oye!" he throws a hand over his lip and jumps from his chair. "I said I will do it when I have time. I am busy now." His voice is muffled behind his hand. He grabs a broom and starts sweeping.

"Did your father not teach you to shave, Antonio?"

"He was going to. Before I left. Just like he taught my brothers to shave when they were old enough."

"But I can teach you."

"No, no, no. My Papà will teach me when he returns. That is the way my family has always done it, and that is the way it must happen now. It is our tradition, and everything would fall apart without it."

"But your Papà is in America." Antonio glares at him as if to ask, "So?" Zio Pietro does not ask again.

"Loyalty is at the root of our profession," Zio Pietro decides to preach one day from behind the head of a customer. "Once a man chooses a barber, he must invest in them. The one who cuts hair is family. Who among these men would ever think of seeing a different barber after investing all this time?"

He gestures to the full shop and the three waiting customers leafing through Sicilian newspapers along the window. They swear and call him names, and he laughs.

"Once, a French priest came in for a haircut, Francois Miquet, you know him? I do a good job, he tips well, we are friendly. And the next month? Nothing. I don't see him again for four whole months," he holds up four fingers. "I talk with the barber on Rue de Paris, and he says the same thing, that a certain Father Francois Miquet left him cold for six months. The Frenchman had been going to a different barber every month, in a rotation. The philanderer!"

To win and keep customers, Antonio learns, a barber must add entertainment to the customer's experience. On Saturdays, when business peaks, Zio Pietro pays the goat herder Leonardo Ribaudo to play the accordion on the stool by the window, and he pays another goat herder to blow into the zampogna. He also imports lemon soda from a cousin in Partinico who grows the lemons himself. He keeps the bottles in an ice box that he says attracts sweating customers in the summers. When Zio Pietro cuts hair, he places a record on his gramophone, and the static-crackling voice of Enrico Caruso crinkles from the brass funnel. Zio Pietro breaks out into opera and sings along while trimming the hair.

Antonio is not sure if he approves of all the extra frills his uncle attaches to the barber shop—the musicians, the shoe shiners, the soda. He should be focused on one thing only—cutting hair. Antonio's family has been cutting hair since before Italy was a country, and they managed it without the ice box or gramophone or electric lightbulbs. Antonio could do without electricity altogether, with all honesty. Electricity is a fire hazard, and it makes their work too easy. Cutting hair is supposed to be difficult, Antonio knows, which is why only the masters can do it. Electricity saps work of its nobility.

Antonio's upper lip continues to fuzz and soften over the course of the winter until he can count each hair individually, and they stray into his mouth when he eats his spaghetti.

"I cannot hold my tongue anymore, Antonio," Zio Pietro has him sit down after work one day. "Your mustache is damaging my reputation as a barber. You cannot wait for your father to teach you to shave it. Your father is not coming."

He rests a hand on Antonio's neck.

"Change is the engine of life, *carissimo* Nino."

"How dare you misuse my papà's words," Antonio says. "Obligation is the engine of life. The only person who will teach me to shave is my papà."

That night, Antonio tosses in bed. *Change is the engine of life*, his uncle's words resound. Images meld on the edge of sleep—the coal-powered ship that brought him to Tunis, the ice box, the gramophone. He imagines taking his slitted hatbox full of coins to Sicily and buying back his father's barber from the bank, to return to the old days, to cut hair alongside his brothers. *Your father is not coming*, his uncle's words repeat, and then a new image appears in his dreams—the girl Anna DiNicola who laughed at his hatbox, who laughed at his plan to return to Sicily. In his dream, he is cutting her hair and failing, and every time he snips at the wrong strand of hair, she tells him to find a new dream. A new dream. Anna DiNicola's hair is perfectly curled, with the waves ending at a single curl hugging her left cheekbone, and she sits in the barber chair, telling him to find a new dream.

Antonio's eyes flash open.

"What is wrong with me?" he mutters to himself. He is not sure if this is how a normal person behaves. He does not even know what normal is anymore.

He walks to Zio Pietro's room, where his uncle sleeps on the floor beside an empty marriage bed, a portrait of his deceased wife nearby. He nudges his uncle awake.

"I am ready to shave, Zio Pietro."

In the wash closet, Zio Pietro keeps a special straight razor that folds out of a walnut sheath. Raindrops *tap tap tap* the window pane. Zio Pietro shows him to run the tap water on the shaving soap, to scrub it with the brush until it lathers. He presses the brush into Antonio's hand and has him lather his upper lip, which Antonio fights to keep from trembling. Antonio asks to pause and swallows the lump in his throat. Holding the razor with the perfect amount of firmness, they scrape the fuzz off Antonio's lip, wiping the razor on each side with a cloth. His lip-hair pours down the drain of the wash basin. Zio Pietro pats him on the back, yawns, and then returns to his sleeping pallet.

Just like how the hair washes down the drain, Antonio knows that his family in Sicily has washed away—two brothers and a father in America, a mother in Sicily, himself in Tunisia. Why did it have to happen this way? From under his bed, Antonio takes the slitted hatbox where the coins have accumulated for the day when he would return to Sicily and work in his father's shop once more. He moves the box to the hallway storage closet and tucks it in the furthest, deepest shelf, where he will never have to look at it again.

15. STRAIGHT STITCH

Every morning, Anna meets with Zia Rosa at the dinner table. She sits cross-legged on the cushions on the floor, and the low table is laid out with all sorts of fabrics and needles and spools of thread. Zia Rosa lowers herself down onto the cushions and with shaky hands gives Anna a needle and thread.

"The first lesson is to thread the needle," Zia Rosa says.

"I already know how to do that," Anna says, and yet it takes her several attempts until she finally slips the wobbly thread through the eye of the needle.

Zia Rosa gives Anna two scraps of cotton fabric.

"I will teach you to make a basic stitch," Zia Rosa says, showing her how to loop the thread through the fabric, not too close to the edge of the fabric.

Anna repeats the motion, but she keeps veering off to the side, and her stitches come out crooked. Before Anna has the chance, Zia Rosa starts pouring new information on her—blanket stitch, slip stitch, back stitch, chain stitch—Anna never knew there were so many stitches! She struggles to keep up until finally, exasperated, she drops the cloth and needle into her lap. "Don't go so fast! I can't keep up."

"But we've only just begun," Zia Rosa laughs.

Zia Rosa can make a perfect stitch even with her shaky hands, yet the task is difficult for Anna. She has a red mark on her thumb from the needle, and her hands are cramped.

"Have you made any new friends in Tunisia?" Zia Rosa asks while they work.

"It's easier to pass through the eye of a needle than to make friends here," Anna says. "It'll take me years to learn French and Arabic so I can make friends with the local girls. I only speak English and Italian, you know."

"What about that girl from the barber shop? She speaks Italian, right? And she is your age?"

"You mean Giuseppina?" Anna asks. "I know of her."

"Why not invite her over?" Zia Rosa suggests. "It is important for a girl to have friends her age."

"I don't know if she would like me," Anna says. "It's hard to force friendships."

Zia Rosa laughs and swats the comment away with her hands.

"Of course, you can force friendships," Zia Rosa insists. "Friendships of necessity are the best kind. I will invite her for you."

That night, Anna lies awake in bed and all she can think about is sewing, imagining new strategies, and practicing. Her sisters back in America are working in factories right now while she is sitting in a mansion learning to make a hundred different kinds of stitches while being waited on by servants. *I must get a job as a dressmaker,* she tells herself, *so I can save up money and one day live in a mansion just like this. Only I will have earned it. And nobody will ever look at me as a sickly girl to be pitied. Never again.* Suddenly, she feels a great pressure on her chest, a race against the clock that sends her heart fluttering. *I have so much to learn!*

In the morning, Anna cracks open her eyes to see Fatma at the door.

"Do you have any clothes that need mending, love?" Fatma asks.

Anna walks to her wardrobe and holds up her stockings, where a rip is growing at the heel.

"I don't want you to mend it," Anna says, "but I would like it if you taught me to mend my own clothes."

"You don't want me to mend your clothes?" Fatma asks, wounded.

"I don't want to be served," Anna clarifies.

"But that is my job, Anna. It's what I get paid for."

"Yes, of course," Anna says, "but it's just that you have a lifetime of experience mending clothes, and I'd like to learn from you if you're willing to teach."

Fatma exhales.

"Don't tell your zia," Fatma says.

Fatma takes Anna to the mending room, a little closet off the side of the courtyard, and she lays Anna's torn stockings on the table. Fatma takes a wooden, egg-shaped tool and settles it under the ripped heel.

"This is a darning egg," Fatma says. "I find a thread that matches the stockings, and I stitch a grid over the egg until the rip is filled."

Anna nods and practices.

She watches Fatma do it easily.

When the time comes for Anna's next sewing lesson with Zia Rosa, she walks into the courtyard to find another girl there—Giuseppina.

"I invited a friend for you, Anna," Zia Rosa says, a wide smile on her face.

"Ciao," Giuseppina gives a little wave, meek and quiet. But Anna notices the girl steal judgmental looks around the courtyard, at the elaborate arches and pillars and the flowers and orange trees, her nose scrunching in disgust. "Aristocrats," Giuseppina says under her breath. "Always trying to show off."

Anna is surprised at the mumbled outburst but says nothing, and they proceed with the day's lesson. Zia Rosa teaches them to do some more stitches, just to build the muscle memory of stitching in a straight line.

Zia Rosa stands up for the bathroom, and while they are alone, Giuseppina asks, "Do you have sisters, Anna?"

"I have four," Anna sighs, "Anastasia, Rosaria, Marie, and Marietta. They all live in America."

"You must miss them terribly," Giuseppina says. "I don't have any sisters. You are so lucky—you can wear your sisters' old dresses and ask them to style your hair. I don't even know how to French braid my hair. No one ever taught me, and I don't think my papà or brothers would know."

"I'll teach you the French braid if you teach me the French language," Anna says, and a meek smile breaks over Giuseppina's face.

"Do you read very much?" Anna asks.

Giuseppina shakes her head no.

"I'd loan you my book collection," Anna says, "except they're all in English. They're such great stories. *The Wonderful Wizard of Oz. Little Women.* Oh, and my favorite is *Anne of Green Gables.* It's about this girl who has the same name as me—or close to it at least—who is sent to live in a faraway land where she gets into all kinds of trouble—also like me. She bakes a cake with liniment oil. She even smashes a slate over a boy's head. I wish I could be as adventurous as her."

"She sounds scary," Giuseppina says. "If that's what adventurous means, then I'd rather stay home."

Anna laughs.

They smile while they work, and by the end of the day Anna holds up her fabric scraps to see a perfectly straight stitch binding the two cloths together.

"Anna, it's perfect," Giuseppina gasps.

Anna beams.

16. WINGED LION

In the waxing hours before dawn, a winter fog steams in from the sea. The streets are blanketed waist-high in mist, darkening the damp paving stones, sizzling away into nothing by seven o'clock under the sun's bleary red eye. While Antonio stirs in his bed, he can hear the clanking garbage carts making their rounds outside and the goatherder blowing his horn for the milk delivery.

In their kitchen, they have a white tile oven with hot coals beneath, and from the shuffling of the copper *cezve* pot, Antonio can hear Zio Pietro boiling water, and soon the smell of Turkish coffee—with the added goat milk, sugar, and cardamon—wafts through the house. Antonio does not understand why his uncle prefers Turkish coffee to the Italian espresso, but he is afraid to ask. After all, he has sworn to obey his uncle in all things. His uncle is generally a happy man, vital yet relaxed in the Sicilian manner. At lunch, he usually drinks two glasses of wine then challenges his children to a wrestling match. Vincenzo and Pete and Giuseppina usually dogpile onto him, tackling him to the carpet, laughing. Sometimes, before he shaves, he will press his chin into their faces and tickle them with his stubble. He will go to any lengths, Antonio realizes, to appear a fool in front of his children.

In the washroom, Antonio turns the faucet and splashes soap and water on his face, which is increasingly spotting with pimples. He carefully gels his hair and combs it in a perfect part. His morning routine of styling his hair has become a tradition, and his papà would always say that traditions are the cornerstone of society. A world without traditions is chaos, he thinks, admiring his haircut.

In the midst of his grooming, he sees in the mirror that Giuseppina is tip-toeing past the washroom doorway, clutching an envelope to her chest. His heart sinks when he realizes what she is up to.

"It's too early in the morning to be looking so suspicious," Antonio says, shutting the water off, returning the washroom to silence.

"You shouldn't be prying," Giuseppina hides the envelope behind her back.

"Giuseppina, you know the Duke won't answer your letters. He never does."

"That's why I'm trying something different. I think I've sent it to the wrong address—,"

"Why do you want his approval anyway?" Antonio asks. "I doubt he even approves of himself. Not since feudalism was abolished, anyhow."

"I'm not just writing to the Duke, I'm writing to the whole House of Grifeo. I have aunts, uncles, cousins, grandparents, people I've never met. If even one of them answers, that would be enough. I'm sure they don't all share the same opinion of us. I have to think some were sympathetic of Mamma, and they would have some influence. I'm sure we could make amends."

"They'll never answer," Antonio shakes his head, sighing.

"What do you know of it? You're not a Grifeo. My Mamma came from a very respected house, you know. Papà told me they owned all the land from Terrasini to Partinico, a giant territory called Tenuto dello Zucco."

"Tenuto dello Zucco doesn't exist anymore," Antonio says. "Their palace in Terrasini was turned into a storehouse for wine, and the palace outside Partinico is in worse shape than the ancient Roman ruins. Trust me, I've seen it, and it's a sad thing. The Duke still clings to his title, though his clothes become more threadbare every year."

Giuseppina stares from the doorway to the letter in her hands, as if deciding whether or not she will drop it in the mailbox for delivery. The postman usually comes to pick up the mail in the morning, so time is winding down.

"Why are you telling me this?" she says, lowering her voice. "I thought you loved Sicily."

"I do, with all my heart," Antonio says, "but it doesn't matter what some old Duke thinks of your family. As long as you're right with God, then you're right with me."

Giuseppina tilts her head, looking at Antonio in a new way. She opens her mouth to speak when—*thud*—a heavy stack of envelopes slides through the slot on their door, landing on the tiles.

"I guess the postman is making his rounds," Antonio says. "Are you still going to mail that letter?"

Giuseppina strokes the letter fondly, then carefully folds it in half and tucks it in her pocket.

"Antonio, someone sent us a letter," cousin Giuseppina pulls up a seat at the breakfast table and lays down an envelope. "It looks fancy."

Antonio cranes to view the envelope and whistles, impressed. The envelope is cream parchment, the size of a chess board, and stamped with a wax seal depicting a winged lion. *Ribaudo Estate,* a calligraphy inscription reads in the upper left corner. Very dignifying indeed. Antonio puffs out his chest, wondering if the letter is for him.

To the Orlando Household:

We are extending an invitation for Sunday dinner at our estate. If interested, please RSVP by Wednesday.

Cordially,

Rosa and Leonardo Ribaudo

"What's this?" Zio Pietro strolls into the room, reading the invitation. "Odd, the Ribaudos never invite anyone to their estate."

"They must be especially lonesome," Antonio says.

"Anna must have put them up to it," Giuseppina says. "She's the only one in that house spirited enough to suggest it."

Antonio nods in agreement. Surely there is no better term to describe Anna apart from spirited. What else could explain the invitation? He imagines Anna begging her zia and zio to organize the dinner party, over and over until they conceded. The thought of sitting at Anna's dinner table, in Anna's house, with Anna's plates and napkins and forks and spoons, ignites a sublime fear in Antonio, like the feeling of standing in line to receive the bread and wine on his First Communion. His heart races and his stomach flip flops, queasy. He does not know why a simple dinner party causes him to feel this way, but it is certainly undignified. He just doesn't know how to make it stop.

17: JUJUBE FRUITS

On Sunday evening, Anna watches the servants set the table in the courtyard under the blood orange trees. They lay down a fine tablecloth of lace and gold thread imported from Milan. They cover the tiles in sheepskin carpets and pillows for lounging. Anna helps to set out name cards for each place, and when no one is looking she moves Antonio's name card across from her, so that he is close but not too close to warrant suspicion.

Anna watches the cook, Fatma, prepare their bread. She mixes semolina, olive oil, water, and rolls out a dozen flat discs of dough, which she wraps in linens and sets on every available surface—the tables, the counters, the beds—to watch them rise. She roasts one of Zio Leo's lambs and steams couscous with its heat.

While everyone is preparing, Anna locks herself in her room and buttons on the new dress she has sewn. The fit is loose and comfortable, and the burgundy skirts swish as she walks. She based the design off a photograph of a Spanish flamenco dress she saw in a book, and the successive layers of skirts are stitched together crooked, not quite ruffled in the way she imagined. She will have to practice flouncing more. In a hallway closet, she discovers Zio Leonardo's sheepskin vest, which she wears on top of the dress, and a red sash that she ties around her waist experimentally. Something about the pairing of all three garments fascinates Anna. The outfit makes her feel like one of the adventurers from her novels. When she steps into the courtyard with her new outfit, Zia Rosa shakes her head.

"What are you wearing, *amore*?" Zia Rosa asks. "Are you from the circus? You have an entire wardrobe full of nice Sunday dresses you could have worn instead."

"Those dresses are the from the 1800s," Anna swats the comment away. "Besides, I like making my own outfits. It's more creative."

"It's *too* creative, if you ask me," Zia Rosa mumbles.

It is nice to feel the cool winter breeze on her ankles, especially under the hot sun. She stands in the courtyard and waits for Giuseppina and her family to arrive, trying to conceal her eagerness at the thought of seeing Antonio and his little fuzzy mustache in her house.

The Palazzolo family arrives through the turquoise carriage doors. Pietro steps in first with Giuseppina and her two brothers after that. They are dressed in their Sunday best, staring at the courtyard and the carved arches propped up by delicate pillars. Finally, in comes Antonio, wearing his taut suspenders, his choking sleeve garters, his hair-part that seems pinned down tighter than an anchor chain. He marvels at the turquoise tiles on the floor of the courtyard.

"Leonardo, you are a goat herder," Pietro says, looking at the tile fountain in their courtyard. "How did you—"

Anna can tell he is afraid to is go on, afraid to ask how they could afford the estate. Surely, he would be embarrassed to know them if told where the money came from, that it was inherited from a duchess in the midst of a famine.

Pietro and Giuseppina sit down on the pillows, where the dinner table is only a few inches off the ground. Antonio stands there, his eyebrows knit in confusion.

"There are no chairs," he says, like nobody else had noticed.

"You sit on the pillows," Anna says.

"Why?"

"Because Zia Rosa and Zio Leonardo are used to eating the Tunisian way."

"But we're Sicilian, not Tunisian," Antonio whispers, glancing at the servants. "Why steal somebody else's tradition?"

"It's good to try new things," Anna says.

Antonio huffs. She watches the boy dip his hands in the water basin, washing his hands along with them. After they say the prayer, Anna scoops up the fluffed, golden couscous with her hands.

"Where are the plates?" Antonio asks. "The forks? The knives?"

"You eat with your hands."

Antonio's eyes widen.

"I'm not getting my hands dirty," he crosses his arms, too stubborn to try this new way of eating.

Anna shrugs and continues to shovel the couscous into her mouth. From another bowl, she tries a triangular pastry stuffed with tuna and parsley, which goes perfect with a squeezed quarter-lemon. For her torn corners of bread, red harissa paste. The adults pass around a bottle of white wine labeled *Muscat de Kelibia,* which makes them roar with laughter for some reason. She digs her hands into bowls of little red jujube fruits and dates, popping them in her mouth.

She tries to swallow the little fruit but feels it still in her throat. She tries swallowing a few more times, still feeling the blockage. Anna wheezes and coughs, and suddenly she is transported back to that winter in Brooklyn when she dreamt about the perfect Nativity costume, when her asthma nearly sent her to heaven. After several months, was she about to relapse?

"Anna, are you okay?" Giuseppina asks.

Anna tries drinking water but has to spit it out because she can't swallow. Zio Leonardo and Zia Rosa notice at this point, and they spring into action. Zia Rosa sprints for the kitchen, while Zio Leonardo leaps to his feet and wraps his arms around her diaphragm, though Anna's real fear is that her choking could trigger an asthma attack. She tries mouthing this, but he does not understand. He pounds on her back, knocking over glasses of wine and bowls of food, staining the imported tablecloths. Antonio and Giuseppina both make the sign of the cross. She imagines her choking triggering an asthma attack, and which of them would know what to do for her? Anna is fighting for every breath, using all her strength to make the thin stream of air pass through, like a straw. Her face feels hot as the blood rushes to it.

"Anna, your face is turning purple!" Zio Leonardo gasps.

Zia Rosa returns from the kitchen with the syringe and adrenalin solution, panting, unfolding the handwritten instructions Mamma had left for her in the event of an emergency.

And suddenly, when Anna thinks she has passed the point of no return, she spits out the jujube fruit, and a stream of air relieves her. Anna heaves in breath. The asthma attack never comes. Slowly, her throat opens, and by the time she looks up again the dinner table is a mess with her food scattered and her drink spilled. Fatma pours her a cup of hot mint tea and has her lay on the divan, propped up by a pillow. When Anna assures them that she is okay, and she thanks Leonardo for helping, the adults cautiously return to their meal, though each of them keep an eye on her.

"I don't need the syringe," she says for the first time. *I don't need the syringe.*

18. FLAMINGOS

After Antonio gives up on being stubborn and eats his fill and after the servants have begun washing the dishes, Zio Pietro nudges him, sloshing a glass of wine. "Why don't you children go out and play? The adults have business to discuss. He downs his Muscat de Kelibia.

They are sitting in the courtyard, and the square of sky has rusted deep red. The orange trees toss and twist in the breeze. Antonio does not leave his chair.

"I would like to stay here, Zio Pietro, so I can discuss business with the adults."

Zio Pietro puts a hand on the back of Antonio's neck. "Antonio, when adults say they are going to talk business, what they really mean is for the children to leave them alone while they get happy on wine."

Antonio frowns. "So, you're not discussing business?"

"Didn't I make it clear?"

"Then the business questions will go unanswered?"

"There never was any business to discuss. *Bedda matri*, you are so serious for such a young boy. Go, relax, play. Enjoy your youth."

Antonio finally stands up and leaves the adults to themselves, happy at least to be out of the mansion. What is the use in having a ten-bedroom mansion, especially since it sits completely empty half the day and only half-empty at night? In Sicily, there were only two groups of people who kept mansions like this—fading aristocrats wasting away in excess until the last of their family fortune dried up and Black Hand mafia captains. The bigger the house, the bigger the target.

Antonio, his cousins, and Anna leave the courtyard while the adults continue to drink and laugh. Anna has brought a blanket with her, which she drapes over her shoulders against the coolness of the coming nightfall. She pulls him around the corner of the estate wall, where nobody can see them.

"Let's go exploring," Anna says. "I know a fun spot we can go, down by the mudflat."

"I'm not much of an explorer," Antonio mumbles, plunging his hands into his pockets. "Also, I don't want to get my clothes dirty."

"Oh please," Anna grabs him by the elbow and pulls. "*Mamma mia!*"

Antonio wonders if Papà would approve of such a thing. Back in Sicily, the streets were far too dangerous for exploring. He keeps his guard up, wondering what Anna's angle is.

Together, they slip outside the turquoise carriage gates of the farm. The winter air is damp and cool, and the earliest hint of night brushes the western hills. He spots the mudflat near Lac de Tunis, which before was dry, is now flush and tossing with dark waves. The water is crowded with ducks and teal and other waterfowl who have migrated south for the winter. Flamingos flap their wings in the water, bathing themselves.

Anna leads him to the far side of the mudflat, away from the outhouse, where the smell of sewage gives way to the smell of olives. The ancient olive trees have twisted trunks wide as a house, resisting the wind for perhaps a thousand years, carpeting the ground in dusty laurels.

"We are now entering the magical forest of Annaland," Anna announces. "Watch out for the elves. They live at the base of the olive trees and don't like to be disturbed."

"Elves? What are you talking about now?" Antonio asks.

"And here are the ruins of the ancient castle of DiNicola, cursed by the wicked witch herself."

Antonio cranes his neck to see a colossus of stone arches running through the olive trees—an ancient aqueduct. It reminds him of the ancient Roman ruins in his hometown.

He follows Anna to the edge of the Lac de Tunis, where Anna kicks her shoes off, lifts the ruffles of her roughly-sewn flamenco dress, and wades barefoot into the mudflat. She looks silly, standing there in her sheepskin vest and her red sash, her dress dark with mud.

"Come on," Anna urges him.

Antonio remains at the water's edge.

"I can't. I'd get mud all over my pants. Besides, we shouldn't be out here anyway," Antonio says. "It's not right to be sneaking out and following each other."

"I'm not following you. You're not that interesting," she laughs, and Antonio is not sure if she is joking. He does not approve of her humor, in any case. A person should always be honest and say what is right. Joking is reserved for children. Eventually, Anna wades back to the shoreline and sits at the base of an olive tree.

"So why did you take me here?" Antonio asks. "Or do I even want to know?"

"If I told you why, you'd probably think it's overly dramatic," she says, and Antonio can hear a tremor of anxiety in her voice.

At hearing her uncertainty, Antonio drops his defenses and takes a seat next to her under the olive tree.

"I wouldn't think it's dramatic. You're the opposite of dramatic; you're, you're—"

Anna tilts her head as he searches for the correct word. "Dignified."

"Me? Dignified?" She throws her head back and laughs. "You have me in stitches. What high praise from the master barber," she says, pulling her blanket about herself. "Here's why I came," and she pulls a device from her blanket—a glass syringe with a needle. Antonio grimaces and fights the urge to draw back from the needle.

"What are you doing with that thing? Nothing unlawful, I hope?"

"It's for my asthma treatment, dummy. But the thing is, I've been in Tunisia a few months now and haven't had a single asthma attack. I can run the hundred-meter dash and climb trees and shout and my breathing is perfectly fine. Maybe it's something about this country, its warmth, but I think I'm healed. That's why I'm throwing this syringe into the lake."

Antonio rolls his eyes. He should have agreed with

her earlier. She was—is—dramatic. All the time. But he notices her eyes scanning his face intently, searching for a sign of judgement, so Antonio forces himself to smile.

"It's always made me feel like a burden," Anna says. "My whole life, other people have taken care of me, and you know what? I'd rather just cut the safety net entirely—just me against the world. If it meant I wouldn't have to watch Mamma dump out her coin purse for my medicine. I hate it, and I'm ready for a change."

"Be careful what you wish for," Antonio says. "You know what they say in Sicilian, *cu lassa u vecchiu cu u novu, sa chi lassa ma nun sa chi trova*—change isn't always a good thing."

"*Se vogliamo che tutto rimanga com'è, bisogna che tutto cambi*," Anna shoots back with another proverb. "If we want everything to stay the same, everything needs to change."

Antonio sighs. Surely, Anna does not know the hard truths of life, as he does. Surely, she has been too shielded by the novelty of America. Antonio imagines her growing up in America with her skyscrapers and monumental bridges, her museums and libraries. Meanwhile, Antonio was growing up watching the Salvia family tormented by the Black Hand mafia, crops burning, houses planted with bombs. Anna does not know that without strong traditions, everything falls apart. But he does not blame her, either.

"Why don't you hang onto the syringe for now?" he says. "Your family paid good money for it."

"Fair enough," Anna finally sets the syringe on the roots of the olive tree.

The wind rustles the leaves, and Antonio sees a few flamingos squawking in the flush mudflat, shaking out their feathers. While he is watching, he feels a sudden soft weight in his shoulder. He freezes. Nobody has ever held onto him like this, not since Mamma back in Sicily. He balances on the roots of the olive tree, rigid, while Anna nestles her flawlessly curled bob into his shoulder. What would Zio Pietro think? What would Mamma think? Antonio is not sure if he is old enough to be doing this, or if this is what Father Vittorio meant when he prayed for the Lord to deliver him from temptation.

"That is a fine dress," Antonio tries to change the subject, pointing to the maroon cotton folded around her ankles.

"I made it," Anna says. "My Zia Rosa has been giving me lessons on stitching, pattern-making, all kinds of things. One day I want to work as a dressmaker."

"What kinds of dresses?"

He watches Anna ponder it for a few seconds.

"Wedding dresses," she finally says, "because they don't have to be practical like work clothes. They only have to be beautiful."

Antonio turns around and glances at Zia Rosa's mansion, with all its intricately carved pillars and colorful tiles.

"You know, your Zia Rosa lives like royalty," he says, "and you would be the sole heir to inherit her fortune. You'd never have to work a day in your life if you didn't want to. Yet you still want to become a wedding dress designer?"

"I'm not like Zia Rosa," Anna shakes her head. "She lounges on the divan all day reading romance novels while her servants wait on her. She's a burden to them. I'm tired of being a burden. My whole life, I've always been the sickly one of my siblings, always falling ill, always watching my parents stretch their budget thin to afford my medicine. I hate it."

"So that is why you work?" Antonio asks. "Because you feel guilty?"

Anna does not reply. She stares at the mudflat, reflecting.

"I think life is happier when we work for ambition," Antonio says. "Not guilt."

"What about you, Antonio? What are your dreams?" she says it casually, with no indication that she is leaning on him with her full weight, her full warmth.

"Dreams are for sleepers," Antonio feels the smooth skin over his upper lip, shaved away without his papà's guidance.

"What about your family barber shop?" Anna asks. "You were going to buy back your papà's barber shop, right?"

Antonio wonders why she doesn't talk with a Sicilian accent. She was raised in a household with two Sicilian parents, was she not? Then why doesn't she talk like a proper Sicilian? Is that how Americans talk?

"My papà is not coming back to Sicily," Antonio says. "There is no barber shop anymore."

Anna scoffs. "You can just adapt," she says.

He's caught off guard. "Adapt?"

"You can still start your own barber shop, but the shop doesn't have to be in Sicily. It can be anywhere, maybe even here in Tunis. You shouldn't be so set on one idea."

"That sounds disloyal," he grumbles.

"Those who dig their heels dig their graves," Anna says with a smirk.

"Digging your grave? Is that what they do in Brooklyn?" Antonio turns to her, and she is looking up at him, her eyes searching his face once more—he does not know what she is searching for.

"Just promise me you will keep dreaming," she says softly.

"Fair enough."

Antonio does not look away from her. Their noses are almost brushing—separated by a hair's width—and Anna continues to search for something in his face, her brow knitting and unknitting, and he graciously allows her to continue her search. Antonio counts one, two, three, four, five. They both exhale.

It all happens so fast. A warm palm on his jaw. His lips change shape to fit hers, just a touch. Antonio counts one, two, three. They both exhale and part, and afterwards Antonio cannot even bring himself to look at her. *What have we done?* He wonders. *Will we have to get married now? Do I need to write Mamma and ask her for permission to see Anna again? Do I need to speak to her aunt and uncle? Ask for their approval?*

They sit at the roots of the olive trees and watch the sun set over the hills. The red sun throws color on the distant medieval walls of Tunis, where the domes and spires of the mosques watch over the flamingo-crowded mudflats. Antonio flinches as the flamingo colony erupts into flight, and he presses his palms to his ears as the rush of rose feathers overtakes him, ascending toward heaven.

19. NOT FROM BROOKLYN

Shortly after sunset, Anna already feels the cloud of shame weigh down on her. The magic of the trees and the evening and the birds, combined with the elation of not needing her syringe, and Antonio being so sweet to her, it all melted together into a lovely hot mess that carried her away. She took it too far. In the moment, she remembers thinking that a quick little kiss was okay. After all, in Brooklyn Anna would hear so many stories of romance from the older girls at school. Practically all the teenage girls in Brooklyn had boyfriends—the dance halls were full of couples twirling each other in circles, and the pier at Coney Island was crowded with teenagers at sunset. But what passes in Brooklyn does not pass in Sicily, and what passes in Sicily does not pass in Tunis. And Anna is from all of those places and none of those places at the same time.

She can tell that concerns of a similar vein are snaking through Antonio's mind by the way he sits petrified, staring at the birds.

"You look ill," Anna finally says.

A few seconds pass before Antonio replies, "I've never done that before."

"What? You've never kissed anyone before?"

"I mean, I've kissed my relatives. But that was just on the cheeks."

"Well, of course. We all kiss our relatives on the cheeks."

"But this was different."

"Maybe we shouldn't do it again," Anna mutters. "It felt like too much of a good thing, like eating too many sweets. I feel guilty somehow."

Antonio nods thoughtfully. "Me too."

"I'm sorry," Anna says.

"No, no. Don't apologize," He raises his voice. "It wasn't your fault."

"So, you liked it?"

"Should I?"

"I think so, but also at the same time, no."

"We should get back to the house," Antonio stands and dusts off his trousers. "Zio Pietro will be wondering where we are."

The world roars with squawking ducks. The earth is soft with mud and carved with fresh rivulets. Anna gathers her blanket about herself and leads Antonio back around the mudflat, to the estate.

20. SCATTERED AND SOWN

Dear Mamma,

Could you tell me the story of how you first met Papà? I am not asking for any reason in particular; I am just wondering how love works. How do you know when you are supposed to marry someone? I am asking for a friend. My friend also wants to know when it is okay to kiss someone. Not that anything has happened. I am just wondering. I wonder about many things.

Love, Antonio

Sweet Antonio,

Your Papà and I were second cousins who grew up on the same street in Partinico. I've known your Papà since I was a crawling baby, and our parents encouraged us to play with each other at family gatherings. We were destined for marriage. Back then, my son, we did not question our parents because marriage was a matter of survival. Someone had to keep the barber shop going, or else our family would starve, and so they could not take any risks with the marriage. They needed to trust that the next generation would be dedicated to the family. Without that, everything crumbles.

Our parents betrothed us to marriage at the age of fourteen, and by age eighteen our families saved enough money for the dowry, which consisted of the barber shop, a house, and a chest full of linens—far more than most received. I was very happy for the stability of a roof and an income. We married in 1894, toward the end of the famine. Our neighbors were sick with hunger, and we did not have any food to serve at our wedding. It was a precious and painful year.

You are right to ask me about marriage, Antonio, for that is always the job of the mamma. You are fourteen, and it is time you are betrothed. I know that you will have a more difficult time than I did, because our family is now flung across the globe, but do not worry. I will take care of everything. I will write to your Zio Pietro to possibly arrange something with your cousin Giuseppina. The Palazzolos are a strong family, despite all the rumors surrounding them. It is true the Duke banished them from Sicily, but they were not to blame.

Love, Mamma

Antonio sets down the letter. He certainly believes in the importance of tradition, and he prays every night for God to make him the best son he can be and to always do what his family needs of him. A year ago, he would have happily betrothed himself to Giuseppina—if that is what Mamma wanted—trusting that his family knew what was best for him, trusting that he was destined for a virtuous life.

But for years now, every answer he has received begs a hundred new questions. At what age will he finally know what his life is for? A creeping feeling grows in his chest. He recognizes it as the same feeling he got when he first decided to shave, to give up on the tradition of his papà teaching him. He certainly benefited from giving up the tradition. Now, the hair on his lip has grown back thicker, and now Antonio sports a consistent dark fuzz, thick enough for him to carefully etch out the thinnest sliver of a pencil mustache, and he is proud of it. Not even his cousins Pete and Vince can grow such a fine mustache.

He thinks of Anna. What is that proverb she always says? *Those who dig their heels dig their graves.* He wonders if she is right. The world has changed since Mamma's time—metal boats cross the Atlantic in a matter of days, electric lightbulbs glint in every window. People no longer have use for mule carts but instead drive automobiles and motorized bicycles. Perhaps the same transformation is happening to marriages.

Antonio dwells on this during Mass when the priest discusses the parable of the sower from the Book of Matthew, where a farmer scatters seeds on rocky ground and fertile soil. Just like the seeds in the story, Antonio realizes his own family is scattered and sown, except this time across America, Italy, and Tunisia. Is he the seed that lands on fertile ground, that takes root and flowers? Or is he the seed that lands on the gravel, that does not lay down roots, and is lost to the wilderness?

PART 3

JULY 1914

21. POLICE BATON

Anna wakes before sunrise to the sound of Zio Leonardo slamming cabinets in the kitchen. Unable to close her eyes and return to her dream, she hobbles into the kitchen, pulling her embroidered satin bathrobe about her.

"I've woken you, haven't I?" Zio Leonardo grunts as he hands her a tiny cup and saucer of Turkish coffee. "Since you're already awake, why don't you help me with the goats this morning?"

Once they reach the pasture, Zio Leonardo's rich baritone fills the air with the operatic strains of a romantic aria. The goats *maaaaa maaaaa* in response, a chorus of voices stirring up a cloud of dust as Zio Leonardo snaps his reed and the animals scurry up the dirt road toward the medieval gates of Tunis.

Trails of smoke drift from rooftops toward the sky as the pungent scents of myriad breakfasts fill the air. Quiet save for the garbage carts and the milk men, the streets feel eerily empty this early in the morning, especially when they reach the sleepy souk. Anna has only been in the souk when the narrow corridors were nearly impassable with shoppers jockeying for space, shouting their orders, bargaining with vendors. Now, with only two or three merchants unloading spice sacks from their carts, it seems lonely.

Zio Leonardo pauses at a doorway, blows his horn, and waits. A woman peers out the window, rubs the sleep from her eyes, and bids him good morning. Moments later, the courtyard gates swing open, and Zio Leonardo leads his flock in, squats down and grips one of his goats' udders to fill the woman's terracotta jugs with frothy goat milk. As they chat in Arabic, Anna tries to follow along.

"Have you heard the news?" the woman asks.

"What news, Shayma?"

"They're fighting again in Europe."

"That's not news," Zio Leonardo laughs, grunting as he bends down to milk the next goat. "They always find something to fight over, and I always try to keep out of their way."

"This time is different," Shayma says, and holds a French newspaper out to him.

"Germany declares war on France!" Anna gasps as she deciphers the headline.

Taking the paper in hand, Zio Leonardo lets out a low whistle and takes off his hat as if at a funeral. "So, everyone is at war with everyone now. Serbia against Austria. Austria against Russia. Russia against Germany." He shakes his head. "And now this."

"Everyone except Italy, *inshallah*," Shayma says, and then she rattles off a string of words so fast Anna cannot translate them, but she does not have to. Anna can understand the intention from her somber tone, as if to say *Your family had better watch yourselves—you do not know what side Italy will take in the war. We might soon be enemies.*

Shayma carries the milk jugs into her apartment and shuts the door, leaving them in the courtyard alone. Anna watches her uncle, who is still staring at the newspaper.

"You look shocked, Zio Leonardo."

He looks up and suddenly snaps his reed to get the goats moving. But instead of going to the next house, he steers them back toward the gate.

"Are we heading home already?"

"Shush, Anna. Keep your head down. We are done for today."

They exit the ancient gates, where the French police officer stands in his starched, blue uniform, following them with his gaze. Anna notices the gun holstered at his side. She shivers and hurries after her uncle, staying in his shadow.

"Have you ever heard of the Jellaz Affair?" Zio Leonardo asks as they walk into the countryside.

"No."

"Well, I suppose it is time I told you. It might help you make sense of the political situation. A few months before you arrived in Tunisia, the French administration made plans to seize Tunis's beloved Jellaz Cemetery for the burials of French colonizers. The symbolism was clear—the French administration wanted to erase Tunisia's history. Thousands of Tunisian protestors showed up to defend the cemetery. Many were arrested, some were wounded, others were shot. By the next morning many Tunisians lay dead, and I remember seeing the young men with so much left unaccomplished, lying on the pavement."

Zio Leonardo clears his throat, composes himself, and continues.

"Shortly after that, an Italian tram driver accidentally ran over a Tunisian citizen at Bab Souika, and that is when the people really started to fight back. There was a city-wide boycott of the tramway and even more arrests. Then riots broke out. In the melee, a stray bullet even struck Pietro's barber shop, shattering his front windows. A nasty affair."

Anna remembers hearing a similar story back in Brooklyn when a parade of women, each of them wearing white dresses that Anna had marveled at, marched through Manhattan with signs saying *New York Women Demand the Right to Vote, Vote Yes on Suffrage, We Protest Because We Are Ignored.* "But did the Tunisians have any other choice?" she asks.

"How could you say that?"

"The French were not listening," Anna says as if it's obvious, "so the Tunisians had no other way to make themselves heard."

"You are young and naïve, my dear Anna. Try telling that to Pietro, who nearly lost his business. If those riots went any further, God forbid, the Palazzolos might not be here. These protests always start with noble intentions, but sometimes they erupt into violence and killing, and us Sicilians are always caught in the middle. The French administration doesn't like us, you see, because we outnumber the French in Tunis. We threaten their grip on the colony, and so they make us do things like registering for French citizenship. Always remember *du' su' i putenti, cu avi assà e cu nun avi nenti*—there are two types of power, those who own too much and those who don't own a thing."

Anna is not sure if she agrees. As they approach home and Zio Leonardo's mansion rises over the horizon, she wonders how he can be a victim. His home is staffed by Tunisian servants who scramble to prepare his food, do his laundry, keep his house clean, and wait on his wife hand and foot. Anna thinks of Fatma, the cook, who has lived on the property for years, never able to start her own family, only allowed to leave on the weekends. How can that be right?

She steps around a pothole in the dusty road. "What would happen if Italy and France take opposite sides in the war?"

"Then it could become unsafe for us here," he says. "We might have to send you back to Brooklyn before the storm breaks."

Before the storm breaks. What would it mean for the storm to break over the heads of the Sicilians in Tunis? When they arrive back at the farm with the goats bustling and bleating around them, all Anna can think about is how exposed and vulnerable their estate is, a lone speck on the massive coastal plain. She imagines a squad of French police officers sweeping across the plain on horseback, arresting all the Sicilians in their wake and carting them off to a prison camp.

Zio Leonardo has a rifle that he uses to put down sick goats, but it would be useless against the French colonial authorities. She shivers and thinks of the bullet that shattered Pietro's barber shop window. And she thinks of Antonio fighting off the police with his broom. She takes in a deep breath and then closes the turquoise shutters over the iron grating and locks the great carriage doors against the looming threat.

22: CRYSTAL PIN

One day while Giuseppina is eating spaghetti, Antonio notices her hair is pinned up in a pompadour; it shines with a mysterious product smelling of lavender. He can tell exactly when Zio Pietro notices too.

"You went to the French salon!" Zio Pietro slams his fist on the table, making the dishes shake.

"He does a far better job than you," Giuseppina sneers.

"The French do not have a monopoly on style," Zio Pietro rants, glaring at the salon across the street. "Pretentious. It's not just good enough for him to be an honest barber. He has to be a *coiffeur*. Yes, he trained in Paris. Yes, he knows the styles preferred by the noblewomen. But I can cut a woman's hair just as well."

Zio Pietro doesn't speak to his daughter for an entire day, after which Antonio takes care to sit on Giuseppina's side of the table for dinner. She is right. Antonio has watched Zio Pietro style Giuseppina hair as if it is as foreign to Zio Pietro as the streets of Paris. He brushes her hair like he is trying to tame a horse's mane, like something to be reined in, and she winces as the brush scrapes and pulls. By the time he finishes, the brush is always tangled with dark tufts and Guiseppina's eyes are always glistening with tears.

The next Sunday morning, with only a few hours to go until Mass, Zio Pietro calls Giuseppina down to style her hair. She stomps down the stairs and drops into the barber's chair, arms crossed, pouting. Zio Pietro observes his scissors. He pauses, knits his brow, and sighs.

"Antonio, why don't you style Giuseppina's hair today. You know the Marcel style, yes?"

"Me?" Antonio asks.

He remembers the horror of snipping off Anna's bangs. He sees his reflection in the scissors—like a frightened lamb being led to slaughter. Pinching the scissors, Antonio holds them to Giuseppina's head. He had been promoted from sweeping floors, even assisted Zio Pietro with a few haircuts, but never had Zio Pietro asked him to cut Giuseppina's hair. His hand quakes with fear at the thought of failure. Zio Pietro looks on, arms crossed, judging his technique. Giuseppina's back rigid. She doesn't move a muscle. Antonio can barely imagine how tense she must be.

Gripping the spray bottle in a shaky hand, Antonio presses the rubber bladder and spritzes her dark hair until damp. A sheen settles on it. *Snip.* The first curl feather-floats to the floor. *Snip. Snip. Snip.* He does not cut straight but rather at an angle so he can control the length of the trim, just like Zio Pietro taught him. When her hair reaches shoulder-length, he ties it at the nape of her neck and pins it above her ear with a crystal hair pin. Zio Pietro grumbles.

When Antonio finishes with the scissors, he draws the curling iron from its holster; its heat rolls sweat beads down his arm. He curls the waves tight, clipping and unclipping the iron on the thick hair. After the right half of Giuseppina's head is styled, Antonio takes a step back. He hasn't done a terrible job. Giuseppina curls the smallest grin, either entertained with Antonio's terror or happy with his results. He cracks his knuckles and dives back into his work, his hands stronger and steadier with each turn of the iron. After thirty minutes, he concludes with the final touch—the single curl that is left to bounce against her right temple.

"It's perfect," Pete whispers from the corner and sets down his broom.

Giuseppina studies herself in the mirror from various angles, breathing a sigh of relief and finally relaxing in her chair. Zio Pietro exhales roughly out his nostrils, gives a single nod, and croaks, "You have surpassed me." And he walks out the front door of the shop, still wearing his white coat.

23. MIRIAM SARFATI

The crowd at Souk El Grana swells with shoppers as Anna hurries to keep up with Giuseppina, Zia Rosa, and Fatma. Zia Rosa, with her nerve difficulties, clings to Fatma, who adjusts the cream cotton cloth around her head. Anna has noticed the other Tunisian women wearing something similar.

"What is this called, Fatma?" Anna asks, pointing to her garment.

"This? This is a sefseri," Fatma says.

Anna admires the drapery of the garment, the way it falls into fashionable folds around her waist. Anna imagines the cream cotton would be thin and breezy—perfect for reflecting the pounding Tunisian sun.

As they peruse the market booths at Souk El Grana, Anna marvels at the fiery spectrum of spices—cayenne, cumin, cardamom—piled in reed baskets, wedding into an aroma strong enough to make her sneeze. Because of the war in Europe, the prices of food have doubled, and Anna must carry a ration book with her, expending her food stamps for limited amounts of sugar, flour, and oil. Anna watches Giuseppina fill a basket with bags of chickpeas, harissa jars, and still-firm apricots.

"You seem awful hungry," Anna tells Giuseppina, pointing at her baskets of food. "Are you opening a restaurant?"

"I'm planning our meals for the week. The food rationing from the war doesn't make it any easier."

"Our meals?"

"Yes, my papà and I do all the cooking for my brothers and, of course, Antonio."

"Sounds tiresome," Anna says.

In Anna's house, the meals are prepared by Fatma and the various servants who rush about the kitchen. The thought makes Anna feel pampered, a word she never thought she'd use to describe herself.

"It's not tiresome. I'm happy to cook with my papà," Giuseppina says as she selects foods. "During the day I work as the cashier in the barber shop, and things are so hectic that I rarely have time to breathe. Cooking with Papà is calming, like prayer. And Antonio always compliments my food."

"You're not Antonio's servant," Anna scoffs. "And Antonio can cook for himself, anyway."

Anna imagines Giuseppina and Antonio working all day in the barber shop together, then sitting at the dinner table, beaming at each other, and the thought lights a fire in her chest. What does Antonio see in Giuseppina? Does he like that Giuseppina would happily spend all her days scrubbing dishes for him? Anna would retch at such a life, and she cannot fathom why Giuseppina would equate it to prayer. Perhaps Giuseppina is right, perhaps Anna has become spoiled, despite all her efforts to fight against it. She frowns and adjusts her dress so that it covers more of her legs, suddenly feeling exposed.

"Your zia is trying to buy your love, you know," Giuseppina points at the bags of clothes that Anna lugs behind her.

Anna remembers the days when she felt pangs of longing for the blue satin of the Virgin Mary's robe, but now Zia Rosa buys her whatever she wants. At the estate, her wardrobe is stuffed with flower-printed dresses. Anna stands taller than Zia Rosa now and wears the latest Brooklyn fashions—a straw cloche hat shaped like a bell, white gloves, a loose, flower-printed dress that ends just below the knee, revealing her calves and ankles and her fashionable pumps, which Zia Rosa *tsked* at but purchased anyway. And that is how Anna knows, sure as ever, that she has become spoiled. The realization is like a hot coal in her chest. How could she allow this to happen to herself?

While Anna fumes, they walk further into the market, and she sees the booths displaying cream veils, pointed cloth shoes, cylindrical red caps, and necklaces strung with gold coins. They stop at a booth walled off by hanging tapestries, where a family is hard at work selling the fine garments.

Zia Rosa and Giuseppina continue to the next booth, leaving Anna alone with Fatma and the vendors. Fatma smiles at the family and embraces the mother in a hug, and the two chat in Arabic while Anna listens. Anna marvels at the garments worn by Fatma's friend—baggy pants bound at the ankle, covered in swirling floral designs. Anna has never seen a woman in Tunis wear pants before.

She wears a cone-shaped head covering tied off with a white cloth around her chin, and the cloth continues to fall past her shoulders like a cape.

"Anna, meet Miriam Sarfati," Fatma says. "She makes some of the finest garments in Tunis."

"I am trying to, at least," Miriam says. "A wealthy patron from Djerba, the Memmi family, has commissioned a wedding shawl. The project is more hours than I thought, and I am worried I will miss the deadline."

Miriam sits at a loom, her fingers expertly weaving and cutting different strands of fabric.

"You're designing a wedding shawl?" Anna says, her heart racing.

"Would you like to take a look at it?"

"Please!" Anna bounces excitedly on her toes as Miriam unfurls a shawl of rich gold brocade. Anna's mouth drops open. The design is so complex, so intricate, it takes Anna's breath away. "This must have taken months of work! Perhaps you could use some help?" Anna blurts out the words before she can think twice. "I'm good with fashion. I promise! Zia Rosa and Fatma can vouch for me."

Miriam Sarfati smiles at Anna's enthusiastic babbling, entertained. "I suppose I could use an apprentice," she says, sounding unsure. "Although you must do exactly as I say. This fabric is extremely expensive, and the wedding is fast approaching."

"Of course," Anna beams. "I'd love to be your apprentice."

"Be warned, you will have to work quickly," Miriam says.

Anna smiles. "A stitch in time saves nine."

"You're going to have to make more than nine stitches."

"It's just a proverb," Anna shrugs. "Something they say in America. Never mind."

"Will I regret this?" Miriam mutters to Fatma.

"Anna is very eager," Fatma shrugs. "She will work herself to the bone if you ask her."

And so it is settled, and Anna marches home from Souk El Grana, fueled with enough pride to generate her own glowing halo. She is an apprentice now! She has a purpose and will truly learn how to sew. She imagines the weeks ahead, working alongside Miriam Sarfati, learning to make the most elaborate golden garments for the wealthy families of Tunis. *From now on*, she thinks smugly, *no one will dare call me spoiled.*

24. TINTING THE SHOP BRONZE

Giuseppina's haircuts are written into the schedule every four weeks, and Zio Pietro often leaves Antonio alone with her after the shop closes. It is a routine now. Antonio unfurls the cape about her. Spritzes her hair until the damp curls shine. *Snip, snip.* Tendrils of hair float to the floor one by one until a bird's nest accumulates on the tiles.

Surely Mamma and Zio Pietro planned these regular haircuts. Planned leaving them alone together. Zio Pietro probably wrote Mamma regularly, giddily describing how their two children were inseparable.

During Giuseppina's haircuts, Antonio glances over his shoulder at Zio Pietro's wedding photograph on the wall. He feels the bride and groom staring at him as he snips Giuseppina's hair. He tries to picture the wedding photograph with his face and Giuseppina's face inserted, wondering what that might look like.

One night he is cutting her hair, and the streets outside burn scarlet as the sun slumps over the Mediterranean, dipping under the sea until the coiled filaments of the lightbulbs are their sole light source, tinting the shop bronze. The windows are open, and a hot summer wind flaps the corners of the newspapers. ITALIAN ARMY ADVANCES AGAINST AUSTRIA-HUNGARY, the headline reads, BATTLES RAGE IN THE ALPS. The war in Europe feels so far away from this little barber shop on the Tunisian coast. If not for the food rations and the endless columns of French soldiers marching in the streets, Antonio could have pretended that for a moment that everyone in Europe lived in harmony.

"Look how shaggy I am," Antonio touches his face in the mirror. "My hair covers my ears. Perhaps I am the one in need of a haircut."

"I can arrange that," Giuseppina says. "Let's trade places."

His stomach churns, but he relents. He sits on the chair, and she throws the cape about him, fastening it at his neck.

"I have never actually cut hair before, you know. Papà never let me. But now that I try it, I find it is far easier than you make it out to be, cousin Antonio."

While she snips, his hair falls away. For the first time in a month, he feels air on the back of his neck. He feels lighter, cooler.

Giuseppina walks to the ice box in the corner and pulls out a lemon soda for herself.

"Do you want one?" she asks.

He nods.

She brings just the one bottle. She pops open the cap and sips, then hands it to Antonio. He presses his lips to it. The glass is beaded with frost, and the sour lemon makes his mouth pucker. The bubbles rush straight to his stomach. The drink is a relief from the hot summer wind blowing in from the empty boulevard.

"Was this your mamma's?" he points to the crystal pin in her hair.

"Maria Minore," she nods.

"She is certainly with the angels now," Antonio passes her the bottle.

"You might think I am imagining things," Giuseppina says, "but sometimes when I'm alone, I feel her sitting in the room with me. I can still picture her face in my mind, though I'm not sure if it is a memory or a dream."

Again, Antonio glances at the wedding photograph of Zio Pietro and Maria Minore that hangs on the wall. The bride and groom in the photograph stare back.

Giuseppina snips some more with the scissors, and then stops. Antonio can tell she is nervous by her twitching movements.

"Were your mamma and papà cousins, Antonio?" Giuseppina asks slowly.

Antonio avoids eye contact. "They were"

"And their families arranged for them to be married?"

"They did it to keep the family strong. I know what you are thinking, cousin Giuseppina," Antonio says, suddenly realizing the eagerness in Giuseppina's eyes, the speed with which she fetched him the lemon soda, how her hands shook with excitement when she held the scissors to his hair.

The setting sun glints through the window and casts a glare on Zio Pietro's wedding photograph, and Antonio wonders if the photograph was placed there intentionally.

"I sometimes wonder if I could ever be as brave as your parents," Giuseppina says. "They married each other for their family. Do you believe that, cousin Antonio? That everything we do must be for the family?"

Antonio wants to say yes, but for some reason he cannot. *You can just adapt,* he hears Anna laughing at him in his head, *you shouldn't be so set on one idea.*

"Antonio?" Giuseppina sets a hand on his shoulder.

"This bottle is empty," he shrugs away from her hand, trying to change the subject. "We should throw it out."

A flicker of recognition crosses Giuseppina's eyes, and Antonio knows that she picks up on his hesitancy.

"Maybe we can talk about it another time," he says, looking away. "I…I don't know how I feel about that yet."

"Okay," she says, her voice almost a whisper. She takes the bottle from him and drops it into the trash. Together, they sweep the remaining hair from the floor and walk upstairs to the apartment. In silence.

25. HAMMAM

A wave of humidity, saturated with the perfume of tart pomegranate, blows Anna's hair back as she follows Giuseppina, Zia Rosa, and Fatma inside the hammam. She cranes her neck at the domed ceiling to marvel at the tile designs of emerald flowers and red starbursts. A fountain bubbles in the center of the hall, where women in towels scrub themselves. Already, Anna feels the beads of water condensing on her forehead.

"Come change into your fouta," Fatma ushers them into a side room, where she presses folded towels into their hands.

After they are changed, Fatma and Zia Rosa lead them through a maze of cramped steam rooms until they reach the innermost room, and Fatma has them sit on the blue-tile benches with their towels. Anna can feel her pores opening as she sweats. A party of mothers and daughters sit on the opposite bench, gossiping in Arabic, occasionally shooting glances at Anna when they hear her foreign accent. They fill the steam room with chatter and laughter. Fatma and Zia Rosa join in the conversation, beaming, while Anna and Giuseppina huddle in the corner. After almost two years in Tunis, Anna can understand their Arabic if she leans forward and listens intently.

"Giuseppina," Zia Rosa says. "The girls over here are gossiping about boys. Tell them about that one boy—you know, the fancy boy at the barber shop who wears the pomade in his hair. What is he called?"

Giuseppina blushes and hides her smile. "Antonio," she says.

Anna's stomach wobbles as the name leaves Giuseppina's lips. Meanwhile, the Tunisian girls erupt into giggles.

"He's very clean," Giuseppina continues. "He doesn't smoke. He always combs his hair. And he makes me feel connected to my family back in Sicily. I'm not allowed to visit my aunts and uncles and cousins, you see, so I like how Antonio brings a little bit of Sicily with him."

"You fancy him?" Anna asks.

Giuseppina's blushing face could have been powdered with rouge.

"Papà leaves us alone in the evenings for haircuts," she says. "Antonio's mamma writes me all the time and says she is happy for me."

Anna feels the heat rush to her face, perhaps from the steam in the bath house, perhaps from the ember of anger that smolders in her gut.

"No. He's your cousin," Anna says.

"Why not? Aren't your Zia Rosa and Zio Leonardo cousins?" Giuseppina asks. "Lots of people in Sicily marry their cousins."

"This isn't Sicily. You have other options."

Giuseppina's smile drops.

"I haven't upset you, have I? Are you jealous?"

"Jealous of what?" Anna crosses her arms. "Jealous of Antonio? Antonio is incapable of making any kind of decision for himself. His mamma steers him like a mule."

The steam room falls silent as her words echo. Zia Rosa and Fatma stare at her.

"That's what I like about him," Giuseppina whispers. "He's completely selfless."

Anna can't help herself. She stands up and excuses herself from the steam room, storming back to the changing room. The air is so humid that plumes of steam erupt from her nose as she fumes. Giuseppina is right to say that Antonio is selfless, but that is not something to be proud of. Anna knows that caring for others does not mean disregarding oneself, and she knows that Antonio would be happier if only he cared about himself the way Anna does.

26: WHERE WE DIFFER

After Mass ends and the priest processes down the aisle, Antonio bends onto one knee and traces the cross over his torso. He files to the baptismal font and crosses himself with holy water, then follows Zio Pietro outside into the sunlight. He spots Anna and her family exiting the church as well, and she quickly draws her lace *mantiglia* over her face, perhaps hoping he won't see her. Underneath the translucent veil, everyone can still see her bobbed hair, which she had curled earlier that week at the French salon. Antonio spots the coiffeur's handiwork from across the square.

"Anna!" he tips his hat as he approaches. "I haven't seen you around. I thought you'd vanished into thin air."

"I did," she nods. "I'm secretly a holy angel and I disappear to heaven on Tuesdays and Thursdays at ten in the morning. Just for coffee."

He laughs. "That sounds sacrilegious, but it would certainly explain some things."

They walk together down the square outside the church, under the shade of the eucalyptus trees.

"Why haven't you stopped by for your regular haircuts with Zio Pietro?" Antonio finally puts words to his thoughts.

"I don't need my hair cut short right now," Anna twirls a finger through her curls. "The weather is getting a little colder these days."

"It's July," Antonio huffs.

"Then I'm afraid we're in for a rough winter."

"If you don't like Zio Pietro's hair styling, you can say so outright. I won't be hurt."

Anna purses her lips.

"So it's not the haircuts, then. There's another reason?"

"Don't put words in my mouth."

"Anna, you're always the first to speak your mind—"

"Thanks for the compliment."

"—and I can't help but notice—"

"You took long enough."

"—that you're coming across a bit guarded," Antonio says it gently because he can tell by her crossed arms that she is feeling backed into a corner.

Anna scoffs because she cannot deny it. "I hear you and Giuseppina are betrothed," she finally says, "and if you really insist on knowing, the thought that you would marry your own cousin just because your mamma told you to makes me want to scream. I thought you were better than that. I thought you would make your own decisions."

They stop on the street corner and wait for an electric tram to pass.

"We have different definitions of love. To me, love means strengthening my family. If I marry Giuseppina, I can bring her to America, become citizens, and sponsor the rest of her family. You think of love like Romeo and Juliet, where two people run off together simply because they make each other smile."

"So you admit it, then?" Anna says.

"Admit what?"

"That I make you smile?"

Anna watches Antonio stutter, flustered.

"My mamma would always say *L' amuri è come a tussi, nun si po ammucciari*," Anna smirks. "Love is like a cough, impossible to hide."

"I can't just worry about my own feelings," he protests. "I don't know how they do things in America, but where I'm from, in Sicily—"

"I'm Sicilian too, might I remind you."

"Not in the way I am. You haven't had to suffer for it," Antonio says.

"Don't preach at me," Anna snaps. "If suffering makes someone a true Sicilian, then you've made me a Sicilian ten times over."

The words land like a slap to the face, and Antonio almost raises a hand to feel where they surely left a mark. They fall silent as two columns of khaki-clad French soldiers march past with bayonets, a reminder that the war in Europe is still raging on. After the soldiers pass, he turns to Anna.

"In Sicily, marriage isn't a personal decision," Antonio puffs out his chest as he moralizes. "It's not just about your *feelings*, you also have to think about the rest of your family."

"You think I don't know that? You think I just fall for men at the drop of a pin? I am not that kind of person."

"You misunderstand me. Anna, if you'd only listen—"

"Despite what you might think, I'm not free to marry solely for love, either. Do you think you're the only one with a family? The same pressures weigh on me as well. But despite that, I will still fight to marry the man I love. And that is where we differ."

She turns on her heel and marches down Rue al Djazira leaving Antonio on the sidewalk, wrestling with that flicker of doubt growing in his chest.

27. FRADJI SARFATI

Anna spends each day, morning until dark, at Miriam Sarfati's workshop, her hands cramping as she weaves the colored weft threads over the tightly strung loom. She wipes the sweat from her brow, glancing at the paper for reference as to which threads go where. Miriam keeps a cupboard with spools of colored thread—red, black, gold, turquoise—which she and her family have dyed themselves. With each weave, Anna pats down the yarn to make sure it is secure, then moves onto the next.

The wedding shawl reaches from head to toe, the red and gold stripes contrasting nicely. Miriam divides the shawl into a grid, and for each row they weave a different motif—diamonds, rectangles, hourglasses. Anna has never done this before, so she waits for Miriam to get started on a motif, and then Anna copies as best she can for the rest of the row.

"We're behind schedule," Miriam says. "The bride-to-be just completed her mikveh today, and the wedding is in three days. I'd appreciate it if you stayed late again to finish the next few rows. In the meantime, I'll make dinner."

"Of course," Anna says.

"You can stay for dinner if you like. I am making pkaila."

Anna nods vigorously. She loves that her work is important enough to warrant overtime. She imagines what the Memmi family will think when they see the finished product, and the thought propels her needle forward, over and over, until another row of diamonds decorates the shawl.

Miriam walks to the kitchen, leaving Anna alone at the loom while olive oil pops and sizzles and the iron smell of spinach wafts, and she realizes the shawl is all hers for the next hour. The responsibility is enough to make her sit an inch taller, to carefully watch where she loops the colored threads. When she first came to Tunis, she could barely stitch a straight line, and now her weaving has nearly caught up to her imagination.

A sudden white flash fills the room, and Anna flinches. When the light clears, Anna sees a boy lower a camera from his eye.

"Fradji! Put that contraption away," Miriam calls from the kitchen. "You will have to excuse my son, Anna."

"I'm trying to figure out the flash," he complains, angling himself in front of a carved archway, and the camera flashes again, exposing the contrast of light and shadow in the workshop. Anna takes note of his dark coils of hair that spill shoulder-length, the kippah on the crown of his head, the sprig of asphodel flowers tucked behind his ear. He is perhaps fifteen, maybe sixteen, not more than a year older than her.

"Madam," he nods at Anna, and it is the first time anyone has referred to her as a woman.

"Are you a photographer?" Anna asks. "I've never known anyone who owned their own camera."

"It's a 1912 Kodak Brownie," Fradji shrugs, holding up the camera, nothing more than a scuffed-up black box with a hole in the middle. It is the size of Zia Rosa's Bible. "I bought my first camera when I was ten. Found it in a resale shop on Rue de Paris for just one franc."

"Don't you have to be a technician to know how to use them?" Anna asks.

Fradji shrugs again. "There's a shop near the post office that processes the film. No big deal. The hardest part is properly focusing the lens and getting the lighting right."

Fradji races down the hallway and returns with an accordion folder.

"Want to see some samples?"

He presses a few black and white photographs into her hands, and Anna marvels at the collection of sepia-tone portraits. In one photograph, a woman sits in the market with a tattoo on her chin and gold coins tied to her hair, peering into the crowd curiously. In another, a man with a bushy beard and a head covering smokes shisha, his eyes weighed down with wrinkles of worry and labor. In a third, a little boy in a kippah grins about some unknown secret. All the photographs are blurred, crooked, swimming with black spots.

"I met these people in the market," Fradji explains. "It's my favorite style of photography—portraits. Everyone carries a story that is written on their face. I want to put a spotlight on the ordinary working people of Tunisia, the kind of people who are never photographed for the newspapers. People like me."

Anna continues to ask questions about Fradji's photographs, for no reason other than to see the passion in his eyes. She remembers hearing stories from her older sisters back in Brooklyn—endless debates over how to tell what a boy thought of them. They would always use the word *signals*. If he sends the right signals, then you know where his thoughts lie. Like a telegraph. Antonio was a dysfunctional telegraph, by any standards. But Fradji is far more talkative, unhooking a boundless stream-of-consciousness monologue about photography. Surely this was the signal her sisters spoke of. But how to respond? Anna racks her brain to think what her older sister Rosaria would do, and then she knows.

"Could you take a photograph of me?" she asks. "I could use a good portrait."

"I don't know," Fradji says. "Processing the film takes a long time. You won't receive it for a while."

"You can mail it to me," Anna says. "Do you have paper and pencil?"

"Of course."

Anna scrawls down the address of Zia Rosa's estate, and then adds for good measure, *Write me!* She smiles for the camera, and a white flash fills the room. And then another flash.

"Is that good?" she asks.

"Yes, perfect," Fradji smiles. "You'll get the final photographs in the mail."

28. EXTRA LOCKS

Antonio has watched and learned the rhythm of the market. On Fridays around four o'clock, the Sephardic men leave work early in preparation for Shabbat, and many stop by to get their shave in before twilight. In the summer, when the city is strung with rainbow Ramadan lanterns and the Muslim families are at home eating Iftar, the shop is particularly empty. As the summer grows old, and the olives and figs are harvested, Berber farm workers venture into the city with their extra cash, and a few stop by for haircuts.

Antonio explains these things to Zio Pietro, his uncle nods in approval.

"You pick up on these things fast, Nino, faster than I ever did. And you have done an excellent job cutting Giuseppina's hair, too. I think you are ready for some real barber work. Would you like to cut hair alongside me this Saturday? You can claim the station with the new mirror, by the window."

Zio Pietro retrieves a white barber's coat from the closet, and as Antonio buttons it, he shivers like he did when the

Bishop anointed him with sacred oil at his Confirmation, when the Holy Spirit came to rest in his soul.

On Saturday morning, when long-time customers stop by for a trim, Zio Pietro grips him by the shoulder and says, "Meet Antonio. He is my nephew, godson, and business partner." *Business partner!* Zio Pietro does not even refer to his own sons—Vince and Pete—with such high regard. Filled with pride, Antonio scrubs his workstation between each customer, spritzes himself with cologne. This is what it means to be a *business partner*.

That same morning, Leonardo Ribaudo enters the barber shop ten minutes late, an accordion strapped to his sheepskin vest. Antonio watches the man kiss Zio Pietro on both cheeks in greeting, then sit on his stool in the corner as he plays some warm-up tunes, filling the shop with musical wheezes. Antonio's customer, whose face is slathered with shaving soap, looks up from his newspaper, swaying his head to the tune.

"Terrible news about this war," Leonardo mutters to Zio Pietro while warming up his accordion. "Let's hope Italy and France fall on the side of the allies."

"You know, my cousin is a government official in Rome," Zio Pietro replies. "Vittorio Orlando, Minister of the Interior. He wrote to me that Italy received competing pacts from both France and Germany."

"Your cousin is the *Minister of the Interior*? I don't believe you."

"You never heard about that? Everyone in Partinico was talking about it when—"

"Listen," Leonardo says, "I haven't been to Partinico in ten years."

Their chatter promptly dies when a column of French soldiers wielding bayonets march past the shop window.

"I might have to request some extra locks on the door," Zio Pietro mutters. "We are so exposed. If Italy and France become enemies, my children and I might have to leave the country."

"Where would you go?"

"I can't move back to Sicily. The Grifeo family put me on their blacklist after they banished me."

"Then you would move to America."

"Me and everyone else."

"What if your sons are conscripted into the army?"

"Pete and Vince are too young for that," Zio Pietro says.

"Antonio is reaching that age, though," Leonardo says in a low voice. "He might receive the orders."

"I'd take every possible measure to avoid that," Zio Pietro says.

Antonio feels a surge of adrenaline at the thought of becoming a soldier. He sometimes admires the soldiers with their smart uniforms and medals. They are defending their country, are they not? What could be more admirable?

The bell rings over the door as the newspaper boy delivers the daily paper. Zio Pietro takes one look at the headline.

"Bedda matri!" he cries.

The headline is in French, and Antonio can't read it, but everyone in the shop breathes a sigh of relief.

"What does it say?" Antonio asks.

Zio Pietro beams over at him. "The Kingdom of Italy has joined the alliance with France!"

"Don't get too excited," Leonardo cautions. "We still have to survive the war."

29. NEW SHORES

Every morning, Anna walks under the keyhole gate of Bab El Khadra, down Rue Souki Bel Khir to the Sarfati household. She says hello to Miriam and picks up on the loom where she left off, and eventually Fradji will wander into the sewing room. He will often gift her one of his photographs, which over time become less blurry and more focused. Her bedroom wall is soon filled with sepia snapshots of camels drinking from streams, the Grand Synagogue, and the soaring arches of the Bey's palace.

"I have some news," Fradji tells her one day, trying to hide his smile. "I am a professional photographer now."

"You got a job?" Anna gasps. "Where? The newspaper?"

"There's a scholar at Ez-Zitouna University who is writing a book on Tunisian wildlife. An uncle set me up with him, and he is paying me to photograph the flamingos at Korba Lagoon."

"Flamingos are my favorite birds," Anna says, remembering sitting at the mudflat watching the flamingos with Antonio.

"Perhaps you'd like to see them in person?" Fradji asks. "Maybe Sunday afternoon? My family will take you."

Anna opens her mouth to speak, but no words come out. She knows by his face that he is serious, signaling that she did not misinterpret. She does not imagine Zia Rosa would approve of her running off to spend time with Fradji, who she only knows as the Sarfati boy and not much else, but it seems his family will be coming as well.

"Let's see some flamingos," she says.

When Sunday arrives and Anna returns from church, she packs a day bag and wraps a white linen scarf around her head to shield from the summer heat.

"Zia Rosa!" she taps on the archway to the entry hall. "I'm going out! I'll be back in the evening."

"You're going nowhere," Zia Rosa raises her eyebrows and puts her hands on her hips. "Not unless you tell me more."

"The Sarfati family invited me to the Korba Lagoon with them. Fradji will be taking pictures of flamingos, and—"

"Fradji?" Zia Rosa says. "Fradji will be there?"

"Yes. He's been hired to take the photographs."

Zia Rosa sighs. "Sit here, *amore*. It is time I taught you an important lesson." She clears her throat. "If you see a man's shoes and slacks, look at the floor. Never look a man in the eye. Abstain from talking to boys outside the family."

"Why?"

"Because you have a reputation to maintain, Anna. The world is very unkind to girls with a bad reputation, and you have to learn to protect yourself from such a thing."

"What about the Sarfati family?"

"The Sarfatis are different. You work for them, so that makes them family. But just remember for when you are older, if a man wants to court you and his intentions are noble, he will ask the family for permission first. He will see you only at the dinner table with the whole family present. Everything will be above board, and the family will decide if he is honorable. That is the way I met your Zio Leonardo, and that is the way you will meet your husband one day."

"But Zia Rosa, that's not how they did it in Brooklyn. In Brooklyn, the boyfriends and girlfriends would go on dates by themselves to Coney Island. They would buy candies for each other and go dancing—"

"I'll have no more of this talk," Zia Rosa winces at the word *dancing*. "This isn't Brooklyn, Anna. We have standards in this hemisphere. *Principles*. If you don't act in a respectable way, then people won't treat you with respect, and I don't want that for you. So, no more talk of dating, please, and especially no talk of dancing."

"Yes, Zia Rosa," Anna finally says, deflated.

"Good girl. Now, go to the Sarfatis. Enjoy your day. But take care and remember what I said."

Within the hour, Anna is skipping under the arches of the Tunis train station, across the street from the bustling port. She slides her francs beneath the brass grating of the ticket booth, folding her ticket into her handbag for safekeeping, fingers shaking with excitement. Determined not to make a fool of herself, she breathes slowly as one in prayer and reminds herself to not let her giddiness overshadow her charm. And there, standing in the platform by the streaking red train with the maroon stripe, is Fradji Sarfati, camera tied around his neck, dressed up in khaki like an expeditionary, and as always a sprig of asphodel tucked behind his ear.

But he isn't alone. His sisters and his mamma, who carries a wicker basket, are standing beside him. Anna follows them inside the train compartment, cramped between Fradji and his mother. Inside, the cabins are dark with wood panels and a maroon carpet. Anna cranes her neck out the window as the train chugs to life, watching the Mediterranean speed by until smearing into a sparkling blur.

Back in America, Anna and her sisters would often look forward to visiting the beach at Coney Island, but the Tunisian beaches are so golden and the water so sparkling that they put Coney Island to shame.

They step off at a rural station with an Arabic sign that she translates as *Korba Lagoon*, and Fradji sets off for the hills at a steady march. Anna wants to race after him, but she remembers what Zia Rosa said and opts for restraint, walking slowly behind with Miriam and Fradji's little sisters.

They follow a shepherd trail through knee-high scrub, palm trees, cypress trees, and jujube trees while the brown plains fall away behind them. Miriam names all the flowers—purple lavender, white asphodel, yellow narcissus. Finally, the lagoon breaks over the ridge, and a salty breeze flutters through Anna's hair.

"*Che bello*," she breathes.

"That's our target," Fradji says, crouching with his camera to snap photographs of the vast, pink colony spread out before them.

The sight of an army of thousands of flamingos, standing, strutting, and squawking across the shallow water is breathtaking, and the noise so overwhelming that Anna presses her palms to her ears. Closest to the edge of the lagoon, flamingos pick over a string of rocks, pecking at the clinging mollusks and leaving a blanket of white downy feathers, eggshells and fish bones strewn across the urine-scented mud.

The birds hover across the water in tight-packed ranks, twig legs racing, spaghetti necks bobbing. They twist and open their wings, flashing alternating black and pink feathers. Two intertwine necks. And as Fradji marvels at the flamingos, Anna stares in the same way at him. She studies his energy and excitement, the bright smile that flashes as he squints into the viewing hole of the camera.

"I admire flamingos," Fradji says, glancing up at her. "They fly wherever they wish, always seeking new lands, new shores. They chart their own course in life. I think everyone should be like them."

Under the strict gaze of Miriam Sarfati, there is only so much Anna can do or say, so she chooses her words carefully. "You read my mind," she says, remaining two paces behind him, standing in the sand and hugging her cardigan about herself.

"Tell me about your work, Anna. What do the wedding garments mean to you?"

"I just like the way they look."

"Oh, come on. You work yourself ragged on that loom. What motivates you?"

"A little bit of magic is involved," Anna admits with a smile. "Have you ever wondered how a garment, when it's not being worn, is nothing more than fiber, but when somebody wears it a transformation happens? The fabric comes to life, speaks an unspoken message, like an expression of the person wearing it. Well-made clothes can transform a person, make them stand taller. Almost like a good haircut."

"You are determined," Fradji says. "I see it in the way you work with my mamma."

His words hang in the air, becoming part of the mist over the lagoon. One of the flamingos takes off at a sprint, unfurling rose feathers over the water, and by the time its feet leave the water, its wings are gliding toward new shores.

30. MAMMA'S BED

Antonio sleeps in the same room as his cousins—Pete and Vince each have their own bed beneath the blue-shuttered windows, the balcony door sitting halfway between them, while he and Giuseppina have separate beds near the door. The setup leaves barely enough room for their wardrobes. No inch of wall space goes unused.

One evening, while Antonio is tucking his blankets beneath the mattress, Giuseppina begins coughin, hacking into her nightgown sleeve.

"You've been coughing all week." Antonio hands her his handkerchief. "Are you sure you are alright?"

During the night Antonio listens to her coughing. At one point, Giuseppina presses her face into her pillow to dampen the noise, but nothing works. Soon, Zio Pietro is at the door, flipping the lights on, and in the new light they see red spots on her pillow.

"Call for the doctor!" Zio Pietro presses a hand to her flushed, shining forehead.

Giuseppina rolls onto her side to spit red mucus into a porcelain washbasin, gasping for breath.

A French doctor soon arrives at the apartment, pressing a stethoscope to Giuseppina's chest, peering down her throat. The doctor pulls Zio Pietro and Antonio aside and says in a low tone, "I'm afraid to say she has tuberculosis."

"Just like her mamma," Zio Pietro says.

A somber hush falls across the room.

"As you know," the doctor exhales, folding his glasses, "there is no cure for tuberculosis. It is an infectious, vicious disease. There are only two outcomes—the body naturally develops immunity, or the body succumbs. You can't keep her in the children's room any longer," the doctor says. "She is infectious now and her siblings might also fall ill. Is there any other bed she can use?"

"We have a spare bedroom that my wife and I used to share," Zio Pietro's voice cracks.

"Don't take me to Mamma's bed," Giuseppina is hyperventilating now.

Zio Pietro slides his arms beneath Giuseppina's legs and back, trying to lift her, but she clings to the bedpost.

"It is only temporary," Zio Pietro says, and Antonio can see the pain in his face as he pulls her hands from the bedpost. "In a week or two, you will be healed."

"Please, Papà, please! No!"

The floorboards creak under Zio Pietro's heavy steps as he carries Giuseppina down the hallway to the other room. Antonio watches them go, his heart plunging, his legs wobbling. In that moment he cannot think of a single thing he could do that would help. He may as well be a picture on the wall watching Zio Pietro and the doctor exchange careful words with their stoic gazes. Antonio is no Zio Pietro, and he backs away, hiding himself in the washroom, shutting the door because he has nowhere else to escape. The sounds of Giuseppina's crying and retching fill the apartment, and he covers his ears.

"What in God's name are you doing?" Zio Pietro finds him in the washroom after the noise dies down. "Your cousin is in need and here you are hiding away."

Zio Pietro grips him by the shoulders—they are the same height now, and Zio Pietro speaks to him as a man. "Giuseppina admires you, Antonio. You are the one person in this household who can calm her spirit. Be at her side, now, and promise me you will always take care of her."

Antonio looks away and, to his shame, he thinks of Anna and her blazing eyes and smart mouth and modern ideas.

"Promise me."

Antonio's heart pounds against his ribcage. He doesn't want to say the words, but they come anyway. "I promise you, Zio Pietro."

Antonio ties a cloth around his mouth and nose to protect him from infection, and he spends the evening sitting at Giuseppina's bedside. Her coughing has subsided for now, and she drifts in and out of sleep. He has never seen himself as a nurturing person, especially since he has always lived under the care of his parents or his brothers or his uncle and has been the object of their nurturing, but when he sees Giuseppina laying there shivering with fever, he envisions himself stroking her hair, bringing her fava bean soup, fanning her with his palm until she is cool. She cracks her eyes open to see he is still sitting at the bedside.

"You don't have to stay with me, Antonio," she whispers through a raw throat.

"I'd like to stay here, if that's alright," Antonio says, feeling his eyes get warm and wet. "To keep you company."

"I would like that. Thank you." Her hand, hot with fever, slips into his.

The next evening, the local priest, Father Francois, stops by for the Anointing of the Sick. Anna arrives to participate as well, rushing to their apartment as soon as news reached her. All of them—Zio Pietro, Pete, Vince, Antonio, Anna—gather around Giuseppina's bed and fold their hands in prayer. Father Francois drones on in Latin as he reads from the red prayer book, tracing a cross on each of Giuseppina's palms and feet using perfumed olive oil. Giuseppina closes her eyes and smiles, and she says she feels a profound sense of peace. After the rite concludes with an amen, after they thank Father Francois and see him out the door, after they leave Giuseppina some time for her *riposo*, Antonio finds himself sitting on the couch with Anna. The shadows are long in the afternoon.

"She will survive this," he tells Anna.

"I know she will. She will get her strength from you. Don't blush now, I saw how you held her hand. Giuseppina adores you, and rightfully so."

With every particle of his being, Antonio is suddenly aware that his knee is brushing against Anna's. He stares down at that place for just a moment and then quickly rises and walks to the kitchen to fill a teapot with water from the tap. Giuseppina will appreciate some calming mint tea when she wakes up. The scent of the mint clears the lump in his throat.

"I promised to care for her," Antonio says, setting the teapot over the stove. "Just like my mamma taught me in the old Sicilian tongue. *Lu rispetto è misuratu, cu lu porta l'avi purtato*—whoever pays respect to others will be respected."

"I don't care what your mamma taught you," Anna says, her voice sharper than she intended. Or maybe not sharp enough. She didn't know.

It is too sharp for Antonio, who seethes at the rebuke. He wonders if Anna has any respect for family at all.

"You shouldn't hang on your mamma's every word," Anna continues. "You must decide for yourself, Antonio. Do you truly love Giuseppina with your heart and your body and your soul, or is this some twisted way of threading the needle between your family's dreams and your own?"

Through gritted teeth, Antonio says, "You are talking like an American now."

"Does Giuseppina bring you happiness?" Anna asks, accentuating her American accent.

"*Happiness?*" Antonio growls.

"Yes, the thing that makes people laugh and smile. Also, keep your voice down or you'll wake her."

"I know what happiness is, and I don't need your sarcasm. I'm just saying, there are more important things than happiness. Happiness is fickle. It comes and goes like the weather. It's not something to build a relationship on."

"Then what is?"

Antonio whips around to face her. "You know what I'm going to say!"

"So say it."

"You'll make fun of me."

"Why do you care? Say it anyway."

"Family!" Antonio shouts. "Family is more important to me than happiness!"

As if an exclamation point, the teapot whistles, spouting a plume of steam. Already, Antonio can hear bedsheets stirring in the other room. They have woken Giuseppina.

"Anna," Antonio lowers his voice, all anger sapped from him at the thought of sickly Giuseppina. "Quit your laughing and help me pour this tea for Giuseppina."

"Of course," Anna's voice also softens at the mention of Giuseppina.

Together, they take the tea into the bedroom and do not speak of happiness again.

31. YOU FIT THE DESCRIPTION

The Indigenous Flamingos of Tunisia. Anna notices the book filling the front table of the bookstore in neat stacks, where she and Miriam *ooh* and *aah* as they open the pink paper jacket inscribed with bold, white Arabic, a defiant contrast against the French-dominated shelves.

Fradji picks up the book for the first time. Anna holds her breath to see his reaction. Brow creased, Fradji weighs the volume in his hands, cracks the cover open to hear the spine creaking, and finally a bright smile breaks across his face like dawn on the horizon.

"It came out well." Fradji's smile grows even wider.

"My son is professional photographer now," Miriam kisses his head.

"I'm proud of you," Anna says, and her voice takes on a high inflection she did not intend. She looks around the bookstore, where a dozen people sit in the various alcoves between the shelves, lost in deep thought on the first page. This is what it was all for. To remind people of Tunisia's native beauty, to remind people of the last word and not the first word in the phrase, *French Protectorate of Tunisia.*

Fradji holds the book up to his face to hide his blush, almost as pink as the flamingos he photographed.

After Fradji and Miriam and Anna fill their bags with copies of the book, they exit the bookstore onto Avenue Jules Ferry, a wide boulevard with a central greenspace of palms and eucalyptus and fountains, where they cross the tram tracks and find a bench for reading. Anna sets her copy on her lap and flips through the pages of Fradji's photographs, carefully lifting the starched archival tissue paper to reveal the glossy black-and-white flamingos in the mudflat. She holds down the pages so they don't blow in the breeze.

Anna wants to ask him so many things—*Was the publisher frustrating to work with? Was it hard to have the book printed in Arabic instead of French? Will you get to do a sequel?* But she cannot bring herself to ask the hard questions, not with his mother sitting at her side.

"Can I ask you a question, Fradji?" she finally works up the courage while they are all weaving through the crowds back to Rue Souki Bel Khir, ignoring the vendors trying to sell them white marzipan donuts.

"What do you want to know?"

"What's the first time you saw a camera?"

Fradji and his mother exchange a smile.

"I was seven," he grins. "A photographer came for a class photograph at school, and he set up a big tripod in the classroom. I kept asking him when the photo would be done, and I think I started to annoy him. Finally, he just gave me the address of the studio, and of course I ran there after class ended. It was like a mad scientist's laboratory. There were dozens of pictures, real life scenes frozen in time, and they were hanging on clothespins to dry. The room had all these red lights like the lanterns they put up at Ramadan but so bright that even your clothes turn red."

Anna listens to him rattle on with the slowly rising smile always in the corner of his mouth. He is simply contagious, but her response can only be as congenial as Miriam's glare will allow. The notion strikes Anna that she could pretend to trip on her shoelace, just so Fradji would reach out his hand to steady her, to clamp his strong photographer's hand around her arm protectively, but she dismisses the thought outright. It would be indecent, and she wouldn't want Miriam or Fradji thinking of her that way.

"I like photography too," Anna tells him. "I just wish it could have some color. That's the one thing a painting has that a photograph never will."

"I guess you're right," Fradji shrugs. "Paintings are best for color, but photographs have their own special trait that makes them just as beautiful. They're…they're, I don't know the right word for it. *Real?*"

Anna laughs.

"They certainly are."

They are rounding the corner past a poorhouse people call Oukala of the Birds, a rambling complex of stacked apartments, staircases, hanging laundry. A block further, and they pass the tanner's workshops where goatskins hang out to dry by the chemical vats, and the street gutters trickle with brown dye that reeks of urine. Local residents are pressing sprigs of mint to their noses to mask the dizzying ammonia of the tannery. Miriam lengthens her stride, and Anna speeds to keep up so they can escape the stench. They turn another corner, where shouts rise. Men are scuffling in the street, stirring up a cloud of dust. Through the haze, she can make out the khaki uniforms of the French police. They are running across the street, pointing their clubs.

"Who are they pointing at?" Anna looks around.

The street behind her has cleared of people—everyone disappearing indoors. There is no one else apart from Anna and Miriam and Fradji. Before Anna can react, the police officers are gripping Fradji by his collar, throwing him against a wall, patting down his pants.

"Where did you get this camera?" an officer asks, dumping Fradji's bag.

His camera, his books, his ticket, all spill onto the street.

"Why are you searching me?" Fradji asks, and Anna can hear the tremor of fear in his voice.

"He didn't do anything!" Anna shouts.

"Shush child, don't escalate things," Miriam clamps a hand over Anna's mouth, then speaks to Fradji in Arabic.

Anna feels the world closing in. Her restful contentment following the bookstore shrivels entirely. She eyes the guns holstered at the officers' hips, and her first instinct is to call out for help. But who would help them, if not the police?

"I don't have a gun, please," Fradji's voice cracks, and his eyes well with tears.

Miriam shouts at him again in Arabic, and Anna imagines she is begging him to stay calm.

Anna remembers when Zio Leonardo spoke of the Jellaz Affair, how the French police had shot untold numbers of young Tunisian men for protesting against the colonizers. Then she sees Fradji's eyes widen with fear, and she feels herself heaving for breath.

"Did you steal this camera?" an officer asks.

"I bought it with my own money. I earned it," Fradji says. "I'm a photographer. Please, please don't hurt me."

"What about these? What are they, earrings?" the officer lifts a set of earrings from Fradji's bag—pink enamel earrings in the shape of flamingos.

"I bought them for her," Fradji looks at Anna, and his eyes fill her with equal amounts of terror and affection.

Anna realizes he had been carrying the earrings in his bag all day, probably intending to gift them to her this evening. No boy had ever given Anna jewelry before.

"We had a report of a robbery," the second officer speaks with the same tone as a waiter announcing the menu. "A thief stole several hundred francs at gunpoint from a shopkeeper, but this boy doesn't have any weapons."

"Maybe he threw his gun in the trash to avoid suspicion," the first officer says, pinning Fradji's shoulders against the bricks.

"Please, he didn't do anything. I've been with him all day," Miriam says, and Anna can detect the forced composure in her pained face.

The officers look straight through her, deliberating in French until finally releasing Fradji, simply walking away, taking the flamingo earrings with them. Fradji wipes his eyes and picks up his camera. The lens is cracked.

"Why did you stop me?" Fradji calls after the police officers.

"You fit the description," is all they say.

Miriam holds Fradji close, cradling his curly head.

"Let's go home," she says.

"I thought they were going to beat me, Mamma."

Anna doesn't know what she can say that will console him. Her chest is tight, her stomach feels sick, like when she threw up on the Atlantic crossing, like when the ground beneath her feet was being tossed on the waves.

"Let's just get you home," Anna adds. "Your family will make things better."

She draws a sharp glare from Miriam.

"No, they won't," Fradji says. "You don't understand. No place in this city is safe from the French officers. They can break into our homes. They can steal from us. They can shoot us. Nobody ever does anything about it. It's like we're not human."

"I'm so sorry, Fradji. Things will improve. We'll talk to a lawyer and you can get those earrings back."

"Anna, I like you, but you don't know what you're talking about. You live in a mansion. You have servants."

During their walk back to Fradji's house, Anna hangs her head. She knows they come from different worlds, and there is nothing in her life at Zia Rosa's estate that could overlap with a single day in Fradji's shoes. But she still wants to help.

"The earrings looked beautiful," Anna says. "I didn't know you felt that way about me."

"It doesn't matter now," Fradji says. "Those earrings will be sitting forever in a drawer in a French police station."

They pass under the medieval gate of Bab El Khadra, finally arriving at the archway to Fradji's courtyard. Anna lingers there, thinking of what to say.

"Will you be okay?" Anna asks.

"I'll see you soon," is all Fradji says, his manner solemn.

Before she can apologize, he disappears into his house, and she sees the mezuzah on its hook above the door. Anna finally turns and walks toward home. Alone. from him and starts walking back home.

32. WRAPPED IN A BLANKET

Antonio sits at Giuseppina's bedside all morning and all evening, and between customers he rushes upstairs to the apartment to check on her. In Mamma's letters, she lists the traditional cures, and so Antonio boils water in a pot and dunks a cloth in it, wringing the cloth out and laying it over Giuseppina's face.

"The steam feels good," Giuseppina says, even though Antonio knows she is in pain by her wincing.

Her chest rises and falls with a gentle cadence of phlegmy wheezing, and through her coughing fits she tries to work the phlegm out, spitting the yellow gobs into a porcelain basin that Antonio holds under her mouth. "You are doing great," he encourages her, wiping her chin. Then he goes to the kitchen to brew more mint tea. Apart from that, there is not much else he can do.

"My head feels so clear," Giuseppina says the next morning. Antonio wonders if she is honest. "Let me look out the window," Giuseppina stirs from the terrain of her blankets and tries to stand, but Antonio places a hand on her shoulder.

"Rest," he says, and opens the window for her.

The fresh sea breeze flaps the corners of the curtains, and Giuseppina fills her lungs. The mere sight of it makes Antonio want to cling to her, to say that he will never let anything happen to her again.

"Ouch," Giuseppina clutches her stomach and winces.

His eyes go wide in alarm. "Your stomach is in pain?"

"It's starved. I've taken nothing but broth for how many days?"

He smiles at that and hurries back to the kitchen. He busies himself with Mamma's recipe, boiling polenta with caciocavallo cheese and, when it'd done, taking a bowl back to Giuseppina's room.

She sits on the bed and spoons it down at a steady pace until the bowl is empty.

"I need more than that."

Back to the kitchen Antonio goes, rummaging through the cabinets to see what he can prepare quickly. He unwraps a loaf of semolina bread dusted in sesame seeds, cutting off slices, stacking them with tomato and what remains of the cheese. Giuseppina devours it, then brings the water cup to her mouth for several seconds at a time, and Antonio runs to refill it from the kitchen spigot. When he returns to her room, Giuseppina is on her feet, standing at the window wrapped in a blanket, the sun casting a golden pattern on her face through the shadow of the iron grating.

"I think I have survived the sickness," she says with a radiant smile.

She walks through the apartment, her legs shaky after spending days in bed, but Antonio is beside her, ready to catch her should she stumble.

"I know of no better feeling than a full breath of fresh air," Giuseppina says with a laugh.

Soon, Zio Pietro sends out invitations for a party to celebrate Giuseppina's recovery. Anna, along with her Zia Rosa and Zio Leonardo, arrive at the apartment with a bowl of pasta, and Zio Pietro sends Antonio running to the baker across the street to pick up a white-glazed cake decorated with bright strips of candied pumpkin and lemon that remind him of the petals of a flower.

By the time Antonio returns to the apartment, Leonardo has warmed up his accordion and is playing a tarantella song, his fingers racing along the buttons while the instrument cranks a zany, winding tune. Zio Pietro, Pete, Vince, Anna, Giuseppina, and Rosa spin in circles around each other, light on their feet, arms raised, clapping to the beat. Giuseppina is the first to drop out of the dancing, and everyone mumbles their agreement that she should go easy, and the dancing ends. After drinking a good amount of limoncello, Zio Pietro does his best impression of Enrico Caruso's opera, and then they cut open the cake to find it filled with ricotta cheese, the sponge soaked in more sweet lemon liqueur. Antonio eats too much and has to rest on the couch, his head spinning.

While shouting and laughter ricochet off the walls, Antonio watches Anna and Giuseppina conversing at the table. For Giuseppina, he feels protective and sorry, like he did when he accidentally locked out the housecat back in Sicily and swore he would never leave it outside again.

For Anna, he feels too many things to name, and that is the difference between them. He knows the truth of the difference, but there is nothing he can do about it.

PART 4

OCTOBER 1917

33. SHABBAT

In the mornings, Anna counts the building numbers until she arrives at the Sarfati household on Rue Souki Bel Khir, down the street from the sunrise-silhouetted gate of Bab El Khadra. Miriam is teaching Anna to dye wool, to let it soak in terracotta pots and scoop out the now scarlet yarns like a forkful of spaghetti. The dye's earthy scent fills the room, and afterwards Anna's hands are stained henna-red. They weave their brocade fabrics on the loom and sing to pass the time, and some days Anna slips into a trance as she works the loom from muscle memory, her fingertips hard with calluses. She learns to love the ache in her hands after a long day's work, and she puffs out her chest with pride as she dresses the booth at Souk El Grana with her handiwork—scarlet and gold shawls, kippot, carma, baggy pants covered in floral embroidery. During the day, the shoppers stop at their booth to admire the garments.

"Is this your daughter, Miriam?" a customer asks, adjusting a sefseri around her head.

Anna laughs at the woman, and to her it feels like a complement.

"Daughter? No," Miriam says to her patrons. "Daughter-in-law? We will see."

"*Inshallah,*" the woman replies after purchasing a roll of brocade and heading to the next booth.

Anna's stomach lurches. *Daughter-in-law?* Her cheeks rouge. Does Miriam expect she will marry Fradji? They usually only discuss the ordinary details of life—work, money, careers. Never romance. Certainly, Anna and Fradji have been sitting together at their Shabbat dinners, and they have exchanged many sweet words, but the thought of marriage never crossed her mind. Perhaps Miriam's words were a slip of the tongue and could really be meant as a complement to how much Miriam valued her. Anna shakes off the thought and carries on with her work.

On Saturday evening, Anna arrives at their house for Shabbat, as she often does. Miriam answers the door, her eyelids darkened with lines of kohl, a *carma* diadem tied to her head with ribbon, bursting folds of fabric that float behind her as she walks. Miriam guides Anna to the table, seating her right beside Fradji, and she folds her legs on the divan. Fradji flashes Anna a smile, and he adjusts the asphodel flower tucked behind his ear. Miriam serves them a stew of oxtail, fried chard, and white beans served over couscous. For dessert, Miriam brings out a plate of sweets—a rolled pastry of date paste and honey, lightly fried, dusted in sesame seeds. She pours out small shot glasses of a milky-white alcohol that Anna can only handle a few sips of. The drink burns her throat and leaves an aftertaste of licorice in her nostrils.

"Drink," Miriam sets down a bowl of goat's milk before Fradji's four sisters, whose cheeks are plump like their mamma's. "You will have to fill in your hips if you want to find a good husband. Who would want to marry such skinny girls? You are like sticks."

"But I am already full from dinner," one of the sisters pats her belly.

Anna watches the girls protest, and Miriam shouts at them and flicks their faces until they finally give in, raising the sloshing bowl of goat's milk to their mouths.

"I do this for your own good," Miriam tells her daughters. "It is very difficult for a skinny girl to find a husband. Not everyone can be as lucky as Anna, who has already found her husband."

Miriam gestures at Fradji, who nods in agreement. The rest of Fradji's brothers and sisters steal secret glances at them together and whisper, and Anna finally understands what they want from her, why they have invited her to their Shabbat dinners, why they have invested so much time into her. She laughs nervously to please Miriam, but inside she feels sick. She is not ready for marriage, not at seventeen.

She always imagined that her future husband would be a family friend, someone possessing the respect of her papà and the approval of her mother. Someone she could laugh with and someone she could truly love. After all, isn't that what she told Antonio? She imagined him now. Making pasta together. Singing in the pews on Sundays. Doing all the things that would make her feel like being with him was like being at home. She knew Antonio would marry would Giuseppina, but she could find another man like him. And they would court throughout her twenties only to finally marry him in her family church back home when she had her life worked out. But Fradji? Now? She certainly likes Fradji, his contagious passion, his bright intellect, his sweet demeanor. Yes, she liked him, but not enough for a ring.

After wrestling with her thoughts for most of dinner, Anna stands up from the divan and says, "I'm so sorry, but I think it's time I go home."

Fradji pauses halfway through chewing.

"Are you sure?" he asks, his voice rising with concern. "We haven't brought out the baklava yet."

"I'm sure," Anna nods. "I…I'm not feeling well. I really appreciate you inviting me, though."

"Can I walk you home?" Fradji offers, extending a hand to her.

"No, thank you." Anna gives him a gentle smile. "I'm fine."

Anna quickly wraps the linen headscarf about her dark coils of hair, says her goodbyes, and steps into the cobblestone alley before Fradji can follow her out. The autumn nights in Tunis are cool, and a sea breeze flutters her dress, nipping at her ankles. She takes one last look at the mezuzah over their door and marches along the winding streets of the medina as night falls.

34. ORDER OF INDUCTION

While Antonio snips the scissors across Giuseppina's hair one morning, an envelope slides through the mail slot on the shop door. He snatches the letter, finding his own name written on it—and what's more—written in Mamma's handwriting, pasted with stamps from Italy. Antonio tears it open and reads the letter, frowning at the final paragraph.

Sicily is unlivable. The family has saved up enough money to send me and the children to America, in the home your papà prepared. In this way, our family has transplanted itself. Our home in Partinico is boarded up, and there is nothing for you to return to.

"What is it, Antonio?" Giuseppina touches his shoulder.

Antonio shows her the letter, and her eyes scan over the looping handwriting.

"If you follow your mamma to America," Giuseppina says, "you will never see Sicily again."

If he follows Mamma, he will have to sit on a boat for ten days. He will have to learn English and prepare a home for himself and Giuseppina.

"Perhaps I could go back to Sicily and maintain my family home. I do not have to cross the ocean to America."

"No one will stop you."

They close the shop for three hours at lunch time, so Antonio takes the time to be alone. He walks along greenspace by the harbor, breathing the brackish air, listening to the water lap at the cracked flagstones, thinking that he has always lived near the sea and that he always must return to it. His walk takes him further, along through Bab El Khadra and into the medina. While the songs of prayer echo from the minaret of Hammam Remimi Mosque, he walks to the empty Sacré Cœur Church, takes off his hat, crosses himself with holy water, drops two francs in the collection box, and lights a candle for the zia he has never met—Maria Minore. While Antonio prays, he thinks that the line separating duty from selfishness is as thin as the wrinkles circling Zio Pietro's mouth, the wrinkles that show the places he used to laugh. Somewhere in heaven, he reasons, Maria Minore knows this, bless her soul. Antonio is kneeling in the pews when Father Francois walks into the empty church carrying a bouquet of roses on some errand.

"What are you doing here, Antonio? It is Tuesday."

"I am praying to Saint Augustine."

"Oh, I see. You pray for his intercession?"

"Only when I have a lot on my mind." Antonio is holding the photograph his brothers sent him, in which they are standing outside their new house in America.

"Saint Augustine was from Tunisia, you know," Father Francois says. "He sailed away from Tunisia when he was a young man. He said goodbye to it."

Antonio pictures his house in Partinico as he knew it, before they boarded up the windows, before the thistles sprang up in the rose garden. He will hoard this memory; he foresees himself becoming drunk off it in the coming weeks when the peals of the transatlantic ship-whistles wear thin and the towers of New York City break over the water. And long after he follows his mamma, long after he takes Giuseppina as his bride and cuts the hair of trigger-happy American cowboys, he will pray to Saint Augustine and know it to be true, that change and obligation are the engines of life just as Zio Pietro decreed. And what of it if he cuts hair on this side of the ocean or some other side, if he is a citizen of this country or some other country— he is the son of a barber just the same, snipping, shaving, styling to the same end. He sees it coming.

Antonio walks to the post office on Avenue de Paris and tells the clerk behind the bronze grating that he would like to register for a passport. His Italian passport is no good because the French government, threatened by the growing population of Italians in their territory, has forced all Italians in Tunisia to register for French citizenship.

"What is your nationality?"

"I am a proud Italian! What do you think?"

Antonio fills out some forms and returns them to the clerk. For his payment, he hands over the fistful of francs, the collective tips from a hundred haircuts.

"It says here you are seventeen," the clerk reads.

"You're never too young to move to America."

The clerk sighs and crumples the papers into a ball. "This is the correct form for you," and he hands Antonio a new paper.

Order of Induction into Military Service of the Kingdom of Italy.

His stomach plummets straight through the floor. "I am to fight in the war?" he looks up at the clerk.

"You are a proud Italian, are you not? They will be expecting you on the frontline."

Antonio rushes back to the barber shop on Rue Pierre de Coubertin, piecing together a story to tell his family.

35. PEWTER MEDALLION

Anna shuts the turquoise carriage doors behind her as she steps into the tile courtyard. Frustrated from the stress of expectations, she stretches her sore hands. Work is not as fun anymore, not with the entire Sarfati family expecting her to marry Fradji, including Fradji. Not that he is unlikeable. She definitely likes him, but she finds it increasingly difficult to do so when her apprenticeship depends on it. What if she says no to him? How would Miriam react?

Zio Leonardo and Zia Rosa are sitting cross-legged at the dinner table, eating their couscous. "Anna," Zio Leonardo pats the cushions. "Come eat with us. We rarely see you now that you are working with the Sarfatis."

She stops where she is. Something is up. She can tell that a secret is in the air. Zio Leonardo and Zia Rosa both shoot glances at each other and fall silent. "Is there something you want to tell me?"

"We have news," Zio Leonardo sighs.

Anna's mind races. Did someone die? That is the impression they are giving her. "What is it?"

"Antonio has been enlisted in the Italian army," Zio Leonardo says. "Pietro told me he is going to fight in the war."

Anna's thoughts leap to the horrible stories from the newspapers, where they say one in ten recruits never make it back home, where the soldiers suffer hypothermia in trenches and flee from poison gas attacks. Her heart races, her chest tightens, her nose prickles, and tears appear out of nowhere. Legs trembling, she backs away from the table.

"He will make it through, *gattina*," Zia Rosa reaches out to her, but Anna brushes her off.

"I have to go to him," she declares. "I have to see him." She turns and runs outside, down the dirt road where the green stubble of esparto grass rustles, all the way to the tram station. She hitches a ride back to downtown Tunis, to the barber shop. While she sits on the tram, her thoughts spiral with fear for Antonio's safety. She has read so many articles in the newspaper about the horrors of the trenches—the poison gas, the bombs, the disease.

The bell rings as she steps inside the barber shop for the first time in three years, and she sees a much older, hairier Antonio with his white coat buttoned up to his collar. When he sees her, his eyes widen like one of Zio Leonardo's sheep at the shearing.

"Anna," he breathes, completely ignoring his customer. "You've come for a haircut? It's been a while."

Anna clasps her hands and is about to reply when Giuseppina emerges from the back room, carrying the cash box. Anna wants very much to wish Antonio well and see how he is doing with his enlistment in the army, to bring him any degree of comfort and listen to his fears, but Giuseppina's presence looms over her like a saint statue, demanding only the most proper of behaviors.

"Yes, I came for a-a haircut," she stutters. "Can you do a bob?"

Antonio rushes through his current customer, and soon Anna is sinking into the cushion of the barber chair, a cloak draped around her. Antonio presses the bladder to spray her hair with water. After a few moments, he says, "Why are you really here, Anna?"

"For a bob," she says, watching Giuseppina counting change for a customer in the mirror.

"You have been going to the French salon for years, and now you are suddenly back here for a haircut? I certainly enjoy having you here, but it strikes me as unusual." His voice is like a low rumble against the back of her neck.

She exhales. "I heard that you were enlisted. I want to hear how you feel."

Antonio snips at her hair and says nothing.

"Is there anything I can do?" Anna asks. "Do you want to talk about it?"

"I have someone to talk to," he says, glancing at Giuseppina.

Snip. Snip. Anna's hairs float to the ground, and she feels the air on her neck. Antonio runs the comb down from her scalp, and she feels his knuckles brush against her ear.

"Do you remember when we first arrived in Tunis?" Antonio asks. "At the harbor? I was frightened, and you gave me a medallion of the Virgin Mary for courage."

"I remember," Anna says.

Antonio digs a hand into his pocket and shows her the little pewter medallion.

"I will carry it with me in the war if it makes you feel better."

"It would," she smiles at him in the mirror.

Anna hands down a few francs for her haircut, says goodbye, and is walking toward the door when she hears Antonio behind her, calling. She turns and waits for him to catch up.

"Anna," he says, "don't feel sorry for me. If there's anyone who taught me not to feel sorry for myself, it's you."

"I will try my best, Antonio."

"Promise me."

"I promise I will try," Anna says before leaving. She does not tell him that he is wrong, that she is in no position to teach him about self-pity. Anna feels sorry for herself all the time, and it is a nagging feeling that she can never cut loose. As a girl, in the tiny apartment in Brooklyn, she worried she was too much of a burden to her family. In Tunisia, in Zia Rosa's estate, she feels guilty to be so wealthy while her servants have so little. And yet she taught Antonio not to feel sorry for himself? How did that happen? How does he see her? What does he think of her?

While she sits on the tram heading back home, she cannot scrub the image from her thoughts—Antonio and Giuseppina together. Ever since Giuseppina's bout with tuberculosis, Antonio has treated Giuseppina like fine pottery that could break at any moment. They go to church together, to the souk together, to the bank together. Surely, they have been discussing his every thought and feeling regarding his enlistment in the military, and he has no thoughts left over to share with her. It made her angry. Truthfully, it made her jealous. And that made her even angrier.

"How did it go?" Zia Rosa asks when she arrives home.

Zia Rosa is sitting in her usual chair reading her romance novel, crunching her salted almonds. Zio Leonardo sits in a rocking chair beside her, smoking shisha.

"He barely even spoke to me," Anna says.

"He's had a shock," Zio Leonardo says. "He'll come around."

"I don't want to sound vain," Anna says, "but I feel like I deserve his time. He was the first person I met when I first came to Tunisia. Am I doing something wrong? Is that why he would rather spend time with Giuseppina?"

"Well, he's betrothed to Giuseppina for starters," Zia Rosa says.

"By his parents," Anna adds. "He might change his mind later."

"Don't dwell on that," Zio Leonardo swats his hand. "No good will come from that kind of thinking. Besides, Antonio is a boy, barely out of the cradle. Why do you want his approval?"

Anna swallows. She cannot form the words.

"You think you love him, don't you?" Zia Rosa says.

"He and I are cut from the same cloth," Anna's voice cracks.

Zia Rosa and Zio Leonardo groan. Anna feels the heat rushing to her face.

"But I thought you had a soft spot for Fradji?" Zia Rosa says. "He's a good man."

"Boy," Zio Leonardo corrects her.

"I'm not sure how I feel about Fradji," Anna tells Zia Rosa. "He's so good to me, but I'm afraid what they will do if I say no. They act like I'm already a part of their family."

"Aren't you?" Zia Rosa asks.

"Stop," Zio Leonardo shakes his head. "This ends now. Anna, I will talk to Miriam Sarfati for you. We will clear up this misunderstanding, and you will tell Antonio how you feel. Make everything transparent. No more of this back and forth."

"That's heavy handed," Zia Rosa says. "Let Anna decide. Anna, what do you want?"

Anna can only think of Antonio, whose face brightened like it was illuminated from the inside, shining with sincerity and longing when he saw her enter the barber shop. She can only think of how he gently ran his comb through her hair, how his voice made her skin tingle when he spoke so close to her ear. She can only think of what will happen if he goes to war and doesn't ever return. Or if he marries Giuseppina and Anna goes home to Brooklyn and they never see each other again.

"Anna?" Zia Rosa repeats. "What do you want?"

36. 40,000 DEAD

Antonio heaves his suitcase onto his bed, clicks it open, and carefully tucks in the shirts he ironed and folded that morning. This is the same suitcase he used when first arriving in Tunis, he recalls. He remembers that day—already four years ago—rushing to fill the suitcase before saying goodbye to Mamma at the Palermo harbor, handing over five lire for the six-hour ferry to Tunis. And now, as a grown man, he can already see himself returning to that harbor, an immigrant no longer. He is not just a barber anymore; he is a soldier of the Palermo Brigade, the 67th Infantry Regiment of the Kingdom of Italy.

"You're packing early," Giuseppina says, standing in the doorway. She clasps her hands and lowers her gaze, despondent.

"I received orders to report to Palermo for basic training later this week," he says. "They're going to teach me to shoot, I suppose."

"The newspapers say we're losing," Giuseppina tosses a newspaper onto the suitcase. The front page is plastered in bold headlines.

CHLORINE GAS ATTACK NEAR
CAPORETTO

DEFEAT AT CAPORETTO
ITALIANS RETREAT TO VENICE

40,000 DEAD, 280,000 CAPTURED
350,000 DESERTED

Antonio swallows. The world spins around him. He has never even shot a gun before. He imagines himself the victim of a chemical gas attack, the soundless cloud creeping across the craters as he runs. The war has careened from crisis to crisis for three years now, with no end in sight. He is used to the constant rationing, the sight of shuttered storefronts, constant propaganda posters telling him to buy bonds. But at the same time, he sometimes imagines himself wearing a uniform, and when the soldiers march in formation past the barber shop, he is filled with a certain admiration. What could be more honorable than fighting for one's country?

Obligation, he repeats his motto, *obligation is the engine of life.* He wonders what Anna would have to say about his thoughts. She is the boldest of them all. Anna. He feels a sudden urge to run to her, to hide with her, to spend the evening listening to her while she discusses her latest sewing project. Anna. Who he misses already.

"Antonio, are you alright?" Giuseppina lifts him from his thoughts.

A pregnant pause hangs between them, and Antonio realizes he does not have an answer for her.

"Antonio!" Zio Pietro's cry suddenly breaks across the apartment. Zio Pietro runs into the room, waving a piece of paper, panting for breath. "You're not going to be a soldier anymore."

"What do you mean?"

"I've just received a letter from Cousin Vittorio at the Ministry of the Interior. He says you have a new assignment—military barber. You're going to cut hair for the generals at the army headquarters. Why aren't you smiling? This is wonderful news."

Antonio's nightmares of the chemical attacks dissipate, but he is not sure if this is a demotion or a promotion. Is it cowardly for him to give up the battle before it has even begun? He imagines the countless thousands of Italian boys who will surely be shot, suffocated, stabbed, while he is safely tucked behind the frontline in a castle, snipping away at royal mustaches. Surely, if Anna were here right now, she would encourage him to accept the new assignment, if only for his survival.

He takes in a deep breath and realizes his hands are trembling. "I guess I will never be a soldier." He clicks his suitcase shut. "I remain a barber."

In the morning, the Tunis harbor bustles with steamships. Columns of soldiers march while the French and Tunisian flags flap side by side in the autumn wind. Antonio breathes deeply, filling his lungs with the salty Mediterranean air. Zio Pietro, Giuseppina, and Anna are there to see him off.

Antonio smooths his uniform—his baggy pants tied tight around the calves, his olive coat, his wide-brimmed hat with black capercaillie feathers. He does not carry a gun in his belt but rather scissors, combs, and pearl-inlaid razors. The other recruits at the harbor, he knows, will soon be bunking at the training camp, learning to throw grenades and to strap on a gas mask in nine seconds flat. Their eyes are wide with fear, surely at the thought of standing against the German bombs, and Antonio tries to ward off the guilt that they could be exposed to poison gas while he cuts hair.

"You've grown so much, Nino," Zio Pietro lays a hand on the back of his neck and pulls him in for a hug. "May God keep you safe."

Giuseppina kisses his cheek, and her face is wet with tears. "I love you so dearly, Antonio."

Anna steps forward next, smiling, and wraps him in a hug.

"Bring yourself back unspoiled," she whispers, pressing something into his hand.

"What's this?" he asks, pulling out a blurry, black-and-white portrait of Anna, smiling in the middle of Souk El Grana. His heart skips a beat as he stares down at it a moment. He swallows and tucks it in his pocket. "Thank you," he says with a nod, his eyes intent on her face as if memorizing her features.

Anna bites her lip and takes a step back. And with that, Antonio pulls away and boards the warship.

37. SHIMMERING MIRAGE

The palm fronds droop hopelessly off the trees. The sun has fried the mudflat into a white-streaked plane of salt where the herders guide camel trains through a shimmering mirage. Anna squints against the sun as she steps outside. With her naturally olive skin, she does not burn easily, but today is different. Today her face is red and she feels a swelling heat in her cheeks as she wraps her head in a white scarf and goes to meet Fradji at the mudflat.

After tonight, she suspects, she will never again be welcome at the Sarfati household for dinner. After tonight, she will never again see the sprig of asphodel tucked behind Fradji's ear. As she prepares to tell him there will never be more between them, a flutter of panic rises in her chest. Will Miriam be mad? Will she lose her apprenticeship? She would miss Miriam, but it is better to be honest no matter what.

But how should she break the news? Should she say it outright? *We don't feel the same way about each other*. Or perhaps start with something more palatable and work up to the critical point? Would Fradji be upset? The last thing she wants to do is hurt his feelings.

She sees him rush toward her. "Anna, I have news," he says and presses a type-written certificate into her hands.

Order of Induction into the Army of the Republic of France.

"My God, Fradji."

He winces. "Do not speak the Almighty's name."

"I'm sorry, I'm sorry. Fradji, I can't imagine how you must feel. Where are they sending you?"

"Somewhere in Italy. I think near Venice."

Anna tries thinking of something to say, but the thought of Fradji in the trenches plunges her heart into cold terror. First Antonio, now Fradji.

"What has France ever done for me? For my people?" Fradji wipes his eyes. "The French fly their flag over the Bey's palace, build tram stations over our sacred cemeteries, reduce us to farmhands and servants. And now they expect me to fight in their war?"

"Fradji, this is awful. They've no reason to do this to you. It's a cruel, cruel thing, and I am so sorry." She swallows and looks away, reminding herself of what she came to do. She opens her mouth to begin the discussion, to say that she does not have feelings for him, but no words come out. *This is not the right time.* After trying and failing, all she can say is, "How much longer will you be in Tunisia, Fradji?"

"Two weeks," he clears his throat. "In two weeks, I leave for infantry training. They will teach me to use a rifle and bayonet. I've never wanted to kill a man before, Anna. I am not capable of such a thing."

"I can't imagine how you feel. It's criminal, what they've done to you, what they've done to this whole country. You don't deserve any of this. Fradji, listen to me. You have to fight through this. For yourself. For your family. You're a tough man, I know you are."

"Anna, before I go to war, I need to tell you something, something I've felt for a long time."

Anna panics, picking up on the loving intonation of his voice. She tries changing the subject, but in her dread, she cannot think of anything else to discuss.

"No, no—"

"I have to say it, Anna."

"Please don't."

"Anna, I—"

"Let's talk about something else. Weather. Politics. Anything."

"I can't keep it to myself anymore. I know you've felt it too. We have to put it in words."

"I don't want to hurt your feelings. Not today, of all days."

Fradji slowly descends until he is bent on one knee, clutching her hands in his. She rears her head back, feeling more trapped than ever before.

"You are in my soul," he says with a sniffle. "If you will have me, I would like us to be betrothed. Before I go to war."

"Fradji, I don't know what to say. You're a nice man, you really are. You're ambitious and creative and good for conversation, but you're not thinking clearly. You're scared about the war. You're jumping to extremes."

"I *am* thinking clearly, Anna. I'm sure of it. Surer than anything."

She pulls away from him and starts walking back for the estate. Fradji stands and walks after her.

"Anna please, don't you have an answer?"

Her eyes well with tears, but not tears of joy. She has no joy. A pit of guilt acidifies in her stomach, and she feels like vomiting.

"Are you sure this is the best time?"

"With all my soul."

"We...we're not well-suited. How would we even do the wedding? You can't get married in a church, and I can't get married in a synagogue. And if we had kids—I can't believe I'm saying this—we'd be in constant disagreement on how to raise them."

"Love conquers all things," Fradji says. "We can make it work. My parents like you, my sisters like you, my brothers like you. They all say we would be happy together."

Anna throws her hands up. "But what do *you* say? And what do you want *me* to say?"

"I want you to say yes," Fradji is whining now, like a hurt puppy. When Anna does not answer, he grips her wrists. "Anna please, give me an answer. I've always felt this way about you, ever since I first met you. You have no idea what it's like to lock that feeling inside you."

"You wouldn't want to marry me, Fradji. I'm headstrong—"

"I love you, Anna."

"I'm pampered—"

"Anna."

"I wish I could love you back, I really do. I'm proud of you, proud of your work, and I like you and admire you, and I admit I have thought of you, but—"

"But what?"

"I can't see myself married to you. It's that simple."

"I'll never love anyone else."

"Don't talk like that. Just don't talk like that, Fradji! You're going to war. You have to focus on survival. Please, just forget about me!"

Fradji looks at her like he has been shot. "I can't forget about you. I'll die without you."

"No, you won't! You're stronger than that."

"I know I will. On my first day in the trenches, I'll be caught in a bayonet charge."

Anna's vision blurs with tears while Fradji continues to plead. She knows that if left to herself she will weep, but as long as Fradji relies on her, she will feign a smile, she will keep him focused on the task at hand. She will do this to help him survive the war. She is obligated, after all, and as Antonio once told her, obligation is the engine of life. Turns out Antonio was right, after all.

Finally, her shoulders slump and she squeaks out a half-hearted, "Okay."

"What?"

"I said okay."

"So you'll marry me?"

Anna crosses her arms over her chest and gives a single nod.

"My dear, my dear, my dear!" Fradji jumps for joy and pulls her close for a hug.

"Keep it between us for now," Anna says, pushing away from him. "It's our secret and we can discuss it further after the war. You just bring yourself back here unharmed, understood?"

"Yes! Yes!"

"I'll see you off before you head to training, okay?"

"Oh Anna. I don't know what to say. You've made me so happy." Fradji dances in a circle, pulling Anna with him. "You must stop by the house tomorrow. I have to finish my chores before Shabbat, and it might be my last day of rest for a while."

By the time Anna finally drags herself away and says goodbye to Fradji and the sprig of asphodel always tucked behind his ear, by the time she is retracing her footprints to the estate, she is sobbing, wiping tears away, blowing her nose on her sleeve, and cursing the idea of obligation.

38. PEPPERED STUBBLE

Antonio steps off the truck, taking off his feathered hat in respect as he beholds the estate rising through the naked nettle trees. He marvels at the marble balustrades that rise to the columned portico, the stucco grottos, peaking at the Italian flag flapping from the terracotta rooftiles. A signpost at the gate proclaims: *Royal Italian Army Command Center, Office of the Chief of Staff, General Luigi Cadorna.*

The sight of the snapping banner—its bars of green, white, and red, its coat of arms—exemplifies both the familiar and the foreign. Where Antonio grew up, the people considered themselves Catholic first, Sicilian second, and only in passing would they mention the Kingdom of Italy, which had declared its sovereignty only within his parents' lifetimes. In fact, every brick in his father's barber shop has seen more come to pass than the Kingdom of Italy in its entirety. He does not feel the stirring of patriotism that he expected.

"Papers?" a guard asks in Italian, disturbing Antonio from his thoughts.

The two men at the guardhouse chat in Italian while Antonio fumbles for his identification papers. In Tunis, Antonio would seize whatever chance he could to talk with a fellow Italian. The muscle memory of the Italian language fills him like a bowl of pasta with sardines, so great is the relief of not having to strain his ears to translate every word from French or Arabic. However, the relief is only partial because of the guard's Northern accent, so guttural that it is almost French, and Antonio has trouble understanding his own language. Perhaps the guard is from Turin. Again, Antonio cannot tell if it sounds more familiar or foreign, and realizes he does not feel entirely at home in his own country.

The guards search his bags, and Antonio withholds a gasp as they confiscate his mustache trimmer. Too sharp, apparently. Antonio notices the guard scratching at dark stubble, and Antonio *tsks* in disapproval. He knows from his training that every soldier is required to have a clean-shaven face, with the exception of mustaches no more than one inch in length so the gas masks would seal. The officers at Villa Molin make a mockery of these regulations.

"You must be the new barber," the guard mutters, taking note of the collection of scissors and razors in his bag. "Let's hope you last longer than the last one."

"What happened to the last one?" Antonio asks.

"He got too comfortable," the guard says as he opens the gate and escorts Antonio to the front door. "Stayed out past curfew in Padua."

Antonio recalls driving through Padua from the train station and seeing the city had been reduced to craters, once-bustling streets resembling the ruins of Pompeii. He shivers at the thought of the poor barber caught up in it.

Their boots track mud and snowy slush across the marble entrance to the villa. Inside, the atrium rises to a vaulted ceiling where Venetian windows cast a golden glow on the frescos decorating the walls. Officers rush up and down the hallways, carrying stacks of papers, their colorful shoulder cords swinging. Every single one of them has a five o'clock shadow.

"Barber! Barber!" a voice echoes down the hallway.

"Looks like you've got your first assignment already," the guard whistles. "And for General Luigi Cadorna, no less."

"Did you say General?" Antonio stutters while the guards shove him down the hallway. "I'm not sure I'm ready just yet. I haven't even set my bags down, you see, and—"

Before he can finish, they have pushed him into the office, and the door clicks shut behind him. Antonio finds himself in the most secure location in all of Italy, clutching a bag full of razor blades—but not his treasured mustache trimmer—looking at the face of his nightmares sitting at a desk across from him. *General Luigi Cadorna*, the nameplate reads.

"Good day," General Cadorna says, and all Antonio can see is the movement of his atrocious silver mustache that bobs up and down when he speaks. It is the most severely overgrown and uneven piece of work Antonio has ever seen. Some strands reach far enough to poke into his mouth. A patchy chinstrap of peppered stubble works its way from ear to ear. Antonio salutes the man.

"Sir, how long has it been since your last shave?" Antonio asks.

"Too long for you to stand there complacent," he snaps. "Get to work."

Antonio paces to General Cadorna's desk, opening his bag. He unfurls a shaving cloth to tie it around his neck, but he is suddenly gripped by fear.

"Sir, is it legal for me to touch your face?" Antonio asks.

"How else would you shave me?" he growls.

Hands trembling, Antonio ties the cloth around General Cadorna's neck. Antonio pours the General's water pitcher into his soap dish and, using his horsehair brush, stirs the soap, creating a foamy lather. He has not felt this tense as a barber since first cutting Anna's hair.

"I'm sure you're happy to see that the Prime Minister is firing me tomorrow," General Cadorna huffs. "It's a partisan stunt he's pulling, that's all. Three hundred and fifty thousand Italians flee the battlefield, and he blames it on me. I'd imprison every last one of them if given the chance. Cowardice has seeped into every level of command while the entire Austrian army is camped only thirty miles away, exposing the King's residence to their range of attack."

Antonio unsheathes Papà's pearl-inlaid, walnut razor and holds it to General Cadorna's neck. What if he cuts the man by mistake?

I am the son of a barber, he braces himself. *I am here to do my duty.* Antonio scrapes the stubble off General Cadorna's check, wiping the foam on a cloth over his shoulder. He works his way to the opposite jaw, and then prepares a heated towel to press against the man's face.

A few flashes of the scissors leave modest silver chevron hugging his upper lip.

"Sir, is this acceptable?" Antonio asks.

General Cadorna chokes the mirror in his fist, and a momentary smile flashes across his face. At the sight of himself, looking sharp as ever, he straightens from his slumped posture, draws back his shoulder blades, puffs out his chest, as if a simple haircut could momentarily shave off months of stress. But only for a moment. The general's expression hardens, and he hands the mirror back.

"The haircut meets regulation," he says.

Antonio cleans up as fast as he can, and the man raises his arm in a salute. Antonio salutes back and scurries from the room.

39. ENTANGLEMENTS

Anna paces across the factory floor, and the clatter of her pumps on the floorboards is drowned out by the rush of electric sewing machines. The walls are plastered with posters urging her to BUY WAR BONDS. French flags flutter from the rafters. Women sit hunched over their work, expertly sliding their fingers across the driving needles in perfect coordination until a heaping pile of khaki trousers amass at the end of the worktable. They are the same kind of baggy, khaki trousers Antonio wore when he stood on the dock and said goodbye, specifically designed for an extended range of movement and durability.

As Anna walks, she catches a few raised eyebrows from the workers, who take in her elbow-length satin gloves and her necklaces borrowed from Zia Rosa's collection. The workers' collective body heat warms the factory, and Anna can already feel the beads of sweat on her arms, threatening to darken her gloves. When Anna reaches the administrative offices at the far end of the factory floor, she takes a moment to gather herself, to draw back her shoulder blades and puff out her chest with confidence. Then she knocks on the office door.

"Come in," a woman replies in French.

Anna creaks the door open to see a woman leaning back at her desk, poring through booklets of schematics, a cigarette between her fingers.

"Are you Madame Beauvoir?" Anna asks.

She nods, not looking up from her work.

"My name is Anna DiNicola. I sent in my application last week, and you asked me to come in for a job interview."

Madame Beauvoir finally sets down her papers and scans Anna from head to toe—her cloche hat, her pearls, her embroidered coin purse.

"You look like you've fallen out of a department store display window," Madame Beauvoir says. "What do you need a job for? I have your application here, yes. It says your only work experience is…a three-year apprenticeship? What in?"

"Luxury garments," Anna says. "I took requests from wealthy patrons in the Sephardic community. Wedding couture, religious attire, that kind of thing."

"Can you use a sewing machine?"

Anna chooses her words carefully.

"I have three years of experience using a loom. I can embroider. I can hand-stitch."

"But you've never used a sewing machine?"

"Is that a problem?"

"I suppose you have the proper skills to learn," Madame Beauvoir shrugs.

Anna sighs and settles into her seat, more comfortably this time.

"But my biggest question," Madame Beauvoir says. "Why this job? You seem like a refined lady, with your necklaces and your rings and the latest styles. Why would you go from an apprenticeship in luxury garments to making soldiers' trousers in a factory? You are over-qualified, to say the least."

Anna purses her lips, and she feels the woman's suspicious eyes on her.

"My apprenticeship was complicated," Anna finally says. "I had too many...entanglements...and I figured it would be best to distance myself from them."

"Entanglements," Madame Beauvoir tries the word out for herself, but she says it with a softer inflection than Anna. Perhaps she has picked up on the meaning.

"And you are sure you won't miss your previous job?" Madame Beauvoir asks. "This won't be the kind of work you are used to."

"I will miss my old job for sure," Anna says. "But this is for the best."

"If you say so," Madame Beauvoir says. "You can start working next week. We will have a sewing machine waiting for you."

40. FLIES HUM

Antonio straps on his helmet, checks out at the guardhouse, and leaves the headquarters, trudging up the road to where the rooftops of Padua break over the nettle trees. Brown slush dirties the road, cold autumn rain *tap tap taps* at the mud.

While he trudges, two columns of soldiers march in the opposite direction, returning from their rotation at the trenches. Flies hum around them, and Antonio smells latrine-fumes and rotting meat. He wants to pinch his nose shut. The soldiers have purple bags under their eyes from lack of sleep, and their uniforms—and their faces—are covered in dirt. Then he recognizes the blue uniforms of the French army. *The French?* He did not know the French had sent troops to Italy.

Click.

Antonio blinks as a white flash bursts, and a wild quail scurries into the trees. One of the soldiers lowers a camera from his eye level, and Antonio spots a familiar face. But that is where the familiarity ends. The nest of curly black hair is shaved down to a buzz cut. The Sephardic kippah that usually covers the crown of his head is nowhere to be seen. The sprig of asphodel he usually tucks behind his ear is gone. His lifeless eyes stare straight ahead as if looking into a different world.

"Fradji?" Antonio calls. "Is that you?"

Fradji looks up from his camera, mouth falling open. "Antonio?"

"In October, France sent a division of troops—the 10th French Army—to support Italy after their retreat," Fradji explains as they walk through the streets of Padua. "We've been shoring up the defenses on the Piave River—laying down sandbags, digging trenches, building bunkers."

The man's voice is gruff and business-like, totally different from the eager artist he once knew. As Antonio studies him further, he notices cuts and bruises all over his face. His neck is so thin it doesn't fill the collar of his uniform.

"I have heard talk that Italy is a beautiful country," Fradji says, "but they are wrong. Give me the Tunisian sun."

"The *south* of Italy is a beautiful country," Antonio corrects him. "The north is the miserable part, yes. It's a curious thing, being back in Italy after all this time. It feels like a foreign country to me. Don't mistake my words, I love speaking Italian, but I can barely understand the accents here. Even the weather is different. If I can't call Italy home, and I can't call Tunisia home, then what do I say when people ask where I'm from?"

"I'm afraid I don't have an answer," Fradji says, and his words condense into fog.

"How long until your next rotation?" Antonio asks.

"I'll be billeting in town the next two weeks," Fradji stretches out his back. "Didn't sleep last night. Marched thirty miles."

Fradji stares ahead at nothing, his heavy-lidded eyes slipping shut, his head wobbling even as his legs keep going. He has, apparently, learned to walk while asleep.

"Do you need to rest?" Antonio says, and he feels like a fool for asking since it is obvious that Fradji is practically comatose.

Fradji makes no eye contact and stumbles forward. Antonio reaches out to steady him, worried that he will faint. The word "food" slips out under Fradji's breath, riding on a sigh.

"Okay, let me buy you dinner."

Antonio takes him to a local restaurant crowded with khaki-clad soldiers. The walls are stacked high with sandbags to protect from shrapnel, and they are seated in a dark alcove. Fradji is awake now and rubs his palms together and pulls his coat around him for warmth.

"I can't imagine what sort of hellscape awaits on the Piave River," Antonio says.

Antonio pictures the enemy armies watching the trenches for any sign of movement, their rifles and artillery carefully aimed on the bobbing French and Italian helmets. The Italians had been continually pushed back, losing ground for about a year, and a thirty-mile buffer zone is all that prevents the collapse of Italy. At the headquarters, Antonio has a warm place to sleep, a meal, and security, all because men like Fradji are risking their lives for him. Antonio feels a swelling gratitude and also a swamping guilt that he got off so easy. But he does not dare put his thoughts into words, afraid that it would send Fradji into a rage.

"I'm glad we have the French on our side," Antonio adds.

"Damn the French," Fradji snaps. "I am half-hoping they lose this war. They take over my country then make me fight their battles. I never asked for this."

Antonio gasps. "But then the Germans and the Austro-Hungarians would win, and that's even worse," Antonio reminds him.

"How? How is it worse? I would just be trading one oppressor for another. That's hardly a difference."

"What about Italy?" Antonio asks. "I wouldn't want to see the Kingdom of Italy fall. I have a cousin who works in the government. His life would be in danger."

"If Italy fell, then you'd know what I have to deal with on a daily basis," Fradji raises his voice. "Don't you understand? Your wars don't matter to me."

"Not so loud," Antonio hisses. "People can hear you."

He peers over his shoulder to make sure no one is listening, but a few soldiers at the bar have glanced their way. Antonio feels a sudden urge to cover his face and leave, to separate himself from Fradji and by extension his opinions.

"Look at us," Fradji scoffs, "coming to blows over some decisions a committee of politicians made. We're just little bugs caught in the tide. Bugs that could be crushed under a boot and forgotten about."

Antonio does not answer. Soon, a young woman sets down two steaming plates of pasta with silver sardines arranged in a starburst pattern, and he relaxes.

While Antonio chews, he searches for a topic of discussion. He did not often speak with Fradji back in Tunisia and he had only ever seen him standing in Anna's shadow with a camera hanging from his neck. Whatever beauty lay in cameras, Antonio cannot see it. To him, all those contraptions do is put painters out of business.

Rrrrrreeeeeee. A singing whistling splits the restaurant, and Antonio cranes his neck for the source. *Rrrrrreeeeeee*

"Do you hear whistling?" Antonio says. "I wish whoever's boiling that teapot would take it off the heat."

"*Shell!*"

Fradji dives over the table, wrenching Antonio by his collar. They hit the floor, their pasta plates shattering. A wave of pressure sweeps through him. The windows spiderweb with cracks, while outside a column of smoke gushes over the rooftops.

"Shell!" someone else shouts, and a warning siren echoes over the city while volunteers run to dig the battered, bleeding bodies from the rubble.

Suddenly, Antonio is a child again in Partinico, hearing the gunshots splitting the night as the Black Hand mafia take their next victim. He tries to hide the feeling but finds himself twitching, jumping, at the slightest disturbance. He traces the cross over his torso compulsively, a reflex now against uncertainty.

Fradji, in contrast, grabs Antonio by the collar with a grip strong enough to choke him, and wrenches him to his feet. They step over the shattered plates and sardines smeared on the floor. In the commotion, Antonio's personal papers have scattered everywhere—his cash, his coins, his identification cards. Fradji helps him pick up the papers before they blow away, and then curls a frown when he picks up one of the photographs fallen from Antonio's wallet.

"I took this photo," Fradji whispers, lifting the sepia photograph of Anna standing in her straw hat, smiling in the souk. "Where did you get this?"

"Anna gave it to me before I was deployed, to keep her in my thoughts."

"I did not know she was in your thoughts," Fradji mutters.

Antonio's stomach lurches. He can hear the trembling rage masked under Fradji's curiosity.

"I think of her as much as any other friend," Antonio does not know who he is trying to convince—himself or Fradji. Surely, Fradji could drop him with one punch if that's what it came to. Antonio can only guess how many Austrian and German soldiers he has grappled with in the trenches.

"She hasn't told you, has she?" Fradji says. "It's supposed to be a secret for now."

"Told me what? What secret?"

"Anna and I are engaged."

41. STARS OF HENNA DYE

With Fradji and his brothers gone, the Sarfati family needs extra help, so on Fridays before Shabbat begins Anna helps Fradji's mother fry the chard and roll the ground beef meatballs between her palms. The pan sputters with olive oil, and when they add the spinach a cloud of steam rises to the ceiling. All the while Anna stares at her bag that sits on the divan. She knows that folded inside her bag is a slip of type-written stationery, a job offer to sew pants for the soldiers. She wonders how she will break the news to Miriam.

"Anna, come with me. There is something I must show you," Miriam tells her after they clean up.

Miriam ducks underneath the family bed and slides out a paper parcel.

"This was my wedding shawl," Miriam says, and she unfolds the paper, unfurling a maroon cloth that reaches to her toes.

"I've never seen anything like it." Anna traces her fingers across the maroon velvet, the embroidered curls of gold thread, the pearls and beads stitched along the waistline. It far surpasses anything she has worked on before.

"I want you to have it," Miriam says, "for your own wedding."

Anna's heart sinks, and she looks back to her bag sitting on the divan with the job offer inside.

"I always imagined myself wearing a white gown and veil," Anna says, "like my mamma and her mamma."

Anna realizes she is channeling Antonio. *I always dreamed of working in my family's barber shop, just like my papà and his papà.*

Miriam does not seem to hear because she keeps talking. "My people's weddings are no small undertaking," Miriam continues. "When I was a young woman, I'd drink several bowls of goat's milk a day to fill in my hips. After my mikveh, my sisters and mother painted my palms and wrists with stars of henna. The wedding takes many months of planning, but I would not trade it for all the riches in the Bey's palace."

Finally, Anna hears herself blurt out, "I accepted a job offer somewhere else."

Miriam pauses, then sets the shawl down.

"I am confused," she says. "You don't want to work with me anymore? Did I offend you?"

"You've done nothing wrong," Anna says, feeling her stomach tie into a knot as she tries to explain. "You've taught me so much, and you've let me into your family, but I can't be your apprentice anymore."

"Why? Anna, please tell me what wrong I have done, and I will change," Miriam says.

"It's not about anything you've done. It's about Fradji,"

Anna says. "I know you want me to marry him, that you want me as your daughter-in-law, but it's too much for me, Miriam. I intend to break it off with Fradji after he returns from the war."

"Why?" Miriam's stare is deadly serious. "That would break Fradji, and you two have been inseparable. What changed?"

"Nothing changed. I'm only being true to myself," Anna says, terrified that she has angered Miriam. "I care for Fradji, but I don't love him like a husband. I can't marry him."

Miriam's expression crumples, and she slowly folds up her wedding shawl, packing it away in its paper and sliding it back under the bed.

"I don't know what to say," she mutters.

"I'm sorry," Anna wishes she could reach out and hug Miriam and express her sympathy, but that would only make Anna want to change her mind. Instead, Anna watches Miriam turn her back and proceed to the kitchen, where the chard pops and sizzles in the olive oil.

"I will still see you again," Anna follows her. "When Fradji returns from the war, I will tell him."

Miriam's face is as solemn as if she is at a funeral. "I understand," she says softly, so softly the sizzling olive oil dulls her words. "Then I will have one less daughter."

42. FILM UNSPOOLING

Antonio stumbles from the restaurant to see a cloud of dust pluming from the collapsed row-houses across the street. The ambulance driver takes his time winding down the road to the field hospital outside town, not even honking his horn. The ambulance is in no rush.

Beside him, Fradji lifts the camera to his only open eye. *Click.* A white flash, and the ruins of Padua are frozen in time, sending yet another painter out of business.

"Drop that camera!" an officer shouts in French, his sleeves studded with the rank of colonel, marching toward them.

"Not again," Fradji mutters, straightening his back and saluting.

"Only government-approved photography is allowed," the colonel says. "Do you have papers for that camera?"

"I…I," Fradji stutters.

"Where are you sending those photographs anyway?" the colonel narrows his gaze, studying Fradji's baggy white pants denoting he is a member of the North African regiment.

The French colonel looks to Antonio, but Antonio holds his tongue, not sure if he is even allowed to report to a foreign officer. Finally, the colonel holds out his palm.

"That camera is now property of the French Republic. Hand it over."

Fradji does not budge, and for a moment Antonio worries he will put up a fight. Fradji eyes the pistol holstered at the officer's side, fists clenching.

"Hand it over."

Nostrils flared, Fradji rips his camera off his neck strap. The colonel takes it, turns his back, and the camera is gone.

"Bastard," Fradji hisses as soon as the officer is out of sight.

That evening, Antonio hurries back to the safety of Villa Molin, where the guards crowd the entrance with rifles and bayonets. Curfew is only ten minutes away. He is surrounded by naked trees and snowy fields and war and Antonio can only think of one thing: Fradji and Anna are engaged!

How foolish of him for not seeing it earlier. The evidence was plain—the only times he had seen Fradji was in Anna's shadow. Since they had started courting, Anna entirely disappeared from her regular haircut appointments.

A stronger question breaks through his swirling thoughts—why hadn't Anna told anyone? Back in Partinico, when two people were set to be married, the entire town knew about it. Is she reluctant? Is she unsure?

Antonio fishes the photograph from his pocket, the photograph of Anna smiling in the souk, which apparently came from Fradji's now-confiscated camera. Anna had pressed the photograph into Antonio's hands with such care, her brow bent with concern, right after Giuseppina confessed her love, casting her aside to watch from afar. He told Fradji that Anna had given him the photograph as a simple a token of friendship. But none of Antonio's other friends wanted so badly to be in his thoughts.

Finally, his thoughts settle on Fradji, and a fire burns in his stomach. Fradji, the man of science who meets with professors and studies photography, who can bend electricity and chemistry to freeze a moment of time onto film. Admittedly, Antonio can understand Anna's fascination. Anna the American who loves all things modern and laughs at the past, surely would find Fradji the peak of excitement, bursting with new ideas. If only Antonio could be as interesting as Fradji.

Arriving at Villa Molin, Antonio stamps the mud off his shoes and takes off his helmet.

"Orlando!" someone calls in a French accent.

In the fresco-plastered atrium, a cluster of officers stand, waiting for him. Antonio salutes, and he recognizes the French colonel from earlier, standing alongside the Italian officers.

"Come with us."

Soon, Antonio is standing inside the general's office, the exit blocked by men with bayonets.

"Sit," he is pointed to a hard wooden chair while the officers stand over him.

Antonio's heart pounds.

"That man you spoke to earlier," the French colonel asks, "he is one of our infantrymen, Fradji Sarfati. How did you know him?"

Antonio grasps for words. He is afraid how much he should say. Surely the officers know something he does not, and Antonio imagines how easy it would be to say the wrong words and incriminate himself.

"Speak."

"I-I used to know Fradji before the war," Antonio stutters.

"You were friends with him?" the colonel asks.

"I knew of him, that's all."

The colonel glances at the Italian officers, nodding.

"We trust you, Orlando," the Italian officers say. "We just want to know the truth. Intelligence tells us this Fradji Sarfati fellow has frequently spoken out against the French government and fits the description of some Tunisian separatists. We even caught him taking detailed photographs of a military encampment with this."

The officer pulls out a weathered Kodak camera the size of a tin of pomade.

"Has he expressed any anti-government sentiments to you? Did you see him disappearing for long stretches of time, perhaps meeting with strangers?"

Antonio wants to gasp. They think Fradji is a spy? The more Antonio thinks about it, the less he can deny it. He knows Fradji hates France—and for good reason. But then he considers how Anna loves Fradji, and if Anna loves him then he could only be the most upstanding, the most virtuous man, more virtuous than Antonio evidently.

"Orlando?" the officer shouts. "If you hide anything from us, we will find out and hold you equally guilty. We know more than you."

"He said, he said," Antonio stutters.

"What did he say?"

"He said that he hopes France loses the war."

Antonio shrinks two inches into his chair.

With a pump of the colonel's arm, the camera smashes on the floorboards, sending its lens rolling toward the exit, its roll of film unspooling across the room.

"Seize him immediately," the colonel says, and the other officers scurry to do his bidding.

Antonio watches them leave, praying for God's mercy. And for Anna's.

43. APRICOT CANNOLI

Anna turns the corner onto the dirt road lined with tall blades of Italian cypress, flanked by pastures of grazing goats and apricot trees and the distant blue sliver of Lac de Tunis. The wedding-cake complex of Zia Rosa's estate waits for her at the end of the road. Home. Or at least the closest thing she has to a home. At this hour, the air is hazy with dust, and the collar of her dress is dark with sweat. She fans herself with her hat, feeling her arms and neck sore after another day in the factory, running the khaki army trousers under the mechanically driven needle, stitching identical seams until the shadows stretch long.

When Anna steps into the entrance hall of the estate, she finds Zia Rosa sitting in her armchair, head buried in a romance novel while the servants bring her a painted bowl of dried apricots.

"Hard at work, I see," Anna nods at Zia Rosa.

"Don't make fun, I've earned my rest. You should follow my example, Anna. No need for you to take a job at the factory when we have all these comforts at home," Zia

Rosa gestures toward Fatma, who brings her a tiny cup and saucer of Turkish coffee. "Sit down, enjoy your life."

Anna feels a flame of irritation in her chest.

"I don't want to be served," Anna says.

"I don't mind the work," Fatma says. "Zia Rosa pays me generously. Because of this job, I can send my son to school. He is studying to be an electrician."

"I'm just saying," Anna backtracks, "you might have other dreams that you've put on hold."

"Of course, I have other dreams," Fatma says, irritated, "but I do the best I can with what Allah gives me. When you are older, you will understand."

"What are your dreams?" Anna asks.

Fatma pauses, and Anna can sense she is growing uncomfortable with the conversation. Anna has never asked her such a personal question.

"I dream of poetry. I have two poems published to my name in a small newspaper," Fatma says. "Of course, I'm no Aboul-Qacem Echebbi. *If a person's soul is small, his dream will also be tiny, then he will not tire or suffer, but whoever has great ambitions will be welcomed by life with the ferocity of a lion.*"

A poet, Anna thinks. *Our cook is a published poet.*

When the sun droops, Anna is splashing water on her face in the washroom, and Fatma knocks on the door.

"You have a visitor," Fatma says.

"At this hour?" Anna ties her satin bathrobe tightly and steps onto the tiles of the courtyard, where she sees

Giuseppina standing, scoffing at the elaborately carved arches and mosaic tiles.

"Giuseppina?" Anna asks. "What's brought you here? It's a long walk from the city."

"I took the tram and walked the last bit," Giuseppina says. "I wanted to show support."

"Support for what?"

Giuseppina raises a tray of cannoli with crumbled pistachio and apricot. Anna creases her brow.

"The newspapers say that fighting has really picked up in Italy," Giuseppina says. "The French and Italians have made a last effort to break the lines of the Austrians and Germans, and to think that Antonio and Fradji are in the thick of the shooting, and it's put me on edge all day, wondering if Antonio is wounded or if he's clinging to dear life in a bunker somewhere. So, I made some apricot cannoli to take my mind off the war. I thought I'd share them with you, since you understand the stress. You probably can't wait to see Fradji again."

Anna accepts the tray of cannoli, but she appreciates it for the wrong reason. She is going to break up with Fradji when he returns, after all. A tray of cannoli would normally be a small thing, especially when Zia Rosa keeps an entire cupboard of sweets in the kitchen, but when Anna thinks of the extra effort Giuseppina went to, her heart warms.

"Come inside," Anna says. "Let's talk about this more."

Giuseppina steps into the kitchen, and they sit cross-legged at the low table and drink Turkish coffee and eat the apricot cannoli. The steam rises from the coffee and fills the room with a sweet cardamon aroma that mixes with the ever-present smell of harissa.

"You're always doing nice things for people," Anna says, pouring out two cups of coffee, "always baking, cooking, taking care of everyone except yourself."

"It is in giving that we receive, and it is in pardoning that we are pardoned," Giuseppina recites the words of Saint Francis that Anna has heard so many times. "I know that might sound like a foreign concept to some people," Giuseppina continues. "A few Sicilian aristocrats come to mind."

"Sometimes you have to serve yourself, too," Anna says, swallowing the cannoli.

"And has that worked for you?" Giuseppina asks. "Serving yourself?"

Anna sets down her coffee cup. She thinks of the hurt in Miriam Sarfati's eyes when she quit her job, the hurt in Fradji's eyes as she tried to break it off with him. She compares herself to Giuseppina, who always seems to know what is right, who always carries an air of gracefulness and sincerity. The thought only makes Anna feel more insecure, and she wonders if she is in the wrong. But she doesn't share her thoughts, not with Antonio's betrothed.

Soon, the cannoli tray sits empty except for crumbs and smudges of cream. The coffee cups are down to their terminal dregs.

"I so enjoyed our talk," Giuseppina beams, "but I have to get back home before it gets any darker."

"You've given me a lot to think about," Anna nods, not returning Giuseppina's smile.

"Actually, I have one more thing to ask. Could you do me a favor?"

"Always," Anna says.

"Could you pray for Antonio? For his safe return? The more people praying for him, the better."

Anna frowns. She already prays for Antonio—she begs the Virgin Mary to intercede for him every day, that not one hair on his well-kempt head be harmed. But she does not correct Giuseppina.

"Of course. I will do my best to pray for him," Anna says through a forced smile, and sees Giuseppina out.

44. BATTLE OF VITTORIO VENETO

Antonio paces his sleeping quarters, pulling at his hair as his thoughts spiral. He knows the French officers are driving to the billets in Padua right now, handcuffs at the ready so they can take Fradji in for questioning.

And he is the one who ratted Fradji out. The guilt weighs like a rock in the pit of his stomach, making him want to vomit. Would they throw Fradji in jail? He can only imagine Anna's despair at receiving the news. Fradji is a good man, and Antonio should be damned himself if he does not want to see Anna happy with him. Antonio cannot stay at the headquarters, complacent and safe while Fradji is arrested. He must go to Fradji.

Antonio catches a ride to the billets on an ambulance, telling the driver to hurry. They arrive in Padua, and Antonio hurries across the piazza to the repurposed hotel, the façade stacked with sandbags, where the French soldiers are staying, where he knows Fradji is staying. He sees a commotion outside where a group of French officers are scuffling, Fradji among them. He is pinned on both sides by a French soldier, their trench coats flapping against the cold autumn rain. One of the officers looks up and sees Antonio. His eyes narrow in anger.

"Did you follow us? Why are you here?"

Antonio opens his mouth to say something—he has no idea what—when a high pitched *rrrreeeeeee* fills the air. Antonio has heard that sound before.

"*Projectiles incoming! Evacuate!*" A hoarse shout echoes from across the piazza, and a loud *boom* rattles Antonio's bones. The piazza fills with screams. Soldiers swarm in every direction.

"Evacuate, soldier!" an officer pushes against Antonio, and he breaks out in a run.

The sirens are blaring *aaaaawwwwooooo*. The same French officers about to arrest Fradji are piling onto a line of trucks, which squeal skid-marks on the bricks as they lurch for the headquarters at full speed. Antonio runs to one of the trucks, but a soldier takes one look at the lack of patches on Antonio's uniform.

"Officers take the priority!" he shouts. "Lower-ranking soldiers are to head for the bunkers!"

Before Antonio can respond, the world flashes white, and a wave of heat throws him onto his back as the truck flips onto its side. Pillars of fire erupt over the terracotta rooftiles, and he can only hear the ringing in his ears. Time deteriorates into nothing, and he feels like he is observing himself from some space outside his body. He tries to stand, but his legs wobble. The French officers are splayed across the stones, dark rivulets running into the cobblestones. He is lying on his back in the wide-open piazza, totally exposed to the whistling shells that light up the sky.

A rough set of arms lifts him to his feet and points out the sand-bagged bunker across the street. Antonio hobbles toward the entrance. Stumbling over a tangle of limbs, he is about to duck inside the bunker door with the others, when he turns and sees a man lying on the cratered pavement, his legs pinned down by the flipped truck. He recognizes the man he betrayed—Fradji, bleeding out in the street.

In a few minutes, Fradji will be lying there unmoving, his soul dispersed into vapor, the very man who is engaged to marry Anna. *Love is something worth fighting for, and that is where we differ,* Anna once told him, and he sees her standing in the souk, running fingers through her immaculate bob. The image catches fire and curls into a charred smoking mess, and Anna melts.

Before Antonio can think, he is running on wobbly legs back across the piazza for Fradji, throwing his shoulder against the truck, but it barely moves. The truck's canvas cover is on fire, and the metal is hot to the touch. He peers under the vehicle, finding that it is balancing precariously on the smashed driver's cabin while the truck bed teeters on Fradji's legs.

The rooftops of Padua light up, and pillars of smoke fill the skyline. Another piercing whistle vibrates his bones, and Antonio dives behind the truck for cover, throwing his arms over his head as a shell explodes across the piazza. A spray of rubble and cobblestones torpedo in all directions, embedding in the dented metal of the overturned truck. Fradji screams.

Antonio grabs the bumper with both his hands, lifting with a burst of power he never knew he had, and the truck wobbles slightly. By now his hands are covered in blisters and cuts and soot. The truck is teetering on Fradji, but soon it will collapse completely and there will be no hope of rescuing him.

Antonio cannot lift it even now, and there is no one nearby to help him. His arms are too thin. He never trained in the boot camps where soldiers carried hundred-pound sandbags over their shoulders through obstacle courses. He is just a barber. Fradji continues to scream, and the truck continues to teeter. *I have to think!* Antonio looks around for a tool that he can use as leverage, like a crowbar or a plank of wood. In an upside-down compartment of the truck, he finds a tire jack. Perfect.

Another shell lands nearby, this time on his side of the truck, and there is no cover. He throws his body over Fradji to cover him, and Antonio cries out as a brick slams into his side. But then the falling debris stops and, hands fumbling, Antonio jams the jack under the truck. He fits the crank and rotates the bar with all his strength. The truck bed rises a hand's thickness, enough for Antonio to drag Fradji out from underneath. His pant legs are dark with blood, and Antonio does not have time to think of the damage.

"Hold on!" Antonio lifts Fradji onto his back, and Fradji clings to his shoulders, still moaning. Antonio's feet slip in the blood covering the paving stones and he trips over the debris of nearby buildings. He stumbles and nearly falls because he never trained for this. He has no idea know how to properly carry someone. But still, he keeps moving. Running as fast as he can across the piazza to the bunker, diving through the doorway just as the next bomb falls.

45. BRUISE LIKE WATERCOLORS

Every morning Anna ties on her satin robe and walks to the kitchen, squinting against the light. Fatma prepares her a tiny cup and saucer of Turkish coffee, and she sips while the postman's truck stops outside the courtyard gate to deliver letters from Fradji. Even when Fradji writes in Arabic, the French censors still black out the key terms.

Fradji does not write much of the war in his letters, only that he is in good spirits, which Anna knows is a lie. He mostly writes about memories of Tunisia—the flamingos, the Shabbat dinners, the Grand Synagogue. She is okay with this, though. The relief of knowing he is still fighting, still burning with an inner fire, still breathing, is enough for her.

But one day, Anna is sipping her Turkish coffee when the mail truck rumbles right past the estate. The postman has no mail for her.

The next day passes, and still no mail.

Every night, she prays for Fradji's safety in addition to Antonio's, and she walks to the church to fumble over the beads of her rosary, whispering Hail Mary after Hail

Mary. On the third day, someone knocks on the turquoise carriage doors, and Anna gathers her skirts and rushes across the courtyard tiles, only to find Fradji's mamma standing there.

"Miriam?" Anna asks. "What is it? What's happened?"

Anna pretends she does not know, but she has heard too many identical stories not to know. She feels lightheaded; her chest seizes up.

"Fradji is alive," Miriam says. "Do not panic—I will tell you the whole story. Yesterday, some French soldiers came to my house to tell me that Fradji is in the hospital. He was staying in Padua when the city was bombed, and he was hit with shrapnel. He damaged his spine and has lost sensation in his legs, but he is alive. They are keeping him in a field hospital near Genoa and are sending him home by the end of the month."

Anna feels the world spin.

"I think I need to sit down," she says. "I can't imagine how you must feel. Your son—"

"The Almighty has delivered him," Miriam says. "This is all that matters."

Anna steps forward to hug Miriam, to give her some comfort, but the woman turns away from her, rigid.

"How much time will you give my son?" Miriam asks.

"What do you mean?"

"How much time will you give my son before you break it off with him?"

"I'll wait until he has recovered," Anna says, "he deserves that."

"He deserves far more than that," Miriam says, spinning around and slamming the gate on her way out.

On the day Fradji returns, Anna wears her cloche hat, her white gloves, and her maroon dress. She takes the tram to the harbor where she meets Fradji's family.

"*Fradji!*" the Sarfati family erupts in cheers as the man rolls off the warship and onto the pier in his new wheelchair. He wears the blue uniform of the French military, a colorful array of medals decorating his chest.

Anna throws her arms around him. He gives a forced smile, his mouth twitching. He checks over his shoulder even though nobody is there. They push him down Rue de Paris, into the medina, and he flinches as they pass through the bustling crowds.

"What would you like to do first, Fradji?" Anna asks. "Visit the souk? See the flamingos?"

"I just want to sleep," he says. "I'm sorry, I don't need—I don't want a celebration."

Once in the safety of the Sarfati household, Anna helps Fradji out of his wheelchair. He clings to her shoulders, and she slides her arms under his knees and back, lifting him like the Virgin Mary lifted Christ in the Pieta, setting him on the family bed. Anna has never held a man in her arms before. He is thinner and softer than she had imagined, and it terrifies her.

"I can't sleep on this," he says, his voice low and flat. "It's too soft."

He crawls onto the tile floor and curls up into a ball. He has them close the window shutters so nobody will look inside and spy on him, which Anna thinks is paranoid, but she does not say anything. She drapes a blanket over him and leaves him curled up on the tile floor, in the dark.

In the kitchen, Miriam shushes Fradji's brothers and sisters, who have laid out the table with plates of fried date rolls dusted with sesame seeds, tiny white donuts of marzipan and rosewater, a dish of baklava shining with honey.

"Let him rest," Miriam says, throwing a cloth over the desserts.

Miriam does not speak to Anna, does not even look at her. Anna sits with Fradji's siblings around the table, saying nothing, knowing that she is not welcome. Eventually, she walks back into the bedroom and sits on the floor at Fradji's side. After a while she realizes he is awake.

"Do you want to go anywhere?" she asks him.

He starts to speak, but then closes his mouth.

"Fradji?" she asks. "Maybe you'd like to take some photographs? Like old times."

"With what? I don't have a camera anymore."

"You lost it?"

"The officers destroyed it so they could control the propaganda."

Anna rests a hand on his shoulder, wondering what else was destroyed in the war.

The next day, Anna visits the camera shop before visiting Fradji. Once she arrives, she sits beside him and hands him a new camera, wrapped in brown paper. The device is silvery-metallic, slender enough to slip inside a pocket, an improvement from Fradji's old box camera, and she bites her lip in excitement as he tears the paper, anticipating a smile to break out across his face.

"Fradji?"

He does not acknowledge Anna but only stares at the camera, face blank like one transported to another world.

"Did I buy the wrong camera?"

By now he is hyperventilating, sweat pouring down his temples. Anna fears he will vomit, so she moves to take the camera away, and in a flash his fist closes over her wrist, twisting her arm in a way it has never moved before.

"*Fradji!*" her arm shoots with pain, and she yelps.

A pump of his other arm, and the new camera sails through the air, crashing against the wall. "*Fradji!*" Anna pulls away from him, rattling his wheelchair, but he grips her wrist more tightly. "Let me go!" She considers striking him, but she cannot bring herself to use force against him. In one glance, her fiancé changes from the gentle photographer to a hardened soldier.

Hearing the commotion, Miriam rushes in from the kitchen. "Fradji!" She wrenches Anna's wrist from Fradji's grasp. Purple patches on her wrist bruise like watercolors.

"What did you do to him?" Miriam snaps.

"I don't know what happened!" Anna steps away, rubbing her wrist. "I bought him a new camera and he didn't like it, and—"

"Perhaps it would be best if you leave. Fradji needs to rest."

Confused and sad—and angry—Anna gathers her things and shuts the door behind her so hard the mezuzah shakes on its hook.

46. VICTORY

Public announcements circulate through the headquarters at Villa Molin, and Antonio pores over the pamphlets decrying the new threat—the Spanish Flu—and how to avoid it. *Everyone at Villa Molin is now required to wear a white medical mask,* the pamphlet says. In the basement barracks, soldiers spread the sleeping cots two meters apart and erect canvas dividers between them. Entire days pass when the only time Antonio sees a human face is to trim an officer's mustache. The senior officers frantically fill out paperwork, arranging logistics, and unfolding maps that show enemy units camped only a brief drive down the road.

After surviving the bombing, Antonio only leaves Villa Molin when absolutely necessary, and leaving is an ordeal in itself. He must scrub his hands—his fingernails, the crook of his fingers, his wrists—put on gloves and a mask, make sure he doesn't stand within two meters of anyone, and carry his identification papers with him. And always, the ground rumbles with nearby explosions.

My Giuseppina, Antonio writes that evening. *One crisis splinters into thousands, and I cannot keep track anymore. I sometimes feel that everything mankind touches, they ruin. The pine forests of northern Italy are reduced to bombed-out husks of smoking tree stumps and craters. The skies are criss-crossed with airplane exhaust as pilots dogfight overhead. I am not sure whether to be more afraid of the bombs or the influenza. It seems the world has simply erupted into a permanent state of crisis—not just Italy, but everywhere. Is this how history is supposed to work? Did God design the world to sour with age? In all my history lessons, I cannot remember a time as chaotic as this. There are too many people on this planet, Giuseppina. Far too many.*

Antonio considers crumpling the paper and rewriting because he does not like how pessimistic he sounds, and he knows Giuseppina does not like hearing this kind of talk. Antonio sometimes has sentiments that are too raw for her, sentiments he cannot share with her.

"Delivery," an officer wearing a medical mask steps into the sleeping quarters and tosses a packet of letters onto Antonio's cot. The envelopes land with a hefty *thud*.

"There must be a mistake," Antonio says. "These letters can't all be for me. Giuseppina just writes me once a week."

"These aren't from a Giuseppina," the officer says.

Antonio snatches the packet from him, seeing the familiar looping handwriting scrawled in green ink across the paper.

Anna DiNicola. Antonio counts eleven letters. "Why are they just now coming?" he asks.

The officer shrugs. "Probably lost in circulation."

Using his shaving razor and his practiced steady hand, Antonio cuts the envelope open, careful not to damage Anna's writing.

Dear Antonio,

Please come back soon—my hair has grown past my shoulders, and you know that isn't a good look for me. You should see the absolute state of the hairstyles back in Tunis. The men all have five o'clock shadows, and Zia Rosa's lip fuzz is growing longer by the day. No, we won't get our cuts from Pietro because his default is to give us a bowl cut every time, and I've resolved to stop visiting the salonier, too. Nobody can style my hair quite like you.

Antonio laughs. He can hear Anna's voice—the one voice that would criticize him and admire him in the same breath—as he flips through each of the pages. While stationed at Villa Molin, he has heard the soldiers express their longing for home, and they give poetic descriptions of Genoa, Florence, Rome, Palermo. Antonio can never relate to them. Yes, it is true he certainly pines for home at times like this, but if asked he could not name where home is—he no longer feels the gravitational pull of Italy, not even to Tunisia. No images spring to mind of quaint villages or bustling cities. For him, home is not a place, and if it cannot be a place, then perhaps it is a person.

He reads Anna's letters deep into the night.

PART 5

MAY 1921

47. A BAD DAY

"I've given everything for a country that's not even mine!"

Fradji's shouts bounce off the walls. "Don't you know how hard this is for me?"

"It's been six years since you were injured!" Anna yells back. "The war is over!"

As always, Anna tries to gently goad him into leaving the house. They go to the souk one day for food, sure to wear their masks to protect from the Spanish Flu that she reads about in the newspaper, but Fradji's eyes dart from person to person, and she can tell the stimulus overwhelms him. Vendors wave bags in his face—roasted chickpeas, dried figs, dried apricots—and he flinches. The pressure bursts when they see some of Fradji's old friends walking down the street, and he veers around the corner in his wheelchair.

"Why don't you go talk to them?" Anna chases after him.

"It would be too difficult to explain."

"Fradji, just go say hello."

"I'd rather not."

"They'll be happy to see you."

"I don't want them to see me like this!" He explodes again, cursing and calling her all sorts of names, and Anna does not know what to do other than stand there in the street and take it, crossing her arms defensively, feeling like she has shrunken along with her dignity.

The other shoppers watch the outburst, and Anna feels the heat of embarrassment rise to her cheeks. Anna hears a shopper dismiss it in passing, "He's just having a bad day." Through the crowd, a French police officer approaches them.

Fradji quiets down.

"Hello, Officer."

Fradji mentions he is a veteran of the Great War, and the officer ends up shaking Fradji's hand and thanking him for his sacrifice, never even addressing Anna.

"Please forgive me, Anna," Fradji says to her that evening, and he hands her a bouquet of roses with a hand-written card. "I'm having a difficult time readjusting. I made a fool of myself at the souk today."

Anna's heart swells, and she accepts the card and the flowers, reminded for a moment that the version of Fradji from before the war—the wide-eyed photographer with the soul of a poet—still breathes somewhere deep inside this stranger. She knows Fradji means no harm. He is not a bomb that could go off at any moment. Most of the time, he approaches the world quietly and kindly. Like the shoppers said, he was just having a bad day, and Anna knows that it would only be right to stand by him.

"Have you considered going to the hospital?" she asks.

"I already went to the hospital. They gave me medicine to manage the pain in my back, and—"

"I'm not talking about your back," she says as gently as she can. "I'm talking about your brain."

"My brain is fine," he fumes, nostrils flared.

Anna walks back to Zia Rosa's estate and lays in her bed that evening, contrasting the rose-red bouquet against the purple bruises on her wrist.

48. RIGHTFUL PLACE

When Antonio steps onto the pier at the Tunis harbor, Zio Pietro and Giuseppina are waiting to greet him. He buries his face into Giuseppina's thick hair, inhaling the familiar lavender perfume. The entire harbor is packed with men in uniform embracing their families.

Antonio still wears the military-issued cotton face mask. Already, the newspapers say, more people have died from the Spanish Flu than from the entire Great War combined. Antonio is sure not to brush against any strangers, and he holds his breath when passing through the crush of the crowd. Zio Pietro pulls him onto the tram, and they ride into the medieval section of Tunis.

"We have passed the barber shop," Antonio says. "Where are we going?"

"We have a surprise for you," Giuseppina says, and she presses a heavy key into his palm.

The tram stops at the square outside Sacré Cœur Church, where the piss-smell of the goat market marries the incense from the church, blanketing the whole neighborhood with a sickly-sweet honeysuckle atmosphere. Zio Pietro leads him further down the road and stops at an apartment building across from Hammam Remimi Mosque.

"Welcome to your new home," Zio Pietro says, and opens the door.

Inside, the apartment is already furnished. He has a blue tile stove with coals stoked below, hanging with an array of copper pots and pans. The table is set under a tray of cannoli with chopped apricot and crumbled pistachios, candied lemons, a sparkling bottle of limoncello. Leonardo Ribaudo plays the accordion in the corner.

"For now, this is your bachelor apartment," Zio Pietro shouts in his opera voice, a glass of limoncello sloshing in his hand. "But not for long. Think of it as a preemptive wedding gift, a future love nest for my two lovebirds."

"You've drunk enough of that," Giuseppina reaches for the limoncello, her cheeks scarlet.

Antonio rises in the morning and walks to the barber shop on Rue Pierre de Coubertin. It feels strange to be commuting from a different part of town and not just walking downstairs to the shop.

"Morning," Antonio says as he rings the bell over the door.

Antonio washes his hands under the faucet with soap and puts on his white coat and face mask to prepare for the day, looking like a surgeon in the mirror. Zio Pietro is humming an opera tune while Leonardo Ribaudo wheezes his accordion in the corner, just like old times.

"Did you hear cousin Vittorio is stepping down as Prime Minister after the war?" Zio Pietro says, tapping the newspaper.

"I suppose it's for the best," Leonardo shrugs. "This new man they're talking about, what's his name, Mussolini? Now there's a politician who shows some potential."

"You take that back," Zio Pietro snaps.

"I mean it," Leonardo replies. "Our allies cheated us during the war, kept us from growing to our full potential. The intellectuals and the city-dwelling folk who hate Italy—they're all conspiring to keep the country down. And now that we have won the war, we are somehow even poorer. Mussolini promises to restore Italy as the greatest nation in Europe. Our rightful place."

"The greatest nation in Europe? Italy was already falling apart before the war," Zio Pietro waves him off. "You're chasing a fantasy I guarantee you that another war is around the corner—and don't give me that look, Leonardo. Mark my words, Mussolini and his thugs want nothing less than another war to distract people from the awful shape the country's in."

"What do you think, Antonio?" Leonardo asks as Antonio is setting up his station for the day.

"I think Italy peaked long ago," Antonio says. "I used to wish we could return to those days—as a boy in Partinico, the crumbling villas and Roman temples would remind me of the glory days. But those days are over. It is better to embrace the future and not dig our heels in."

And he hears Anna's voice in his head, saying *those who dig their heels dig their graves*.

"Bah," Leonardo swats the air in defeat.

"Embrace the future indeed," Zio Pietro laughs. "I never thought I'd hear you utter those words, Antonio. When you were a boy, you were as stiff as dry pasta. What is the future for you?"

Antonio has never fully considered his future. Before the war, he was preoccupied with the past. During the war, he was preoccupied with surviving. When he casts his thoughts forward like a fishing line, all he can see is a foggy notion of himself cutting hair in his very own barber shop.

"Maybe I'll move to America," Antonio suggests. He imagines the bustling skyline of New York with its radio antennae, its electrical wires blocking the sun, its chugging factory smokestacks.

"I doubt Giuseppina would like that," Zio Pietro says. "She'll want to stay closer to home."

"You're right," Antonio mutters as a lump catches in his throat. "Maybe America is too big a dream for now."

49. SILVER RING

When Anna finally looks up at the great clock hanging over the worktable to discover that her shift has ended, she stretches out, rising from her sewing machine. She slaps her canvas patterns in the pile with the rest, then picks up her skirts and races a mile in the sweaty May heat for Rue Souki Bel Khir. She has fallen into the habit of wearing a white cotton medical mask everywhere she goes now. She hurries past Hopitâl d'Israëlites, which these days is always besieged by the homeless. The Spanish Flu has burned through the neighborhood, and the poor souls lay under the front façade, hacking violently. She spots a young man carrying an old woman in his arms, begging the hospital workers to treat her.

"The hospital is at capacity!" a man in a suit says, struggling to hold the door closed.

In the winding medieval section of the city, such sights are commonplace, yet Anna knows that closer to the coastline the European colonists are sheltering comfortably in their gated estates, attended to by their own home nurses should they fall ill. Every day she swings between anger at the injustice and the guilt that she is part of the problem, that every franc locked in Zia Rosa's bank account means one less bed in the hospital.

Anna traces a cross over her chest, a reaction against guilt. She makes a note to pray for these people and drops them whatever coins she has in her purse. She remembers the terror of her own asthma, of not knowing when her next breath would come.

Soon, she arrives at the Sarfati household and knocks on the door.

"Where were you?" Fradji answers, pulling open the door. "You usually come around five-thirty."

"I had to work a little overtime," she says, wiping the sweat off her forehead, unwrapping her headscarf as she enters. Already, the smell of harissa snakes through the house.

"Have you left the house today, Fradji?"

"Yes," he says, and Anna knows it is a lie. The shutters are closed. He wears the same clothes as the day before, and the day before that. According to his mamma, he did not go to the synagogue last week, instead sitting inside the house in the dark.

During dinner with the Sarfati family, Miriam does not even speak to Anna, not after Anna ended her apprenticeship on the premise that she would break up with Fradji, only to still be engaged to him six years later. Miriam instead glares at her.

When dinner ends, Anna pushes Fradji's wheelchair around the courtyard for fresh air, between the dripping water pump and the outhouse. They do not make eye contact, and they do not dare hold hands. Such contact is not allowed until after marriage, and she can see Miriam watching them through the window.

"How much longer?" Fradji asks.

"Until what?" Anna tils her head.

"Until the wedding? We've been engaged six years now."

Anna stutters as she tries to find her words.

"You know, thoughts of marrying you carried me through the war," Fradji says. "I would have died without you. Please don't hurt me, Anna."

Anna forces a smile through her irritation. Hurt Fradji? Anna knows she has done nothing but care for him. Before she can respond, Fradji pulls something from his pocket and presses it into her hand. A silver ring. Again, her anger dissipates, and she reminds herself of the profound wound hiding just under Fradji's skin, and the lengths he has gone to show his appreciation for her.

"We have to solve some major issues before we can consider marriage," Anna sighs.

"Like what?"

"Like religion, for starters. I've heard of interfaith couples who had to flee the country, and I don't think your mamma would like it if I skipped the mikveh and the tallit and the henna."

"You could convert," Fradji suggests.

"So could you," Anna scoffs.

"Don't hurt me, Anna," Fradji repeats, and his voice takes on a ragged edge.

When she hears the hissing in his voice, Anna flinches, feeling the bruises on her wrist. In the years since returning from the war, he has taken to wearing his hair close to his skull, and oftentimes he does not wear his kippah during the day. His head looks rough and scarred and intimidating without his curls and the sprig of asphodel tucked always behind his ear.

"Don't you see where this is headed, Fradji? If we married, one of us would end up resenting the other no matter what."

"So, you resent me?" Fradji raises his voice.

"You know that's not true," Anna snaps, raising her voice as well.

"You're ungrateful," Fradji seethes. "I wasted away in that trench for months, dreaming of the day when I could hold your hand. I watched my friends shot, their limbs blown off before my eyes. I even—I even killed. I killed so many men—shooting, stabbing, shelling. You have no idea, Anna, and I did it all for France—France! The very people who seize our land, who grind my family into the dirt!"

"The war is over," Anna mumbles, and she knows right away she had said the wrong thing.

"*Over?*" Fradji's spit flies. "I've been at war my whole life! From the day I was born, I have been marked as a target. It's because of my name, because of the way I pray, because of the way I look!"

Anna stops pushing his wheelchair along the courtyard. Fradji is red-faced, a web of veins snaking down his neck. He clenches the arms of his chair in a death grip.

"You know the thing they told me in training," Fradji says. "The French kept telling me, 'This isn't boxing. This will not be a clean fight. A merciful man is a dead man.' And I am finally starting to agree with them. I wish I had been brave enough to turn my aim against the French, against every last one of them. And what about you! I was merciful to you, Anna. I gave you so many chances. I let you string me along for six years!"

"Fradji, you're scaring me," Anna says.

Fradji snatches the silver ring from Anna's hand and hurls it at the outhouse. The sudden violence of his movements fills Anna with fear, and she steps back, but again Fradji's hand clenches around her wrist, gripping the spot that is still sore from the last time. The neighbors poke their heads out the windows, attracted to the commotion.

"Fradji, stop this!" Miriam is running into the courtyard.

Anna wrenches her wrist from his grasp and runs from the courtyard, slamming the gate behind her.

50. PLATINUM BAND

Antonio holds Giuseppina's hand as she gathers her dress and steps off the tram, onto the gravel road. Plumes of spring rainclouds hang over the Mediterranean as the wind whips the blue sea into chopping black waves and hurls sheets of sand over the road. Antonio raises an arm to shield his face against the salty wind, squinting.

"We should hurry before the clouds roll in," Giuseppina says. "This shouldn't take long."

She holds a jasmine bouquet and adjusts her black veil. Antonio takes her arm, and they hike down the road, passing the neat rows of apricot trees, orange trees, olive trees which are each budding with constellations of little perfume-worthy white flowers. "Maybe now that the war is over, we can return to Sicily," she says.

"Or I could continue to work for Zio Pietro a few years," Antonio says. "Hopefully I can learn English."

"What do you need to learn English for?"

Antonio pauses, not sure if he should tell her. "I've thought of moving to America," he mumbles, "to open a barber shop."

"America? Why not work at the barber shop in Sicily? Isn't that what you always wanted, to cut hair alongside your family?"

"I have taken up a new dream," he says. "Zio Pietro is content to stay in the same shop his whole life, but a bigger world sits outside this city. This is what I discovered in the war. Why stay in Tunis when I could start my own shop in the heart of Manhattan, with all the modern novelties?"

"I would rather be close to family," Giuseppina says. "I've been dreaming of Sicily too long, Antonio. I've lived in exile in Tunisia my whole life. I just want to settle in one place where I can walk down the street and see my family. You understand?"

"I understand," Antonio says, and he does not mention America again after that. Instead, he reaches inside his pocket and feels the cold metal, his heart thumping. Hopefully, they can finish this before the spring rainclouds break. Finally, they arrive at a small church perched on a rocky outcrop, overlooking a beach below. Antonio guides her through the metal gate, into the yard of headstones.

Giuseppina sets the bouquet of jasmine flowers at a white mausoleum chiseled under the name *Maria Minore Palazzolo.* Antonio touches an index finger to his forehead, stomach, and shoulders, tracing a cross. The waves crash, and the violently tossing palm leaves threaten to ruin the moment. Again, Antonio digs his hand in his pocket and feels the smooth, rounded surface of cold metal, the jagged points of diamonds.

"Ciao Mamma," she touches the engraved letters on the mausoleum. "I wish I could take you with me."

Antonio hopes that her mamma in heaven approves of him. In his prayers, he likes to think that the angels are all-seeing, that Giuseppina's mamma was watching him when he was at war, that she judged him for all his vices and praised him for his virtues. Surely, he could not hide anything from such an angel. Perhaps her mamma would approve of him after this, after Antonio includes her in the biggest decision of his life.

Antonio bends onto one knee, on the gravel path in front of Maria Minore's grave and takes Giuseppina's hands.

"Giuseppina Palazzolo," he says, holding out the Maria Minore's ring. "Grow old with me."

Giuseppina slides on the ring and marvels at it—a platinum band crowned with a swirl of three diamonds. Antonio notices her lower lip tremble, and he worries she is upset. A cold prick strikes his face, and the terracotta rooftop of the church soon taps with raindrops. Distant thunderclaps threaten their moment. Finally, Giuseppina nods.

"I will, Antonio. I will. Until my last breath."

She puckers her lips to kiss him, but Antonio steps backwards.

"What is it?" she asks.

"The Spanish F-Flu," Antonio stutters. "I wouldn't want to accidentally pass influenza to you if we kissed."

"The pandemic is on its way out, Antonio. It has been for a while now."

"There's still a chance."

"Well, influenza can't pass through this," Giuseppina digs through her bag, pulling out a handkerchief and smoothing it over her mouth like a mask. The handkerchief is diaphanous, and he can see the outline of her smile through the cloth.

"*Amore.*" Antonio chuckles at her ingenuity, and he feels warm despite the Mediterranean wind that flutters his hair.

Holding her waist as gently as he would a cracked vase, Antonio presses his lips to the other side of the handkerchief. One, two, three, four, five, he counts. Just long enough for the cloth to cling.

51. ELBOW-LENGTH WHITE GLOVES

Anna and Zia Rosa and Zio Leonardo receive an invitation to a gathering at the outdoor café by Place Halfaouine. Upon their arrival, they find Antonio, Giuseppina, and Zio Pietro sitting around a table under the shadow of the octagonal minaret of Saheb Ettabaâ Mosque, which stretches over the eucalyptus-lined greenspace where a fountain gently bubbles. The nearby souk swells with shoppers, and Anna can only spot a handful of them wearing protective masks. By now, the threat of the pandemic is fading—the death statistics have dropped such that the newspapers stopped printing them on the front page, then the second page, then altogether, and medical masks have disappeared from the cafés as well.

Anna hugs Giuseppina and kisses her on both cheeks, and in passing she notices a diamond ring glittering on Giuseppina's left hand. Anna's stomach drops, and she knows now what this party is for.

"Thank you everyone for coming," Antonio calls them to attention. "I invited you here for a special announcement. Giuseppina and I are engaged."

Zia Rosa claps her hands in excitement. Zio Pietro kisses the newly engaged fiancés on their cheeks, though Antonio wrenches himself away, reminding them of the influenza threat. Anna fakes a smile and shakes their hands with a limp palm. For most of the party, Anna says nothing and orders a mint tea while Antonio and Giuseppina are describing the proposal at the cemetery, puppy eyes locked together.

"Anna," Giuseppina says after the laughter subsides. "I want you to know your friendship has been so important to me. You're really like an older sister."

Anna gives her a weak smile. "That's a really nice thing to say."

"Could you be my maid of honor?" Giuseppina asks. "You're the only person I know who could pull it off."

"What a compliment."

"You're my closest friend, Anna," Giuseppina goes on. "Also, it would make me and Antonio very happy if you wanted to sew my wedding dress. We are willing to pay, of course, because I know that's a big ask."

Anna feels insulted, but then she realizes that Giuseppina was not capable of insulting someone, and her request must be sincere. She cannot deny the elation on Giuseppina and Antonio's faces, the way they gaze into each others' eyes. "Of courses," she nods. "I'll be your maid of honor, and I'll make your wedding dress if it will make Antonio happy."

"It would."

"Here, I think I have a pencil," Zia Rosa digs into her pocket, pressing a pencil and an envelope into Anna's hands. "You can sketch the dress on that."

"I'm looking for a more traditional wedding dress," Giuseppina says. "None of that art deco stuff you see in the magazines. No beads. No long train. Make the neckline modest, with a veil that goes to my elbows."

"Are you sure? I might—sorry, *you* might—want something more ritzy." In her mind, Anna imagines something tall and loose-fitting, with elbow-length white gloves, lots of fringe, and a train that stretches three feet behind her.

"Make it modest," Giuseppina repeats. "Antonio will like that."

"Okay." Anna frowns. "I'll see what I can do."

Anna presses the pencil to the back of the envelope. She can see the design in her mind, but it is fleeting. Suddenly Anna envisions herself—not Giuseppina—walking down the aisle. Papà, regal as ever, six feet tall, is walking her up to the altar where a groom in a tuxedo waits for her, a groom with a pencil mustache and hair parted with pomade, a groom named Antonio.

"Are you stuck?" Giuseppina asks, noticing that Anna has not begun to sketch.

Anna forces herself to pencil in a measly line, and then she suddenly crumples the paper into a ball. "Why do you love him?" Anna asks before she can think the words through.

Before Giuseppina can respond, a waiter brings out two cup-and-saucers of mint tea, breaking up their conversation. The tea is steaming hot, yet the cooling minty scent cuts clear through to her sinuses. Anna takes a sip, and the garnish of pine nuts and mint leaves clink against the ceramic of her cup.

"I love him because he's honest. He takes care of himself and others," Giuseppina rattles off, then looks off into the distance, lost in thought, stumbling on a deeper answer. "The first time I heard my cousin from Sicily was coming to live with us, I was starstruck. Anything relating to Sicily always fascinated me, you see, because it was the one place I was never allowed to go, not since the Duke banished my parents. Papà would always tell me that Sicily is the most beautiful land in the world, and he told me about my grandparents, my aunts, my uncles who lived there, and I always felt cut off from them, like I wasn't a part of the family. I wanted so badly to live with them, to attend their weddings and baptisms and celebrate life. So, I suppose that was my first fascination with Antonio. He was from Sicily. He made me feel, for the first time, like I was a part of my own family. Like I belonged."

Anna nods solemnly. "That's a very good answer."

Again, Anna presses her pencil to the paper, more confident this time, and begins to sketch the wedding dress in earnest.

52. THE WRONG HEMISPHERES

In the storage closet at Sacré Cœur Church, Antonio clips on his suspenders and tightens his sleeve garters. He pulls on his black jacket and folds a silk cloth in his breast pocket. In the mirror, he draws back his upper lip to carefully trim his pencil mustache and slick his hair into a pompadour. Perfect.

Cracking the door open to peer into the church nave, Antonio sees that he has only enough guests to fill in the front two rows of pews. In the traditional weddings from his childhood in Sicily, the churches would be packed with hundreds, entire family trees rooted to the pews. At the reception they would host a band with an accordion, tambourine, mandolin, and zampogna, and everyone would dance in a ring to the rapid-fire tarantella music. But in Tunisia, he cannot say the same. He spots Vince and Pete, Leonardo and Rosa, the barbers and shoe-shiners employed at Zio Pietro's shop. Antonio does not even have a close friend to name a best man. Zio Pietro is the most finely dressed of them all, wearing a tan suit with a green paisley cravat, sporting an expertly curled mustache like King Victor Emmanuel III. Zio Pietro only had one piece of advice to give Antonio that morning, the same piece of advice he had always given him—to relax and enjoy.

Antonio knows that in another storage closet at the other end of the church, Giuseppina is stepping into her white wedding gown and veil, assisted by Anna, her maid of honor.

"Don't even think about looking at the bride before the wedding," Rosa Ribaudo spots him, and he quickly shuts himself away.

While Antonio waits, he sits on a chair in the storage closet, tucked between saint statues with chipped paint, dusty wreaths of advent candles that wait for next Christmas. He always imagined his wedding would be far more nerve-wracking—he has heard stories of grooms outright fainting at the altar—but it feels like a regular day at work. He is here to do his duty to the family.

A gentle knock alerts him at the door, and Antonio turns the doorknob.

"Anna?" he says, and suddenly his cool reserve breaks, his heart pounding beneath his pocket square.

She wears a veil of her own, except it is deep blue and only brushes her shoulders, and in her hands she clutches a bouquet of flowers—white jasmine flowers, of course, that perfume the little closet with a vanilla-and-licorice scent.

"Don't faint yet, I'm just the messenger," Anna says. "Giuseppina had to tell you something but the bride can't see the groom before the wedding, so she sent me."

"What's the message?"

"She wants you to know the reception hall is running late because of a funeral, so the dancing will start an hour later than planned. It will be a rolling schedule."

She does not even make eye contact.

"You are so somber, Anna. When's the last time we spoke?"

"I have been busy with Fradji," is all she mumbles, staring at her shoes. "Sorry."

Antonio frowns. The girl who used to make fun of him for being too rigid, who had crossed the Atlantic with a smile on her face, who had launched herself on a city that did not even speak her language, now apologizes and shies away.

"Fradji is taking a toll on you, Anna. Anyone can see that."

"It's not about me. I want to show that love conquers all things, Antonio. With enough care, Fradji will return to his previous self. I know it."

"But love cannot conquer all things, Anna. In fact, love cannot conquer anything at all. Love only embraces."

Anna crosses her arms.

"What ever happened to obligation?" she asks. "You always say obligation is the engine of life. Does Fradji not count now that it's inconvenient?"

"I was young and naïve when I believed that," Antonio says. "I have changed since then. I dream of moving to America now."

"Then we have finally switched places," Anna says.

"What do you mean?"

"Now you are the modern one," Anna fakes a smile. "Look at you, dreaming of moving to America. Me, on the other hand, I've tied myself up in the past and given up my future in the process."

Antonio wants to assure her, but he feels a weight on his chest. He knows that the real reason he wants to move to America is because of Anna. He cannot go back to Sicily and he cannot stay in Tunis because he will never be able to truly love Giuseppina so long as Anna is in his orbit. But he cannot tell her this.

"Perhaps you're right," is all he manages to say. The pipe organ starts humming, and the priest emerges from the sacristy to light the candles. "You should go, Anna," he says. "They've started playing the organ. I will be walking down the aisle soon."

"Congratulations again, Antonio," Anna says before leaving. "I want you to be happy."

She closes the door behind her, leaving Antonio alone in the storage closet.

53. A NEW MUDFLAT

Love cannot conquer anything at all. Love only embraces.

Anna can hear Antonio's words replaying like a broken record player, every rise and fall of his syllables engraved in her thoughts. After midnight, she and Zia Rosa and Zio Leonardo meander home from the wedding reception in the cricket-roaring brushlands along the lagoon, her thoughts buzzing from a tonic of wine and sleepiness. Her calves are sore from dancing, and she collapses into her bed, pulling off her pumps.

So many emotions stratify in her mind now that she is settling from the stir of the party—regret for not telling Antonio how she feels about him, jealousy for Giuseppina's happiness, dissatisfaction with her job at the factory, concern for Fradji—too many sentiments layered upon each other to begin to dissect.

She envisions the loving gaze that Antonio and Giuseppina had shared during their first dance at the wedding reception. It leaves Anna feeling tender-hearted in the same way that beef is tender after being pounded with a mallet.

She hears the crunch of salted almonds and knows that Zia Rosa is sitting in the hall nearby, enjoying a late snack. Should she tell Zia Rosa her thoughts? The thought of sitting down with someone and explaining this whole situation raises her blood pressure.

"Anna? What are you doing up so late?" Zia Rosa sets her bowl of almonds down as Anna approaches.

Anna's throat swells, and she cannot find the words to say what she means. She pulls up her sleeves to show Zia Rosa.

"*Carissima nipote!*" Zia Rosa gasps, pulling Anna into her embrace and kissing her cheeks. "It's Fradji, isn't it? You told me once that you wanted to break it off with him. I should have known." Zia Rosa strokes her hair and peppers her cheeks with some more kisses. "Don't worry anymore, *amore*, I am getting you out of this mess. Marriage is out of the question."

"Fradji is very hurt, Zia Rosa, in his body and mind. He needs me to help him recover. If I break off the engagement, it will ruin him. I'm afraid he might—" Anna collects herself—"I'm afraid he might kill himself."

"My dear niece, it is okay to let Fradji go, cruel as it sounds. Fradji has his own family, and they will help him seek treatment, but not you. You cannot give him what he needs, and you will destroy yourself if you keep trying. I hate to see you this way, love."

Zia Rosa holds Anna's hands.

"I will tell Fradji myself if you want me to," Zia Rosa says. "He doesn't scare me."

Anna's thoughts run in circles between Zia Rosa's advice and her own desire to support Fradji, and she does not know whose advice to follow. She just feels so sad for Fradji and his suffering.

"I will tell him," Anna finally says. "It is my responsibility."

Anna settles on inviting Fradji to a stroll on the esplanade, a half-mile stretch of greenspace along the harbor where manicured blades of cypress trees cast dappled shadows on the grid of gardens and sandy promenades. Old men lounge, legs crossed, on benches reading French newspapers. Well-to-do couples stroll with umbrellas for extra shade. The gardens are public enough that Anna can call for help if needed, with enough shrubbed-in alcoves to save Fradji from embarrassment if he reacts badly, if she breaks his spirit. There is even a tram station nearby if she needs to escape.

Fradji pushes himself in his wheelchair down the cypress-lined esplanade by the harbor as Anna searches for any kind of small alcove where they might stop. Finally, she settles on a bench overlooking the harbor where, in the distance, she can see flamingos flapping their wings, migrating to a new mudflat.

"I always thought flamingos were the most beautiful of creatures," Fradji says.

"Would you take a photo of them?" Anna asks, hoping that he will somehow be lulled into activity.

"There's no point," Fradji shrugs.

They spend a minute or two just staring at the Mediterranean, while Anna stifles her inner panic. She tried breaking up with him before the war, and he had begged and begged until she was worn down. She feels that he will do the same thing now, and that any kind of discussion would devolve into sniffles or shrieking. Or both. What if she finally marries him? Would it really be so awful? She could return to making dresses with Miriam, and maybe she could try to be happy. That is the only reality Fradji would understand, the only reality that would heal his wound. No. He is wounded, yes, but allowing herself to be wounded will not heal him. Some wounds need to be cauterized. She is the only one strong enough to do it.

"I can't marry you, Fradji," she finally says.

Fradji stumbles on a string of half-words, fast as his racing thoughts. "I loved you, you know," he says finally.

"Yes, I know," Anna nods, "and you were special to me. Your passion. Your imagination. Your creativity. And your family was so welcoming."

"Not welcoming enough though."

"That's not the issue."

"Then what is?"

"You already know."

Anna can tell Fradji is trying to buy time, to stall her with his questions until she forgets why she came. She can hear the panic rising in his voice, and Anna realizes this conversation could simmer for hours if she lets it. She feels a burning resolve in her chest, to finally be done with this. To release him from her false promise. To release herself from her false obligation. To not worry about him anymore.

"I'm going to leave now, Fradji." She stands and looks down at him.

"I'll still see you tomorrow, right? We should keep talking about this."

"No," she says gently. "I am not going to marry you. I have to end this."

He grabs her hand, his grip strong, forceful. "Anna? Wait. No!"

"I gave all my time to you!" She wrenches her hand back, a fire of newfound strength igniting within her. "I told you before the war that I did not want to marry you. But you pleaded, and I gave in. Since that moment, I gave in every time you asked me to. I gave you *all* my time, for six years. I won't give you another second of it."

Before Fradji can explode, Anna turns her back and walks briskly toward the tram. As she takes a seat, she watches the city fly past in a blur of white lime and turquoise. The sea breeze is a reassuring kiss on her face. A weight lifts from her shoulders, and a sense of elation floods through her. She doesn't have to dread every new day. She can live for herself again. She breathes in the fresh air and resolves to embrace the future.

54. WHEREVER THE DONKEY FALLS

In his dreams, Antonio hears the whistle of the falling shells, looks over his shoulders for the bobbing helmets of the Austrian and German soldiers, knowing that even the simplest activity like eating pasta could instantly plunge one into a life or death struggle. But every time, his dreams fizzle out, and he finds himself again in bed, in Giuseppina's arms, and the troubled waters are again calm. From what Antonio has read in the newspaper, nightmares are completely normal for returning soldiers, so he does not dwell on it. Not that he was a soldier. He was just a barber, and only experienced a fraction of the trauma of a soldier in the trenches.

Fradji was a soldier. Antonio remembers the sight of Fradji bleeding out in the piazza while the plumes of rubble and fire launched men into the sky. The poor man. Antonio can only imagine Fradji's suffering, and he still feels a creeping guilt considering how he had ratted him out to the French officers. If the officers had survived the attack, they would have arrested Fradji on false charges of sedition. Mamma would have told him in the old Sicilian tongue, *t'avissi a mettiri na màschira*, that he ought to be wearing a mask to hide his shame. Antonio often prays for forgiveness, but he knows prayer is not enough. He must act. He must help Fradji through his recovery.

One day after work, Antonio goes to visit the Sarfati family household on Rue Souki Bel Khir, down the street from the gate of Bab El Khadra. He did not announce he was coming, since he and Fradji rarely spoke, so he hopes someone from the Sarfati family is home.

"Hello?" an older woman answers the door.

"My name is Antonio Orlando," he replies to her in Arabic. "I'm a friend of Fradji. Is he here?"

"I don't recognize you. How do you know him?"

"We were stationed in Italy together in the war."

She gives a slow nod to show that is enough for her "He could use a friend right now," she says. "Go and talk to him."

From the kitchen, Fradji wheels into the sitting room. When Fradji sees a new person in his home, his entire body flinches in surprise, like he has just turned the corner to see a poisonous scorpion.

"Hello Fradji," Antonio says. "How have you been?"

"Have you come to threaten me?" he asks.

"Threaten you? Why would I do that?"

"To defend Anna's honor."

"Wait, what happened with Anna? No one told me anything."

"She broke off the engagement," Fradji says. "I have no one, Antonio. No one. My friends and family shun me. Everyone thinks I am a ticking time bomb, that I cannot be trusted because of my fits. Sometimes I just lose control of myself, and I feel like I'm back in the trenches. Everyone thinks I am dangerous."

"I don't think you're dangerous, Fradji," Antonio says. "You're a good man, and I know what you're going through. I often have nightmares of the war, and the sight of an airplane sends my heart pounding with terror. I think we both have a bit of shell shock."

"It seems to affect you less though," Fradji says.

Antonio shrugs.

"Anna kept telling me I should seek treatment," Fradji says, "but I already have. I went to Hopitâl d'Israëlites, and all they did was prescribe pills to calm me down."

"That sounds like a start. Take the pills," Antonio says. "I read in the newspaper that you can get electroshock therapy for it, too."

"Electroshock," Fradji sneers. "It sounds like torture."

Antonio takes a seat on the divan at Fradji's level, trying to take a more understanding approach.

"Your family loves you, Fradji," Antonio says, quiet and serious. "You're not alone, and you never will be."

"I *know* that," Fradji says, "but I don't *feel* it. Not since Anna left. She was the only one who could calm me down, who could make me feel like the person I was before the war. I believed that if we married, I would be happy again, back to my old self."

"Anna is only human. She can't take away your shell shock."

"Then who can? A doctor? A rabbi?"

"I don't think it is something to be taken away. It's more like something to be managed, like shaving every day so your face doesn't get too scruffy."

"Of course, you would make a reference to shaving," Fradji gives a rare laugh. "I guess there's no going back to the way things were."

"You will find happiness again, Fradji. In Sicily we have an old saying, *unni cari, u sceccu si suse*, wherever the donkey falls it also stands up. The only way to go is forward, to make the best life you can with what you have, and you have a lot—a family, a garment business, a talent for photography."

Antonio lets that last word hang in the air, and he can tell by Fradji's silence that he is thinking on it. Through the window, a few rays of sun trace dust motes, slanting down from the curtains to the table, where Antonio can see Fradji's battered camera—it smells strongly of glue, and a brush sits on a linen cloth nearby, along with a screwdriver and a roll of film. Had he been repairing the camera?

"I used to do nature photography for a professor at Ez-Zitouna University," Fradji says. "He published my photographs in a book about Tunisian wildlife."

"And?"

"The professor spoke about publishing a sequel, but I never followed up on it. I'm afraid he forgot about me."

"You know what you have to do, Fradji," Antonio says. "Go to that professor, tell him you're back in the business of taking photographs. Make some art."

"Yes," Fradji picks up his camera, and Antonio watches his finger hover over the shutter button, a smiling growing. "Yes, I know you're right."

Fradji asks him to stay for dinner that evening, and as they eat a stew of fried chard and white beans on couscous, the conversation turns to business and family history.

"My great-grandfather worked at the shipyards of Livorno in Italy," Fradji says.

"I had no idea you were Italian," Antonio says with a big smile.

"We have family there still," Fradji says, "and we visit them for weddings and funerals. The Sephardic community in Livorno is still very strong."

"Then you probably knew of my cousin, Luigi Orlando," Antonio says. "He ran the shipyards in Livorno for a time."

Fradji's mother nods thoughtfully. "The name sounds familiar."

They sit and talk late into the evening, sipping from glasses of cloudy white arak and eating dried figs. Finally Antonio looks out the window to find the city in darkness.

"I stayed too late," Antonio leaps to his feet, downing the last of his arak. "I have to wake up early for work tomorrow, and Giuseppina will be wondering where I went off to."

"Then I guess this is goodbye." Fradji wheels himself to the door with Antonio.

By his serious tone, Antonio can tell that his goodbye is not just for tonight, but for every night here out. Perhaps it is for the best. Antonio knows he has no right to friendship with the Sarfati family, not after what happened in the war. Surely, Fradji is ready for a new chapter in his life, to close the book on Anna and her friends. They have nothing left to say.

"Goodbye," Antonio says. "Please know that my door will always be open to you."

With that, Antonio steps out into the night and hears Fradji shut the door behind him.

55. HORNS

After the breakup, Anna spends her evenings alone, parsing through her thoughts. When her days at the factory end, she goes on long walks along the shore of Lac de Tunis, often not arriving home until dark. Having time to herself is a breath of fresh air, and her emotions settle like the calm waters of the harbor.

During one of her walks, she travels all the way to the Tunis docks, and with no more land left to traverse, she sits on a bench by the pier while people walk by. Anna admires the spectrum of outfits on parade. She spots a Maltese tram driver leaning against the wall on a smoke break, a red flannel sash tied around his waist. A group of French-speaking businessmen in crisp cream suits tuck folded sun-umbrellas under their arms while checking their pocket watches. Two Tunisian women carry baskets of vegetables, their white sefseri billowing in the Mediterranean breeze.

Unlike her first day in Tunis, not a single wooden ship is docked at the harbor, only the hulking steel ocean liners that herald the changing times with their horns. Finally, she spots an American flag flapping off the stern of an ocean liner, and the passengers stream down the pier, just like she and Mamma had done nine years ago.

Perhaps she should hop on the ship and sail back to America.

Anna considers the idea more and smiles at the thought of being with her family again, wondering how they are doing. Nine years has passed since she last saw them. Besides, what is left for her in Tunisia other than memories and dead ends? Could she really spend the rest of her life in this city? She would constantly be checking over her shoulder, worrying about encountering Fradji on the street, earning a pittance from her factory job, watching newlywed Antonio and Giuseppina build a life together.

And if she returns to America? Would that grant her a fresh start in life? After all, America has plenty of job openings for fashion designers, more job openings than existed in Tunis. She has outgrown her asthma, and at age twenty-one she could take off at full sprint down a dusty road only to suffer a few light coughs. Surely, she could return to Brooklyn without worrying about her health.

Tunisia's climate has healed her asthma. Its bustling marketplace has taught her a trade. Its people have taught her to take ownership of herself. Now, she realizes, Tunisia has given her everything it has to give, and it is time to follow the example of the flamingos and migrate to new shores.

Yes. Anna knows this is the right thing to do. She inhales the sea breeze, gathers herself, and walks a few blocks down to Rue Pierre de Coubertin, to the barber shop on the corner, where she looks through the front window to see Antonio trimming away at a walrus mustache. A sudden instinct tells her to walk inside the shop, the ringing bell announcing her entrance. She walks right up to Antonio while he is working.

Antonio's eyes widen, and his cheeks flush. "Anna, how are you?"

"I need to talk," she says. "Would you mind meeting me by the mudflat outside Zia Rosa's estate? This evening?"

"Of course," he says.

56. BITTER

Flush with water from the spring rains, the brackish mudflat plays host to newborn white flamingos whose eggshell fragments and down feathers are scattered among the reeds at the water's edge. Drawing in a lung full of air scented with mud and olive wood, Antonio stares, hands in his pockets, across the water to the grove of olive trees and the ancient aqueduct where he and Anna first kissed so many years earlier. He can still feel the press of her head against his shoulder. He draws in a long breath and turns toward the dirt road where he sees a small figure walking from the estate. As she grows closer, Antonio can make out Anna's bobbed hair. When she is close enough, Antonio allows himself to walk toward her.

"Anna." He says her name as if that is enough. As if her name is everything.

She stops a few feet away and then looks out across the mudflat. "Could you do me a favor?"

"Of course. Anything. Are you okay?"

"Can you check in with Fradji?"

"I visited him yesterday. He told me your engagement is off."

She nods and finally looks at him. Really looks at him.

"Fradji has agreed to undergo the proper therapy," Antonio says. "I believe he will recover in some way, though I don't know what that will look like."

"Thank you. You were good to do that."

Antonio takes a step forward. "But what about *your* recovery? You look exhausted. I can see the bags beneath your eyes." He watches her rub her eyes as if suddenly self-conscious and thinks back to when they first met, both new arrivals in Tunisia. She wanted to see and do everything, to explore and experience every facet of the country, but these days she looks like she is tired and sore right down to the marrow in her bones.

"I've been thinking," she croaks, then clears her throat. "I think it is best if I return to my family in America. I need some time to rest and to think about what I'll do next."

Everything in Antonio's body freezes. He feels like he just experienced a blast of the electroshock therapy he told Fradji about. Then his body seems to go slack, like his knees might fail him. He feels his nose tingle. His eyes go blurry. His fingers twitch. He'd thought about going to America to get away from Anna so he wouldn't risk seeing her, wouldn't think of her constantly, compare his wife to her constantly. But now? The thought of being separated from her forever…? He wonders if this is what a fish feels when it is gutted.

He swallows hard and tries to speak. Nothing comes out. He swallows again. "I hate goodbyes, Anna."

"Then let's make it bittersweet and not just bitter." She reaches for him and loops her arms through his, pulling him close. She smells the pine-resin pomade that slicks his parted hair. "I couldn't stay in Tunisia even if I wanted, not when I have to be second in your life to Giuseppina. Do you understand?"

He nods. "I'm sorry if I ever caused you heartbreak." Antonio whispers.

Anna laughs softly. "Thank you for saying that, but it doesn't make me feel any better."

They stand like that for a minute, just holding each other. Then, finally, Antonio steps back, and Anna's arms drop to her sides.

"Goodbye, Antonio," she says a final time, and he stands and watches as she walks away until fading from view, until he is left all by himself, staring across the lapping mudflat toward the olive grove.

PART 6

JUNE 1921

57. THREE-INCH FRAME

Anna has never crossed her family's threshold before. When she left Brooklyn all those years ago, their new house was nothing more than a plot of grass near Coney Island where Papà had dug the foundation and laid down bricks. Now, the three floors of red brick masonry tower up to a spouting chimney. They keep a little plot of greenery, barely enough to stretch her arms, where Papà has built a workshop and a bubbling fountain made from broken dishes.

Anna, sore and yawning after her journey across the Atlantic, steps inside and sets down her bags.

"Ciao?" Anna calls.

The house communicates its indifference to her through silence, and Anna walks down the hallway, not even recognizing the musk of hot tomato and basil that drifts from the kitchen. Family photographs decorate the hallway, and half of the faces are strangers to her. In the hall of sepia portraits, Anna can only find one picture of herself, from age six, a three-inch frame hung on the periphery like an afterthought. This is the first time she has stepped foot in her own family's home, and she feels more Tunisian than Sicilian, more Sicilian than American.

"Welcome home!"

A chorus of voices make her jump, and she steps into the kitchen to see her family gathered around a table of lasagna.

"Oh!" Anna reaches out her arms, tears springing to her eyes as her family rushes her, peppering her cheeks with kisses.

"Is that you, Anastasia?" Anna asks.

Only Anastasia's glasses, nose, and mouth are visible under her veiled black habit. A heavy wooden cross hangs over her chest. "It's Sister Saint Stanislaus now," she chuckles.

Anna hugs her sister Rosaria, who wears a gold wedding band and introduces a man who must be her husband—Anna's brother-in-law, a complete stranger, she realizes with horror. Mary, Andy, and Marietta are grown adults, though she has not seen them since they were swaddled babies. And lounging at the table, another batch of children Anna has never seen in her life stare at her, shy at meeting her. They are her brothers and sisters.

"Tunisia has made you so glamorous," Rosaria says, touching Anna's white gloves, her necklace, her bob.

"Zia Rosa has spoiled her," Mamma laughs. "She is a princess now."

"Now Marie has competition for the princess of the family," Rosaria teases.

"I'm no princess," Anna protests "I work hard."

Her sisters study her like a museum exhibit. Anna does not see any blush or lipstick on them—their faces are pale and lined with worry-wrinkles, and their hair is tied back in tight buns.

Mamma sits her down for dinner, and with the size of the family they barely squeeze around the table. Anna pokes a fork at her piping-hot rectangle of lasagna.

"Why aren't you eating, Anna? Mangia," Mamma gestures.

Anna wants to say that she hasn't eaten lasagna in years, and the fact sends her deep into thought, but she only nods and digs her fork into the layers of spiced sausage and ricotta pooled in marinara.

"Now that you're home, I'm sure you'll be reading through the classified section," Rosaria says, shoveling down forkfuls of lasagna from the other end of the table. "Didn't Zia Rosa teach you to mend clothes?"

"She did," Anna says, "but I had an apprenticeship, and the servants taught me as well."

The dinner table chatter hushes at the word *servants*, and Anna only hears the clatter of forks on plates.

"I'm not entitled," Anna says. "I made the dress I'm wearing now. See these embroidered roses? I finished them in under an hour. Name any fabric, I've worked with it."

"Rosaria, don't hound your sister," Mamma snaps. "And who are you to gawk at talk of servants—you are in charge of thirty women at the pants factory, no?"

"You work at a factory?" Anna asks.

"During the war I worked at a factory that made uniforms for nurses," Rosaria nods. "I climbed my way to position of forewoman, in charge of overseeing the second shift."

"And they are hiring," Mamma adds.

"Mamma, I don't have the power to hire people," Rosaria says, cutting herself a second rectangle of lasagna. "It's not that simple. My manager—"

"Oh, be a Christian and give your sister a job!" Mamma waves her hands. "She comes all this way from Tunisia, and she has had the most difficult time."

"I'll put in a word with my boss," Rosaria finally says. "That's the most I can do."

"Thank you," Mamma says on Anna's behalf, though Anna does not know how grateful she should be.

After dinner is over, Anastasia, Rosaria, and Mary kiss her goodbye and put on their coats. Along with their husbands, they step out into the cold and catch a taxi, leaving Anna sitting in the front living room, imagining the factory workstation that awaits her. She pulls off her white gloves and her jewelry, stowing them in her bags. She will not be needing them anymore.

58. SPAGHETTI & CHOPPED EGGPLANT

In the morning, Antonio finds Giuseppina lightly snoring, her arm draped over him, and the sight still surprises him. He cannot decide whether he is in her bed, or whether she is in his bed, or whether the bed belongs to neither of them and is the family's bed. Every night for the first few weeks, they disappeared under the sheets for the unspeakable act that married folk often do, and afterwards he would lay shocked into utter silence by the foreign holiness of it. Antonio recalls when Giuseppina first moved her possessions into his apartment, when an elderly woman in the neighboring apartment had asked for her name, and Giuseppina replied with his own name, *Orlando*.

While she snores, Antonio feels that her arm is damp with sweat, an inevitability in the summer heat. He reminds himself to buy her a lighter night gown for the summertime. He folds back the covers and fans her with his hand to cool her down, and she stirs until waking.

"Thank you," she smiles, and reaches for him.

They have created a miniature Sicily in their apartment. The walls hang with family photographs, a crucifix, a wooden icon of the Blessed Mother and Saint Anthony of Padua. Giuseppina keeps a wardrobe with her mantiglia veil just like his Mamma did, for when they walk to church and hear the Latin prayers. The two of them together, in this way, have created a bubble where they can temporarily close their eyes and be returned to Sicily, the old country, to charge forward into the past.

They wrap around each other, and she slides a hand under his shirt to feel his heartbeat. They hold each other like that, drifting in and out of sleep, until they hear Leonardo Ribaudo blowing his horn in the street to signal the morning milk delivery.

"I will get it," Giuseppina sighs.

"No. You rest," Antonio steps out of bed before she does, fluffing the pillows for her.

"Are you sure?" she rises, but Antonio lowers her onto the mattress.

"You rest. I'll get the milk."

Antonio runs into their building's courtyard and pulls open the iron bars of the gate, letting Leonardo Ribaudo guide his herd of goats onto the pavement. Antonio lays out his empty terracotta pots, and Leonardo squats down to milk the goats on the spot.

"Have you been in good health, Leonardo?" Antonio asks to fill the silence.

"We have an empty nest back now that Anna has left for America. Rosa isn't taking it well."

"Have you heard from her?" Antonio asks.

"Who? Rosa?"

"No, Anna. Has she written you since she arrived in America?"

"I haven't heard from Anna since she stepped on that boat at the harbor," Leonardo says, "but I trust she is with her family. It's for the best."

"Yes," Antonio frowns. "It's for the best."

At noon, the shops close and the Arabic call to prayer echoes from minarets around the city. Antonio and Giuseppina put their work on pause and return to the apartment for their *riposo*. They prepare a steaming pot of spaghetti with chopped eggplant and crumbled ricotta cheese. The smell stops him in his own shadow as he ladles it out and sits at the table across from Giuseppina. Antonio looks onto his plate at the chopped tomatoes bleeding into the eggplant.

"I haven't eaten Sicilian spaghetti in ages," Antonio says. "I think I've grown to prefer couscous, to be honest."

"You should reacquaint yourself with spaghetti," Giuseppina says. "We will be eating a lot of it when we return to Sicily."

"Return to Sicily?" Antonio sets his fork down.

"You used to always talk about one day rebuilding your family's barber shop. Remember as kids you would both save your tips in that little hatbox? Well, now that the war is over and we have some money, we can start planning our return."

Antonio frowns and looks away from his plate.

"I don't know, Giuseppina."

Antonio remembers his little hatbox full of coins that he used to save up for exactly that purpose—buying back his papà's shop, carrying on the tradition. But he has seen more of the world now. He has lived through war and plague and famine. He has seen the craters and ruined cities on the Piave River where the beasts of artillery fired over and over again, and never once did he see the Piave River flow in reverse. Rivers only flow forward.

"I don't think it's possible to go backwards," he finally says.

"You think Sicily is backwards?" Giuseppina puts down her fork and says in disbelief. "It is *backwards* that I had to spend my whole life in exile. You at least grew up in Sicily until you were thirteen. You had your cousins, grandparents, aunts, uncles. You had a sense of belonging. Me, on the other hand, I've never once known that feeling. Ever since my parents were banished for their marriage, the nobles in Sicily have pretended we don't exist."

"Then why do you want to return?" Antonio throws his hands. "The Duke doesn't see you as a legitimate member of the family. When you write him, he sends your letters back. He doesn't want you."

Giuseppina gasps, and Antonio knows he has said the wrong thing. His heart sinks as he contemplates her hurt, and he knows he will have to ask her forgiveness. At the same time, he feels a steely resolution, that he must save Giuseppina from further heartbreak by the Duke and also remind her that he has dreams of his own.

"I just want to know who my family is!" Giuseppina shouts like a pipe bursting from too much pressure. "Papà's side, Mamma's side, I don't care. It's so hard when you don't know your family tree—you saw how empty the church was at our wedding. Our guests didn't even fill up the first two pews! Antonio, it made me so sad that you didn't even have a friend to name as best man. So yes, I've had enough of our isolation. I want us to return to Sicily."

"I can't," Antonio's heart races, this time with fear, as he observes the pained expression of the woman he loves.

"Why? What has changed?"

"I want to start my own chain of barber shops," Antonio finds himself saying. "Not in Sicily, but in New York where the whole world is watching. In Sicily, our shop was just chairs and mirrors. I want to make my own shop, with all the novelties of the twentieth century—electricity, radios that play music. I want to be at the heart of the action."

Giuseppina's fork clinks against her plate, and he holds his breath as she gathers her words.

"Since the day I first laid eyes on you," Giuseppina says, "you have told me that you want to return to Sicily. Now, after surviving the war—thank the Good Lord—we finally have a chance to do it. And you want to abandon that dream?"

"That was the dream of my childhood," Antonio says, terrified of hurting her, but resolved all the same. "Now, after surviving the war and becoming a man, it would be a shame if I did not follow my new dream."

59. SEMOLINA FLOUR

Anna walks down the rows of seamstresses hunched over their sewing machines, expertly sliding their fingers within a hair of the pounding needles. Only one of the sewing machines sits unattended. Her sewing machine.

"Anna, you're late!" her sister Rosaria shouts above the mechanical whir of the machinery.

Rosaria's shirt is dark with sweat in the June heat, her sleeves rolled up and her hair tied in a bun. She clutches a clipboard to her chest. Rosaria sits Anna at her workstation.

"You know how to use a Singer, yes?" Rosaria asks.

"That's it? No introductions or anything?"

"Welcome to the working world," Rosaria says. "Despite what Mamma says, I can't give you any special treatment in these walls. Arrive on time, meet your quota, and nobody will bother you."

Anna glances at her coworkers—blank-faced women whose hands race faster than the Tunisian darbuka drummers who would play in the souk. She can see no hesitation as they make their stitches between the two panels of cotton, slapping it down in a pile as soon as they finish and racing to the next. In the rafters, an American flag billows from the waves of heat.

By noon, Anna stretches out her back and walks for the exit.

"Work isn't done yet," Rosaria shouts from across the hall.

"It's noon," Anna says. "I'm going out for my *riposo*."

Rosaria laughs.

"Nobody takes naps in New York, Anna. You can take a bite of your sandwich in the break room, but then it's back to your sewing machine."

After work, Anna emerges from the factory into the summer sun. She stretches her back, wrists, and neck, all sore from hunching all day over the machine. While walking back toward the train station, she catches sight of a dry goods store on the corner and stops in her tracks. Tempted by her stomach, she steps inside the store to browse through the shelves of boxed grains and canned foods. Normally, she would be sitting down to a steaming bowl of lamb and couscous about now.

"Do you have any couscous?" she asks the grocer at the counter.

"Cous-what?"

Evidently not. The thought makes her ache. "I'll just take some semolina flour then," she sighs.

Anna cradles the sack while she sits on the train, trying to avoid eye contact with the other riders. Arriving home in Brooklyn after her family has already eaten dinner, she pours out the semolina flour, rolls it into clumps with her hands. She steams the grains over cooking lamb, like the servants had taught her in Tunis, and the grains hydrate into pearls of chewy couscous.

Anna sits alone at the kitchen table, while outside the night is inked in and the cars honk in the dark. She swallows spoonfuls of the hot couscous and lamb, closes her eyes to pretend she is in Tunisia again, thinking of the endless hours at Miriam Sarfati's loom, watching a wedding dress form beneath her hands. The work of dress design is magical to her, the only thing that makes her feel like she is using her whole mind. Not factory work.

With all the ceremony of a priest at the procession, she washes the last grains of couscous from her bowl, dries it, and stows it away in the cabinets, climbing the stairs to bed.

60. APRICOT PRESERVE

Antonio hobbles into the apartment, heaving a basket of apricots onto the tile countertop of their kitchen. The sun-bright fruits are soft enough to bruise in his hands. Giuseppina saunters over and plucks the apricot from the top of the pile. She bites into it, and the juice runs down her hand. "These are so sweet. They'll be perfect for preserving."

Antonio pauses, about to remark that her voice sounds hoarse, but she seems fine so he shrugs and carries on. Using the knife set from their wedding, they chop the fruits into little cubes, toss them together in a bowl, and throw away the pits. Street performers outside beat darbuka drums, and they bounce to the rhythm as Giuseppina brings out the ceramic sugar pot and their collection of jars. She grumbles a few times to clear her throat. Again, Antonio considers making a remark, but it seems too trivial. They dump the mountain of sliced apricots into the saucepan, sprinkle in the sugar and the lemon juice, and strike a match for the oven. The kitchen soon sizzles with the floral citrus scent, and Antonio closes the window shutters so the smell doesn't attract flies.

"Do you feel hot?" Giuseppina asks suddenly.

"Only a little," Antonio shrugs. "Why, are you—"

Antonio turns to look at her, and her cheeks and forehead are bright red as if she had suddenly powdered herself with rouge.

"Darling, you're like a tomato. I think you have a fever. Why don't you sit down and rest? I'll finish up here."

"Are you sure?"

"Yes, go to the sitting room. Take a rest."

By the time Antonio has poured the fruity orange mush into the glass jars and sealed them away, he returns to the sitting room to see Giuseppina hunched in her chair, holding her head in her hands.

"Darling," he sinks to the floor beside her and wraps an arm around her shoulder.

"I feel nauseous."

Antonio runs to fetch the porcelain basin, and she grips the sides to vomit into it, her entire body heaving. He holds back her coils of dark hair.

"You must have eaten spoiled food," Antonio says.

"I'm fine."

"Giuseppina—,"

"I'm fine, I just need rest. I will take my *riposo* now," and Giuseppina disappears into the bedroom, saying nothing more.

Antonio dumps the basin into the courtyard bathroom and rinses it with soap and water from the spigot. By now his thoughts are racing faster than the tram cars on Avenue Jules Ferry. What if she is dehydrated? What if the Spanish Flu isn't over yet? What if some new pandemic is starting that the health authorities are not yet aware of? He scolds himself for not scrubbing down the kitchen with soap and feels the shame rising to his face.

While Giuseppina is sleeping, he steps into the street and hurries down Rue de Mars, weaving through the crowds of shopkeepers returning for lunch, hoping he can catch the druggist before he closes. He races under the shadow of Sacré Cœur Church and the wide plaza where French workers are paving bricks over the old Islamic cemetery, past the goat market where the flies swarm, finally arriving at the drug store on the corner. Panting, he pushes through the door.

"I was just about to close for the afternoon," the druggist says from the counter.

"Please, my wife is sick," Antonio leans on the counter to catch his breath. "She was running a fever this morning. She's vomiting. She's exhausted."

The druggist raises his eyebrows.

"Your wife, you say?"

"Yes," Antonio nods.

"And you are how long married?"

"A few years."

The druggist smiles, and his happiness confuses Antonio.

"Have you considered that she might be having morning sickness?"

"You can't be serious."

"Are you ready to be a father?"

Antonio's stomach drops. Already, he can see the next ten years unfurled ahead of him. He imagines their curly-haired baby, stumbling through their first steps, babbling *Papà, Papà*. And he knows they will not just stop at one child, and soon the apartment will be full. The color rises to his cheeks at the thought of being called Papà.

"Grazie a Dio!" Antonio shouts to the heavens, and he gives the druggist such a handshake that he pulls away.

With new energy, Antonio races back across the plaza, his coat flapping in the wind. The goats at the market *maa* at him as he passes, and the herders laugh at him. He stops under the steeple of Sacré Cœur Church to trace a cross over his chest and thank the Good Lord. A child!

He wonders how Giuseppina will react, unable to decide if she would express her joy through tears or shouts. And he would have to tell Zio Pietro as well. His uncle would break out into opera and dance across the room. What if it is a girl? Antonio already knows a name— Anita. A perfect name. And if it is a boy? His thoughts are moving too fast, and he is off the subject of names and onto how they might celebrate the joyful news. He is climbing the stairs two at a time, bursting through their apartment door.

"Giuseppina!" he calls, rushing into the bedroom where his wife is sitting up in bed, hacking a yellow gob of mucus into the basin. A handkerchief sits crumpled on the nightstand, speckled with flecks of red. She is coughing. He has heard the terrible coughing before, when she was a teenager with tuberculosis, and Antonio knows that she is not pregnant, that there is no child.

He deflates instantly, stunned at the sense of loss that washes over him followed by a punishing gut punch of guilt.

"What's going to happen to me, Antonio?" she asks, eyes wide with fright.

Antonio finds himself transported to his teenage years, when Giuseppina had fallen ill with tuberculosis for the first time, and Zio Pietro had pulled him aside. *Promise me you will take care of her*, he had said. *I promise*, Antonio had replied.

61. TEN-CENT DANCE

"Don't worry, Anna. I'll pay for your admission," Rosaria says, dropping a dime into the donation box. "I've been too hard on you at work, and I know you've had an awful hard time adjusting to New York, so it's about time I've treated you to a night out."

"Our birthday present to you," Mary adds. "Twenty-two is a special year."

The dance hall throbs with zigzagging trumpet blasts. Rainbow streamers string along the ceiling and sway with the waves of body heat. Under the lights, the air is humid with rose and lilac perfume, like a greenhouse. Her sisters Rosaria and Mary, along with their husbands, float onto the dance floor and join the girls and boys who hug close and move along to the Charleston, neckties and necklace beads flying to the jazz tunes.

Anna walks to the chairs and takes a seat at the dance floor's edge, hugging her arms around her chest. She wears a heavy wool sweater over her dress to cover herself from prying eyes. While her sisters dance, Anna reaches for the camera that hangs around her neck. *Snap*. She captures the moment—the smiles, the dizzying motion as the dancers twirl, elated. She captures the moment because she cannot have it, storing it away to process and frame on a wall at a later date. Her photography collection grows now, quickly enough to replace Fradji's photographs.

"Can I punch your dance card?"

Anna turns to see an Italian man holding his hand out to her. The thought of letting another man drag her out to the dance floor, to spin her in circles without end, forms a pit in her stomach. She rubs her wrist in the spot where Fradji had wrenched her arm and wishes she knew where to find the old Anna amidst her memories.

"I'm with someone," she finally tells the man. "I can't dance with you."

"Who are you with?" he cranes his neck. "I don't see anyone."

"I just can't dance with you," Anna sighs.

The man frowns, turns away, and disappears back into the crowd.

In a flash, Mary and Rosaria are at her side. "Anna, he was sweet on you. Why'd you send him away? Did he say something untoward?"

Anna clutches her camera and fiddles with the knobs and buttons.

"I just don't feel like dancing."

"Listen," Rosaria bends to Anna's eye level. "You've been like this for weeks now—not feeling this, not feeling that. I want to see you laugh. Could you just try dancing with someone? And take off that coat; this place has heating."

"If you want to cheer me up, don't make me flirt with strange men. You and I have different ideas of fun."

Rosaria and Mary nudge Anna onto the dance floor, and together they spin her around, dancing in a sisterhood triangle linked by held hands. While Anna watches the dance hall fly in circles, she cannot bring herself to smile. The act of dancing is stressful to her. Men stare at her from the corner of her eye, track her movements, and she knows they are trying to maneuver to her end of the dance floor. She does not have the energy to take their flirtations, their pithy jokes.

"Talk to me, Anna," Rosaria finally pulls her aside. "Do you want to go home? I thought the dance would cheer you up."

"I thought it would, too," Anna says morosely. "But it's just too stressful, with all these men wanting to spin me in circles. I'm burned out on love, Rosaria. How do I know they're honest or kind or…"

"Is this about Fradji?"

Anna cannot speak. Of course, it was about Fradji.

"You've made your point," Rosaria grabs her coin purse, calls for Mary and their husbands. "Let's go home, Anna. I'll make you some pasta."

62. SPARED FROM SUFFERING

It's been over a week since the coughing started. For the second time in his life, Antonio ushers Father Francois into his home. He watches as the priest unpacks his glass vial of holy oil from his robes. With their heads bowed, Father Francois reads from his red prayer book, and with the balsam-perfumed oil traces a cross on Giuseppina's eyelids, ears, nose, mouth, hands, and feet, each time droning the same Latin refrain. They thank Father Francois for his time, and the priest heads back to the church.

"The blessing made me feel very peaceful inside," Giuseppina says in between coughs. "I think I could be brave enough to accept my fate now, whatever should happen."

"You will recover very soon," Antonio assures her, swallowing the lump in his throat, "just like when you were younger. You defeated tuberculosis once, you can do it again."

"This time is different," Giuseppina spits a gob of mucus into the porcelain basin. "I feel so much worse now than the first time. I've lost ten pounds, Antonio."

"No," Antonio shakes his head, feeling his face heat and his eyes pool with tears. "You will recover. God would not allow anything else."

Throughout the night, Antonio lies at her side and listens to her hacking. He helps her to raise a glass of herbal tea to her lips and to take her medicine with a few crusts of focaccia bread. The medicine temporarily quiets her coughing, and she gains a few hours of much-needed sleep while Antonio clears away all the blood-flecked handkerchiefs. Her cheeks are sunken like a skeleton. Her olive skin has gone pale and clammy.

If only she had not gone to Souk El Grana last week, or even if she had visited a different souk, she would not have contracted the infection. Instead of suffering in bed, she would be spreading the first of the apricot preserves on toast with Antonio for breakfast. Why hadn't Antonio stopped her? Why hadn't he protected her?

His fists clench in anger at himself for not intervening earlier. After all the dangers they had weathered—tuberculosis, the war, the Spanish Flu—a simple trip to the market erased all their good fortune. While she sleeps, Antonio paces the bedroom, fuming, overcome with anger, wrenching the bedposts until his hands are sore, swearing at pillows, weeping silently so hard that his forehead throbs.

He knows that nature has no favorites, that whatever happens will happen, he just doesn't wants her to suffer. That is the best he can hope for. The realization leaves him foggy-headed, unable to focus on account of the hole in his heart.

By the time he collapses into bed at Giuseppina's side, his blood pressure again lowered to acceptance, he feels like he did when his brothers and papà left for America, how he had screamed and railed against them, and how no amount of anger could prevent that ship from leaving the harbor. He cannot change fate. He cannot change Giuseppina's tuberculosis. His only prayer is that she will be spared from suffering.

When Antonio opens his eyes again, he sees Giuseppina finally fast asleep at his side, her chest rising and falling peacefully, and that at least is a comfort. He walks to their balcony, which is just big enough for one person to stand and lean against the swirling iron grating, and watches the blocky rooftops of Tunis stretch onto the horizon. A soft blue light brushes the medieval facades, and in the West the hills are reeling back the darkness. He does not want to guess at how many—or how few— hours he slept last night, so he suppresses the thought on his way to the kitchen, setting a kettle on the stove for mint tea. This morning is unusually normal, and Antonio closes his eyes, breathing deep, believing for a moment that Giuseppina would recover, that the last week had all been a hallucination.

"Antonio?" her call echoes from the bedroom.

He sprints down the hall, thinking that some disaster has happened. She is lying there, still pale and sweating, but with a curling smile on her lips.

"I had the nicest dream," she says. "I was in Sicily. The fields were lush with olive groves, grapevines, almond trees. I saw Partinico, and all the houses were freshly coated in stucco so that you can't see the stones beneath. They were painted the colors of coral and lemon, and the balconies were decorated with blue tiles and hanging roses. All the families had full pantries, and the church bells rang out in tune with the birdsong. There was no mafia to speak of, no sulfur mines, and the poorhouses were all empty. My family was there—cousins, grandparents, aunts, uncles—and I was meeting them all for the first time. The Duke and the Duchess were there, and they even apologized for what they did to Mamma. They took me into their castle and told me stories about Mamma, and I cooked pasta with them. It was so real, Antonio, I could have sworn I was awake and everything was right with the world."

Antonio strokes her hair because he has no words. These days, he feels like he is always on the verge of crying, feeling sharp sorrow stabbing in his chest. He reminds himself to ask the druggist for any medicine that could calm his nerves.

"Do you remember when we were little?" Giuseppina asks. "I would send all those letters to the Duke, and he would just send them back?"

Antonio nods. He keeps his composure for her sake and rests a hand over his mouth so she cannot see his trembling.

"I never told you, but I kept the letters even after I stopped writing. They're stored away in Mamma's jewelry box," Giuseppina points to the bronze box on the dresser. "I'd like to read them."

"Are you sure?"

"Yes, can you get them for me?"

Antonio lingers at her bedside, reluctant. The letters would only remind her of the life in Sicily that she never had, a hopeless glimpse at an impossible dream.

"I don't think they would do your heart any good," he says.

"Antonio, I'm a grown woman. I can handle it," she says, her voice more forceful. "Please bring me my letters."

"Of course."

Antonio walks to the dresser and cracks open her mother's jewelry box. Inside he finds the letters, which by this point are yellowed with age. He can see her life chronicled in her handwriting, which starts out shaky and trails off in crooked lines, aging into the cursive of her later years—tight, controlled, organized. He brings her the letters, and Giuseppina spends most of the morning poring over them, her brow knit. Antonio wishes he could help her, but all he can do is bring her mint tea and painkillers while hours grow old.

63. WE CALL THE MOUSE REASONABLE

Anna walks to Saint Bernadette's church after work, creaking open the door into the echoing cavern of a nave. The church has come a long way since she was a girl. The parishioners have built an additional wing onto the church with a courtyard and rose garden, where they run a school and a food bank. Instead of using a cheap garden trellis as their confessional, the parish can now afford a proper mahogany booth.

She admires the fourteen wood carvings depicting the Stations of the Cross along the walls and thinks about her life. For months, she has carried a soul-sapping weight on her chest, and who can she tell about it? Her sisters, who she has just now spoken to after nine years? They are strangers to her now, or at least they will remain strangers until better reacquainted. She does not have Giuseppina or Antonio or Zia Rosa or Zio Leonardo—none of the people who truly know her. Who else remains? She does not leave the house except to work and pray, and the English language—her birth language—feels rough on her tongue after nine years of speaking French and Sicilian and Arabic. She desperately wants to tell somebody how she feels, somebody who will not speak over her or try to solve the problem, somebody who is required to sit quietly and listen to her without comment.

Anna slips inside the mahogany confessional booth and pulls the curtain shut.

"Anna?" Father Elmo asks from the other side of the grating.

"Ciao," she says.

Father Elmo barely reaches his snow-haired head over the grating inside the confessional booth.

"One second, let me get my encyclopedia," the priest grunts, setting a stack of books on his chair, climbing up until he is at eye level with her. "That's better. What troubles you, Anna?"

Anna sighs. "Where to begin? I broke off my engagement recently."

She expects Father Elmo to say something witty like *That's not a sin*, but he says nothing and sits there silently, nodding.

Anna tells him everything—her feelings for Antonio, her engagement with Fradji, how she tried to break up with him. She talks about Fradji's enlistment in the French army, how he returned a changed man, and how he hurt her.

"I had to break it off, Father Elmo, but Fradji could not handle the shock. Instead of supporting him, I abandoned him."

She expects the priest to rebuke her, but he just sits there silent for a long moment. "You've done the right thing, Anna," he finally says, somber. "How are your living arrangements now? Secure? Does your family support you?"

"Yes, I moved in with my parents," Anna says. "I feel very comfortable in Brooklyn, at least in a material way."

"Good, good," Father Elmo nods. "But I see the guilt still chases you. Do you blame yourself for what happened?"

"Very much," Anna says, and she feels a rush of heat to her face, and her voice cracks. "I know Fradji hurt me, but he was still the kindest, most thoughtful person. The war changed him. It's the war's fault, not his. Given enough time, I could have brought him back to his former self—I know it. I told him that I loved him, and then I left him."

"But you say that the cracks in your relationship grew even before the war," Father Elmo says.

"No I didn't."

"I am repeating your own words. You mentioned religious differences."

"Well, yes, we had some religious disagreements. First off, his family wanted me to convert to Judaism. I guess that's a big disagreement, actually."

"Did you ever talk to him about your own faith?" Father Elmo asks.

"I did take him to church a few times. He hated it. I suppose I was secretly hoping he would convert to Catholicism."

Father Elmo gives a single, slow nod, making his point.

"You probably think I'm a fool," Anna says.

"We're all fools. Take me for example, I chose to become a priest," Father Elmo laughs, tugging at his collar.

Anna smiles.

"What happened with Fradji is nobody's fault, Anna. When a mouse runs from a cat, we don't call the mouse foolish. We call the mouse reasonable. And you did not abandon him—I'm assuming this young man still has his family to look after him. Your needs are equally important. You cannot fill another person's cup when your own is empty."

"I know all of this," Anna nods, "but it doesn't make me feel any better. My thoughts send me in circles."

"In time you will grow past this, Anna. When you feel low, pray to the Blessed Mother. She will keep you strong."

Anna nods and feels a shiver run down her spine. Wiping her eyes, she leaves the confessional and sits in the pews until she is calm. The familiar surroundings of the church transport her to nine years earlier, when she was a little girl and the wheezing of her first asthma attack echoed off the walls. She remembers the terror of the moment. She worried she would never live to adulthood, and yet nine years later she finds herself sitting in the very same place, the place that sent her on her journey to Tunisia.

Tunisia. The land of her first job, her first kiss, her first love. She thinks of Zia Rosa teaching her to stitch in a straight line, of all the hours spent embroidering wedding dresses for Miriam, of all the evenings spent repairing torn pants for the soldiers in the Great War. And this is how Anna knows that her years in Tunisia, though buried and gone, were not wasted. They prepared her for this moment, so she would be strong enough to own herself, to be no one's burden. She has spent enough time wallowing.

Feeling a sudden gleam of intention, Anna rises from the pew, crosses herself with holy water, and leaves the church. She buys one of each newspaper from the street vendor and takes them to the deli, poring over the classified sections. After an afternoon of scanning, she circles a few job openings at the high-end fashion companies—so elite that she doesn't believe she is qualified for them—and begins to write applications. As they say in Sicily, *cu nesci arrinesci*—who leaves their comfort zone succeeds.

64: PEACE

A knock on the door, and Antonio opens his apartment door to find Zio Pietro and Pete and Vince standing in the hall, solemn like at church. They set up their three sleeping cots in the sitting room, the same kind Antonio had slept on during the war.

"Get some rest, Antonio. We will look after Giuseppina for a while," Zio Pietro says, setting a hand on his neck.

"I can't rest, Zio Pietro. It wouldn't be right for me to rest while Giuseppina is like this. After all, it's my own fault."

"It's nobody's fault."

"I shouldn't have let her go to the souk."

"The risk was so small. Nobody could have guessed this would happen."

"But—"

"Antonio, I know the stress of caring for a sick spouse, and I know you need your rest. I took care of Giuseppina for eighteen years. Trust me."

It is a small relief, as small as relief can be, but Antonio leans into his reading chair, stretching out his sore back and throbbing head. These days, his thoughts are in a constant haze, a haze that soon fades into sleep. His eyes slip shut.

By the time Antonio wakes, he sees Giuseppina standing before him in the sitting room. She clings to Pete in one arm and Vince in the other, and her legs are thin and boney, her eyes are sunken with exhaustion.

"I'm too tired to walk," she pants in protest. "You'll have to get me a wheelchair like Anna's fiancé."

While her brothers are looking after her at the apartment, Zio Pietro takes Antonio to the prosthetics store by the gas works. The dingy shop is lined with shelves of wooden legs and arms and glass eyes. The veterans from the Great War frequent this shop often. Fradji had recommended it. The clerk hands Antonio a catalog of wheelchairs, and he flips through the pages, arriving at a realization. His concern is no longer about whether Giuseppina will recover. His main concern now is providing her comfort. It is such a cruel thing to make a man choose.

"A wheelchair isn't a prison," Zio Pietro nudges him, perhaps noticing his stress. "It will give her some extra mobility when she is feeling up to it. You'll be able to take her to the gardens."

Antonio's stomach squeezes, his forehead pounds, and he feels a dagger of stress in his chest. Finally, he just chooses the softest wheelchair and hands over his money. The whole time in that shop, surrounded by the prosthetic limbs, Antonio feels like he is being strangled. He wants to vomit. He wants to scream, to cry, but he knows any kind of outburst would be unfair so long as Giuseppina is suffering. He will not allow himself the luxury of an outburst.

They bring the wheelchair back to the apartment. It has leather cushions two inches thick—the seat, the arms, the back. Giuseppina doesn't fill it in. She is so thin and shivering. They drape a blanket over her for warmth.

"Take me to the seashore," Giuseppina says. "I want to listen to the waves."

Her father carries the wheelchair downstairs while Antonio gathers her in his arms and follows. Once they are on the ground floor and she is settled in, they push her through the winding streets to Avenue Jules Ferry, and from there to the shore of the harbor, by the esplanade. She holds her blanket close, and the stares of the pedestrians make him want to yell.

"Are you comfortable?" he asks, and she nods her reply.

The waters of Lac de Tunis are calm and lap gently against the esplanade, so close that Antonio could untie his shoes and dangle his feet in the salty water. The branches of the eucalyptus trees and the cypress trees rustle in the fishy breeze. Giuseppina closes her eyes and inhales, and the wind flutters her curly hair. While they are standing there, Antonio watches her pull off her blanket, revealing her mother's bronze jewelry box.

"What are you doing?" Antonio asks.

Giuseppina opens the box and gathers up all the letters inside, each one addressed to the nobles back in Sicily. She winds her arm up as if to throw them, and Antonio moves to stop her.

"No," Zio Pietro touches Antonio on the shoulder. "Let her do this."

With a grunt of effort, Giuseppina hurls the letters into the air, and they balloon into a fluttering cloud that float like feathers, gracefully, to rest on the surface of the water. Antonio, Zio Pietro, Pete, Vince, and Giuseppina stand and watch the papers drift until disappearing on the horizon, out to the port of Goulette and from there to the Mediterranean, perhaps drifting until one day they wind up on the sands of Sicily.

Giuseppina exhales as she watches the letters fade, and a smile dawns on her.

Zio Pietro and Pete and Vince visit Giuseppina every day until they have practically moved into the apartment alongside Antonio. They leave the barber shop under the management of a senior barber for a few weeks, and they do not leave the apartment except to buy food.

Giuseppina's coughing has grown fainter, and her breath comes in wheezes. Antonio sits at her bedside and massages her temples.

Soon after, Father Francois arrives again, to check in and speak with Giuseppina in private, and Antonio knows that she is receiving her final counsel and her final communion, to mentally prepare her for what will come next.

The hour comes, around midnight, when Antonio is curled up at Giuseppina's side. He can see her bones. The handkerchiefs are dark red by this point, and they have no more clean linens. The blood expelled from her lungs amounts to three quarts. She cannot hold down food, and she has no more strength to cough.

Antonio tucks his face into the crook of her shoulder. He fixes his gaze on the bouquet of jasmine he'd set in the vase at her bedside. The snow-white buds had not yet bloomed when he bought them yesterday, but now their petals are partway through unfurling, fluttering in the moonlit wind through the cracked turquoise window shutters.

"Such beautiful flowers," Giuseppina breathes. He can barely hear her.

"You know what the florist told me yesterday, when I bought the flowers?" Antonio asks. "She said they are Arabian jasmine, the national flower of Tunisia, which only blooms when the world is at its darkest. At midnight, they are at their most beautiful."

"That's a nice thought," Giuseppina smiles. "*Chiù nniuri ri mezzannotte nun pò fari*—it can only get brighter after midnight."

Antonio props her on the pillows to make sure she is comfortable and holds her hand to his heart while the white blossoms continue to unfurl.

"Can I ask you something?"

"Anything."

"Why did you throw away the letters?"

"Because I had created a false idol in Sicily, Antonio. My whole life, I begged for God to give me a place to belong, to let me return to Sicily and meet the rest of my family. Then He gave me you, and I thought I loved you because you made me feel closer to my family in Sicily. But I was wrong. I don't need Sicily to be happy," she says. "God did give me what I asked for, but not in the way I expected. All I need is you."

"Oh, sweetheart."

"I have made my peace with God," she whispers. "I am ready to be with Mamma. I love you, Antonio."

He presses his palm to her heart, and all he has the strength to say is, "I love you."

They enter the lonely hours from midnight to sunrise, and Antonio notices that Giuseppina is drifting into and out of consciousness. He calls Zio Pietro and Pete and Vince into the room, and they sit at her bedside in prayer. By the time the sun rises, she is at peace, and the bouquet of jasmine is in full bloom.

65. NO MORE TIME TO WASTE

Every day after work, Anna checks the tarnished brass mailbox on her family's front door, not finding any responses to her job applications at the designer studios. After all, operating a sewing machine on a factory line is a chasm's leap away from the work of a custom designer. In the mornings, Anna walks past the studios on her way to the factory, and she admires the dresses on the mannequins behind the glass, the classic ballroom styles, the modern flapper styles. Their work transcends the everyday use of clothing for cover—these dresses are pieces of art.

"Anna, this envelope has your name on it," Mamma says one evening when Anna returns from her shift at the factory.

Anna's fingers are sore from working the sewing machine all day, and yet she tentatively grips the envelope. *Edith's Custom Bridal Gowns*, the envelope says. Her heart races.

Dear Ms. DiNicola,

My name is Madame Edith Hardy, and I am the owner of Edith's Custom Bridal Gowns. Thank you for your interest in a position as a designer with our team. I have reviewed your qualifications, and your experience designing wedding couture aligns with what we are looking for. I would be interested in an interview at our studio first thing on Monday morning, 9:00 AM. If you have any questions, feel free to write and we will answer promptly.

Sincerely,

Madame Edith Hardy

Anna sets the letter down as if it is a precious gift. Already, her thoughts are racing. What kinds of questions would they ask in the interview? How many people were they interviewing? Who was she competing against? She imagines the other candidates to be the academic sort, who keep bookshelves full of design catalogs and boast decades of experience.

"Who is the letter from?" Mamma asks.

"Just a friend," Anna replies right away. She does not want anybody to know about the job interview, partly to save them from raising their hopes too soon, partly so word would not trickle down to Rosaria and the factory management.

On Monday, Anna calls in to let Rosaria know she will be late for work. She locks herself in the washroom, curling her hair into tight waves like Antonio used to do for her. She digs out her old clothes from Zia Rosa—a cloche hat tied with a blue ribbon, her most professional chiffon business blouse. She descends the stairs into the kitchen, rehearsing possible answers to the interview questions.

"You're dressed like a librarian," Mamma says. "Where are you off to?"

"Work," Anna says.

"Now that's a bare-faced lie, but I'm not going to pry," Mamma says. "You're a grown woman."

Anna takes the train over the Brooklyn Bridge, then walks to 5th Avenue, where Edith's Custom Bridal Gowns is tucked between two gothic-style mansions that surpass even Zia Rosa's estate. Inside the shop, the walls are impeccably white, and designers swarm about dress forms with measuring tapes and sketch pads. Anna feels professional just standing there.

"I'm here for an interview with the owner," Anna tells one of the workers. "Could you tell me where Madame Hardy is?"

Anna is pointed to the back office, where the owner is filling out paperwork. She is a head taller than Anna, her grey hair tied in a scraggly bun that betrays stray wiry strands of hair, and wrinkles of stress mark her eyes. She drinks from a coffee cup and yawns.

"Excuse me," Anna knocks on the open door to announce herself.

"Yes?"

"My name is Anna DiNicola. I'm here to talk about—"

"Oh yes, Anna. I remember your application. Come, sit down."

Anna sits at the chair across from the owner's desk, and she feels her heart racing, though she does not dare show the tightening fear inside. Anna holds her head high and straightens her back, forcing herself to smile.

"Your application said you had spent time as a designer in Tunisia," Madame Hardy squints as she reads off the original letter. "You had a three-year apprenticeship making wedding couture, plus freelance, plus factory work. A little bit of everything."

"I do what I can," Anna tries to play it off so Madame Hardy will not think she is vain.

"At our shop, we receive custom wedding gown requests from all over the world, so it's useful to speak multiple languages. Do you speak anything besides English?"

"Absolutely," Anna smiles, and she counts on her fingers, "I speak English, Sicilian, Italian, French, Arabic, a little Ladino—"

"Any German?"

"Unfortunately, no German," Anna says, and she worries if this disqualifies her. Why else would Madame Hardy ask specifically for German? Anna tries to not think too much about it.

"What interests you about a career in design?" Madame Hardy reads another question.

"My whole life, I've been the sickly child of my family," Anna is not sure if this is the right thing to say in an interview, even though it is true. "I've always been dependent on other people to get by. Design is a way for me to depend on myself."

"So that is why you want this job?" Madame Hardy asks, and by her tone Anna can tell she is unimpressed. "Because you feel like a burden to your family? That's awfully harsh."

Anna pauses and considers it. She remembers what Antonio told her back in Tunisia, in the barber shop. *I think life is happier when we work for ambition*, Antonio had said, *not guilt.*

"I work for my own passion," Anna says. "I have no more time to waste on guilt."

"That's a nice thought," Madame Hardy suppresses a yawn and moves on to the next question.

"Anna, another envelope with your name on it," Mamma says at the kitchen table, raising yet another letter with the words *Edith's Custom Bridal Gowns*.

Surely it is a rejection letter, yet Anna feels her pulse accelerate as she grips the envelope, tearing it open.

Dear Ms. DiNicola,

I am pleased to extend you an offer for a position as a designer at Edith's Custom Bridal Gowns. Your experience working in Tunisia and your knowledge of other languages stood out from the competitive candidates we interviewed. We would be happy to—

Anna does not finish reading the letter. The paper feather-floats to the ground, and she drops into her chair, feeling a swelling pride break over her like the cool waves of the Mediterranean, like the Holy Spirit itself. Her final nagging thoughts about the guilt of abandoning Fradji, the guilt of being dependent on her family, the guilt of not pursuing Antonio, wither into dust. She sees a new future for herself, free from fear, free from dependence. A future in which she is fully herself.

66. WALNUT

Antonio sits on the chair at the visitation, his eyes trained on the walnut-wood coffin before him. The visitors circulate through his apartment, and he nods at them, his temples pounding. He does not even hear what they say, and the hour passes in a daze. He fumbles with the buttons on his coat, and the simple task takes him a full minute.

The guests of the visitation suck on sliced lemon and sample caciocavallo cheese, and he is confused that they can eat like nothing happened. He hears people say, "she isn't with us anymore," and the words do not find a meaning in his head. Giuseppina was only talking a few days before, in this very room. He keeps expecting her to come walking around the corner at any moment, saying his name. He does not know who he is without her.

He sees Zio Pietro wearing a black suit, black shirt, black tie, black pants, staring out the window with blank, shell-shocked eyes. "Nino," he comes near and rests a hand on Antonio's shoulder. It is too much.

Antonio goes into the bedroom where it happened, and creaks open the door. The white bedsheets are tidy and tight, and light slants in from the window, catching the swirling dust motes. Framed photographs of her mamma, Maria Minore, gather dust on the windowsill. Antonio traces a cross over his torso, first pressing a finger to his forehead, then his navel, then his shoulders, then finally to his lips which he pinches shut to keep from bursting. He remembers the children's bedroom, which he had shared with Giuseppina, Pete, and Vince since he was a boy. He remembers every late-night conversation, every stifled giggle as somebody told a joke and Zio Pietro barked at them to be quiet and sleep.

In the misty morning, Rue de Mars clears of shoppers, and its businesses close for the hour. A jet-black carriage shines with wax, reined by three muscled dark horses. In its wake, a marching band follows—Leonardo Ribaudo wheezes his accordion, another man blows into the zampogna, another pumps three fingers on the pistons of a trumpet. The procession winds up the street, to the esplanade by the harbor where Antonio and Giuseppina always held hands on their walks. They wind up the coast, and the houses of Tunis give way to the fields of olive trees, orange trees, and apricot trees that stretch over the hills. While the carriage bumps along the road, Antonio keeps a palm resting on the walnut coffin. He knows from his brothers that walnut is the most expensive kind of wood, used only in the coffins of dukes and duchesses, just like Giuseppina wanted. He spent his savings on it, including every last coin from his little hatbox, the chronicle of their childhood, the accumulated tips from all their years working together in Zio Pietro's barber shop.

The procession ends at a small church perched above the Mediterranean, where Antonio, Zio Pietro, Pete, and Vince together carry the coffin into the newly built mausoleum marked *Orlando*.

Father Francois says the final rites from his book, and they close the mausoleum forever. The crowd slowly files away, yet Antonio does not move, fixed to the spot clutching his bouquet of jasmine flowers, his gaze traveling back and forth between Giuseppina's resting place and the neighboring headstone marked *Maria Minore*.

"Would you like to stay here longer, Nino?" Zio Pietro asks softly.

Antonio nods because he cannot speak.

"I will stay with you," Zio Pietro says.

Zio Pietro does not have to say anything because Antonio can feel his strong hand on his shoulder, the same hand that had helped guide his first scissor-snip. They stand and listen to the Mediterranean waves and the rustling palm leaves. Antonio can feel Zio Pietro's shoulders shake, and his chest heave, and by the time they are both calm, the sound of the waves returns to them, and the sun is slipping below the sea.

PART 7

OCTOBER 1929

67. MEASURING TAPE

Anna is sipping coffee at her breakfast table in her bathrobe when the ringing telephone chatters throughout her apartment. She remembers how proud she was when she first purchased the telephone, with its sleek black metal, its shining rotary dial, its coiled cord. Her brand-new apartment has built-in wiring to accommodate such modern technology. She has finally made it in life, a professional wedding dress designer who can afford her own apartment.

"Ms. DiNicola speaking," Anna answers the phone.

"Ciao."

Anna recognizes her sister Rosaria's voice crackling on the other end.

"Rosaria? You're calling early. How is baby Michelangelo?"

"Difficult," Rosaria sighs. "All I do anymore is eat, sleep, and nurse."

While Anna listens, she paces around her sitting room, where she keeps a few bookshelves filled with wedding dress catalogs. The walls are decorated with woven scarlet-

and-gold Tunisian fabrics and wooden icons of the Virgin Mary. The radiator warms her by the window, where the streets of Manhattan bustle many floors below, where the pedestrians commute to work like crawling ants.

"Anna, would you mind coming over to visit me on Sunday?" Rosaria asks. "Something special has happened, and I wanted to tell you in person."

"Of course, what is it?"

"I won't admit to anything at this point," Rosaria says. "I want it to be a surprise, so come over on Sunday and I will announce it to everyone."

Anna is giddy the rest of the morning as she washes in the bathroom and dresses for work. She walks to Edith's Custom Bridal Gowns on 5th Avenue. Inside, the walls are unbearably white. She sets down her bags and gets right to work for her current client—a millionaire's wife who requested a custom gown absolutely shimmering with thousands of beads in an art-deco pattern. The gown had captivated Anna for weeks, and it sits in the back of her mind day and night. She cannot wait to return to her work.

Throughout the day, the shop swarms with wealthy women in fur coats and satin gloves, most of them gushing about their marriage to a banker or a stockbroker. Anna has a meeting scheduled with a prospective client, a Ms. Jameson who is supposedly connected to the Rockefeller family, who describes in detail what she imagines for a dream wedding dress. Anna listens patiently and sketches her ideas, erasing and re-sketching until she gets a sense of what the woman wants. No matter how expensive Anna warns them the dresses will be, Ms. Jameson does not seem to mind. She simply pulls out her checkbook and fills in whatever number Anna says.

"What did *your* wedding dress look like?" Ms. Jameson asks her.

The weight of the comment hits Anna like a wave, and she has to set down her pencil.

"My wedding dress was very plain and simple," Anna says, "but I never wore it."

"My apologies," Ms. Jameson says. "I assumed you had been married, since you design wedding dresses. It must be hard for you."

"I'm happy with my life," Anna says.

For the rest of the day, Anna's morning buzz deflates. She unrolls her measuring tape and collects the measurements of smiling brides, and their happiness leeches off hers. Anna imagines what it would be like to be in their place, to walk down the aisle with all her friends and family sending their well-wishes, to come home to a man at the end of the day instead of the silence of her Manhattan apartment where she eats dinner alone.

68. JOHN D. ROCKEFELLER

At first, Antonio's grief was fierce and unrelenting. It dug a chasm in his chest and left him in a daze. But ten days on an ocean liner with nothing but calm unbroken water to look at, then stepping off the boat onto Ellis Island, is a welcome distraction. The Statue of Liberty sends it cold, unflinching gaze, betraying not a single emotion, and the absence of human passion offers Antonio relief from the turmoil of his last few months in Tunisia.

Life in Tunisia had grown monotonous, meaningless. The silence of his apartment on Rue de Mars became unbearable, so he had avoided his apartment whenever possible; in fact, he avoided most of his old haunts. It had only taken three months to realize that he had nothing left in Tunisia except old memories.

"Passport, please," the American accent disturbs Antonio from his thoughts.

The line at the Ellis Island counter has shortened until Antonio is next, and he hands over his passport and struggles through their questions with his limited knowledge of English. The American immigration officials ask him to take off his shirt. They pull out a stethoscope and examine his heartbeat, his tonsils, ask him to cover one eye and read letters from a distance. Hours later, they sit him down for questioning.

"Do you have anyone in America to sponsor you?" the official asks.

Since his parents and brothers had moved to St. Louis, Missouri, Antonio said, "Emanuele Palazzolo."

"What is his profession?"

"Finance."

"How do you know him?"

"He is a distant cousin. My Zio Pietro put me in contact with him."

The official pencils all the information onto his clipboard.

"Very well. Welcome to America, Mr. Orlando."

The first week in Manhattan, Antonio takes night classes to improve his English and opens a bank account. He sets up electricity and hot water in his apartment. He feels like he has exited from the other side of a storm, but now that the winds of emotion have cleared, he is left with nothing except the cold, hard reality of sleeping alone. Every night he dreams of Giuseppina and the pressure of her body next to his, her black curls of hair, then wakes to find only quiet.

His Saturday morning is empty without Giuseppina's hair styling session, so instead Antonio pulls out the scrap of paper Zio Pietro had given him, with the address of his distant cousin, Emanuele Palazzolo, who has been working in America twenty years at an Italian-American credit union. With nothing else to do, Antonio navigates to Emanuele's apartment building, and knocks on the door.

"Ciao?" Emanuele opens the door, and Antonio can tell the man has Zio Pietro's bulbous nose.

"My name is Antonio. Pietro Palazzolo sent me to talk to you."

"Antonio! Yes, he wrote that you were coming. Please, come in!"

On Emanuele's wall, a framed photograph of a thin-faced old man watches them.

"Who is that?" Antonio points to the photograph.

"John D. Rockefeller, of course."

"Is he your grandfather?" Antonio asks.

Emanuele laughs. "No, of course not."

"Then is he a saint?"

"In a way. He is the richest man in America. Business-man extraordinaire. And one day I'll take his place."

Antonio nods, and Emanuele brings him coffee and sliced apples, and they sit on his chairs and talk.

"Have you found a job yet? I know it can be difficult finding work in a new country, so please ask if you need any help. I have been living in America twenty years. I know how business is done here, I know who is hiring, and I don't want you to make the same mistakes as me. We Sicilians must stick together."

"I have no intention of applying for a job. None at all."

Emanuele sets down his coffee cup.

"No intention? You're not bohemian, are you?"

"I've never been accused of that," Antonio laughs. "I'm looking to start my own business, a barber shop. I could use your help."

Emanuele raises his eyebrows.

"You're a bold man," he sips his coffee. "There's a barber on every corner already. What makes yours different?"

"Because I understand why people go to barber shops. Emanuele, I have cut hair on two continents, in war and peace, in life and death, and I know that people don't just go to a barber for a haircut. They go for the experience, for the dignity. A good barber can make a man stand taller. Trust me, I am no *quaquaraquà*."

"Fair enough," Emanuele says, "but you'd need quite a sizeable loan to open a barber shop in downtown Manhattan. Do you have the credit for that?"

Antonio has never taken a loan in his life, so he swats away Emanuele's comment with a wave of his hand.

"Listen," Antonio looks Emanuele square in the eye. "I need you to be my business partner. You know finances, and I know barber shops."

Emanuele gulps down his coffee.

"That's a big ask, Antonio."

"You want to be rich as this Rockefeller fellow one day, right?" Antonio points to the photograph. "You'll never get there as an apprentice investment advisor, or whatever it is you do. This is your chance to build something. Whatever happened to Sicilians sticking together?"

Emanuele stares with longing at the photograph of Rockefeller on the wall. A few moments of deliberation pass while Antonio holds his breath.

"Fine," Emanuele says. "I'll see what I can do."

69. WHITE LETTERS ON THE GLASS

Anna arrives at Edith's Custom Bridal Gowns on 5th Avenue. She pulls off her heavy wool coat and gloves because the radiators greet her with a wave of heat. She punches her timecard and walks to her workstation, where Ms. Jameson's wedding dress stands pinned to its dress form. Looking up, Anna notices that, for the first time in her memory, the rest of the studio is completely empty.

"Hello?"

Voices chatter from the break room on the other end of the studio. Anna stands in the doorway. Her coworkers are crowded around a table, reading a newspaper. She spots the owner, Madame Hardy, whose hair is unkempt and frazzled while she speaks to the managers in hushed, worried tones. Anna freezes. The silence, the newspapers, the sudden disregard of daily work—*has another war begun?* Only a few years ago in Tunis, the same sights had announced disaster. What is it now?

Anna pushes her way to the center of the group and reads the newspaper headline in bold.

STOCKS LOSE 10 BILLION IN ONE DAY

Smaller columns and similar headlines plaster the paper.
WALL STREET IN PANIC
AS STOCKS CRASH.

"I suppose it's sad, but it's not a funeral," one coworker says. "Besides, we aren't bankers. Why would it affect us?"

"They say stockbrokers are jumping out of windows," another worker whispers, pulling at her hair.

After work, Anna runs straight to the bank to withdraw her savings, but she is met with a crushing crowd who all echo the same words—the money is gone. All of it.

Not a single client comes into the shop that day, and Anna receives a call from Ms. Jameson, asking to pay a cancellation fee on the custom dress. The studio stagnates, and Anna knows the wedding dresses will never be worn.

When Anna talks to her sisters, Mamma, Papà, they tell her not to worry.

"Our family is secure," Papà says to her. "We owe no payments on the house. After all, I built it myself. We rent out the top floor to tenants, and I have my workshop too. Also, your mamma still delivers babies. We have plenty of income."

But at work, Anna hears rumors of layoffs. The owner's shoes clack onto the work floor, and the sewing machines fall silent.

"Camilla, Angelina, Lucy, I need to speak with you," Madame Hardy's voice echoes, and the three women process to her office.

By noon, the three women have gathered their belongings and are walking down the street away from the shop. The practice continues every day for a week, and the studio becomes more and more quiet, with half the workstations sitting empty. Anna knows she is the least senior designer in the studio; the other women have been working there for decades, whereas Anna has only been there four years. The other women have families who rely on them, Anna knows, she often hears them chatting and sharing pictures of graduations and baptisms. Anna, on the other hand, has only herself to take care of. Surely, she would be among the first to go.

Her fears are confirmed one day, when the owner, Madame Hardy, calls her into her office. Anna braces herself, tracing a cross over her chest.

"Forgive me," Madame Hardy whispers as she hands Anna her notice. "As a business owner, I once promised to look out for my team, to make sure everyone would earn a stable income for their families. I've known many of these designers since they first arrived in this country, and now the economy leaves me no choice but to let them go. What kind of leader am I?"

"An honest leader," Anna says, turning in her keys, somberly gathering her equipment and taking one last look at the studio before stepping onto the street.

At age thirty, Anna is unemployed. She tries to keep from panicking. She thinks of the years of training—the Virgin Mary's blue robe, the lessons with Zia Rosa, the apprenticeship with Miriam Sarfati, operating a sewing machine at the factory. She thought that after a lifetime of climbing the ladder she had reached her dream job—a wedding dress designer for the wealthiest clients in Manhattan, able to afford her own apartment, no longer dependent on anyone, totally self-sufficient. But now things will change. She cannot imagine any other studios are hiring, and she cannot guess how long until the economy recovers from the stock market crash.

In Central Park, she sees homeless families erecting houses of cardboard and corrugated tin. Anna realizes she is no different from any of them. Her savings account at the bank is wiped out, she has no job, and her rent is due in two weeks. Her thoughts start to spiral, and panic sets in, and she feels like she did when she was a girl suffering from asthma attacks. She will have to move in with her parents in Brooklyn. The indignation rises, the anger that after twenty years of work she is right back where she started.

Anna turns off 5th Avenue and walks through Little Italy, where she notices a moving truck parked in the street. They are moving in furniture into a new store, with the windows covered in brown paper to conceal the remodeling inside. Anna feels sorry for the shop owner. What a lousy time to open a business, and by no fault of their own. On the glass windows facing the street, a worker carefully paints white letters on the glass—*Antonio Orlando Barber Shop*.

Anna, her thoughts already racing from unemployment, gasps at the sign. She can hear her heartbeat in her eardrums. Her legs wobble. This couldn't possibly be the same Antonio Orlando—there are a thousand Italian men with the name Antonio Orlando. It could be anyone. She considers writing a letter to Zia Rosa to ask if it was true that Antonio had emigrated. After all, Zia Rosa is the only person from Tunisia who she even occasionally writes to.

But she ignores the creeping feeling and continues walking.

70. GAMBLING

Antonio surveys his barber shop. He had spent the morning in the realtor's office, straining to follow his English, filling out paperwork, with Emanuele co-signing for him. This is the first moment of quiet he has had all day. The grey floorboards are dusty and barren, the plaster walls cracked and spotted with holes where nails used to hang.

"This is *my* barber shop," he whispers to himself, amazed that the words would ever leave his lips.

As the realtor had explained that morning, this property used to be a tavern, and the faint shape of a bar can be seen outlined in dust on the floor. The original water taps from the bar will have to be reworked into water faucets for porcelain sinks, and the walls will soon be lined with mirrors and reclining chairs. When Antonio closes his eyes, he can picture the store, even surpassing Zio Pietro's store. He can even hear the crackling sound of Enrico Caruso's opera playing on the electric gramophone.

When Antonio opens his eyes again, he sees Emanuele through the shop windows, waving his hands.

"Antonio!" he calls through the glass, and by his tone Antonio can tell something bad has happened.

"It's gone!" Emanuele shouts as Antonio lets him into the shop.

"What's gone?"

"My savings—everyone's savings. All gone! The stock markets have crashed, and everyone at the bank was withdrawing all their money. It was anarchy. We have no money, Antonio!"

"I have money from Tunisia," Antonio starts to say. "I have a year's salary saved from my time working with Zio Pietro."

"You don't understand," Emanuele says, pulling his hair. "Our bank is no more. There is nothing. Zero."

"But I worked my whole life to save that money," Antonio says, and his heart sinks as he recalls the long days spent cutting hair, counting every penny. "How could it disappear? What was the bank doing with it?"

"Gambling," Emanuele says.

Antonio turns to view his barber shop again. His barber shop. The phrase has taken on a different meaning now, knowing that this shop is all he has in the world. He has no fall back. Antonio knows that he and Emanuele will have to make this barber shop profitable, or else they will be out on the street. Already, he feels the stress weighing down on him, and he hears his mamma saying *tantu a quartara va all'acqua ca si rumpi*, that the basin filled with too much water will soon break. He sinks into a sitting position against the barren floor, bunching his fists into his hair. He would not be surprised if gray tufts are taking root in his scalp right now.

"Where do we go from here?" Antonio asks.

Emanuele crouches down to Antonio's level. "We get to work," he says. "This shop needs to be open for business by the end of the week, even if we have to work all night. Whatever it takes. It's all we have now."

71. SWEET BAMBINO

On Sunday morning, Anna packs into Papà's car and grumbles through the traffic to Rosaria's brownstone apartment near Coney Island. After cancelling her lease on the apartment, after packing away her possessions, she has moved back in with her parents. No job, no income. Mamma and Papà talk to her softly and every few words say, "You poor thing." Even when they pull up to Rosaria's apartment, Mamma is trying to set Anna up on a date with her druggist's son.

"Rosaria, *comu semu?*" Mamma sets down a glass bowl of sugared almonds and three trays of frozen lasagna, though they cannot eat any of it an hour before Mass.

Rosaria shushes them; she lays on the couch while the baby's chest rises and falls with soundless snores. The walls in her living room are piled high with boxes wrapped in white paper.

"Anna, hold him," Rosaria straightens up and pats the couch, motioning for Anna to sit.

"Are you sure? I don't want to wake him."

"It's important to me that you hold him."

Rosaria sets the baby into her arms, and Anna sits there rigid, afraid to make even a slight movement. Michelangelo stirs. His skin is red and splotchy, his arms and legs covered in little rolls.

"Sweet bambino," Anna whispers.

Everyone in the room stares at her and the baby—Mamma and Papà *aah*. Rosaria unfolds the white silk baptismal gown, just to see if it fits, and together they dress the baby while he is still in the daze of sleep, before he has time to grow hungry and cry. Anna helps Rosaria to pull his rolled arms through the armholes, to tie on the little hat, the little shoes.

"You're very well-suited to take care of children," Rosaria tells her. "You look like a natural zia. Zia Anna."

Anna smiles and continues to rock the baby in her arms as he falls in and out of sleep.

"There's something else I wanted to ask you Anna," Rosaria starts.

Anna can detect a serious intonation in her sister's voice, and she prepares herself.

"I want you to be Michelangelo's godmother."

Anna sets the baby down.

"Why me?" Anna asks. "Mary and her husband already have several children. They own a house and have careers. Why not choose them? Me, on the other hand, I'm no Madonna. I mean, have no husband to be the godfather."

"He doesn't need a godfather. A godmother is good enough," Rosaria says. "And you're plenty nurturing. It's an instinct."

"You're avoiding the question. Why not choose Mary? Why me?"

Baby Michelangelo whines, and Rosaria does not have time to reply. "I have to feed him. I'll be back soon."

Anna watches her sister rush up the stairs to nurse the baby. She knows why Rosaria chose her. The reluctance says it all—Rosaria must have chosen Anna out of pity.

"Anna is struggling," she overhears Mamma telling Papà in the kitchen. "Being a godmother would do her good. She can babysit Michelangelo in the evenings and have something to do now that she's lost her job."

Anna marches into the kitchen, and immediately her mother falls silent, busying herself with the tray of lasagna as if she had not said anything.

"So you want me to be like Zia Rosa?" Anna asks. "Never having any children of my own, no career to speak of, driven to substitute someone else's child for that place in my heart?"

"Less aggression would be appreciated," Mamma avoids eye contact.

"Anna, we just want you to have some love in your life," Papà steps between them.

"Is that it? Love? Or do you just feel sorry for me?"

"*Is there a difference?*" Papà raises his voice for just a moment, then collects himself when Mamma lightly slaps his arm with a washcloth.

"Maybe I'll just reject Rosaria's offer," Anna crosses her arms, feeling a fire of indignation rage in her chest. "She'll have to ask Mary to be the godmother."

"Anna, I know you like to do things your own way," Papà says, this time calmer. "Maybe you're trying to prove you're not a sickly little girl anymore, but it doesn't matter. Rosaria is trying to help you."

His soft inflection reaches Anna, and she uncrosses her arms. She sees the earnest sparkle in her parents' eyes, the same parents who protected her from famine and violence as a baby in Sicily, who cared for her in a dingy ship across the Atlantic, who struggled for years to build a life for her in America, and after all that effort, tearfully gave her up to Zia Rosa because they believed it was in Anna's best interest. Their sacrifice dawns on Anna for the first time, and she realizes that everything they have done in life was for her. Her indignation melts away, and she feels something gentler, deeper, stronger.

She ascends the stairs to where Rosaria is nursing the baby, cracking open the door.

"I'll do it, Rosaria. I'll be Michelangelo's godmother."

Little Michelangelo gurgles in Rosaria's arms.

72. BREAD LINES

The day arrives when the technicians bolt a barber's pole onto the shop façade, and Antonio watches as his hopes sink into a pit in his stomach. The pole is carved from wood and painted with twisting candy-cane stripes, rising past ridges of molding to a glass cylinder, where an electric motor spins the stripes in a hypnotizing merry-go-round. Antonio inclines his head to see the golden glowing bulb that crowns the column, and the sight fills him with love and fear, like an unholy crucifix. It is the only thing he could ever want and yet also the last thing he needs.

He looks past the painted letters on the window, *Antonio Orlando Barber Shop*, to where plumbers are installing faucets and washbasins. Movers install mirrors, carry in the new barber chairs, plug in a General Electric ice box for lemon soda.

Every new item is a boulder that drags Antonio further into debt. At the first opportunity, he would strip the shop to its essentials and sell the ornamentation to meet rent. Yet they are not his to sell. He already signed the contracts which required him to pay monthly installments. If only he had known the stock market would crash, if only he had known his own bank would go under, if only he had known he would lose everything. If only he had stayed in Tunisia.

Around that time, the bell chimes as Emanuele strides into the shop, carrying a shining barber chair. He tracks dirt into the shop, and so Antonio sweeps the floor behind him.

"This might be my biggest mistake yet," Antonio cringes.

"What do you mean?" Emanuele, setting the chair.

"The bank owns the property, General Electric owns the ice box, and the factory down the street owns the chairs. We don't actually own anything in this whole shop."

"That's the genius of it," Emanuele says. "Welcome to the twentieth century."

"What will happen if the ice box is damaged, or the mirrors accidentally crack? They aren't even ours. Back in Tunisia, Zio Pietro at least owned the furniture."

"Antonio, the only way out of this mess is forward," Emanuele says. "When we open the shop and customers start pouring in, it will get easier."

"There will be no customers," Antonio says. "Nobody has any money. The streets are full of bread lines."

"We will have to take it day by day," Emanuele lowers his voice. "That's all we can do at this point."

Antonio feels like screaming. Back in Sicily, being in debt was like a prison sentence. As a boy, Antonio remembers the mafia visiting his family's home and demanding their money, seizing whatever they wanted when they could not pay.

"Times will improve, Antonio," Emanuele says calmly. "You look like you could use a party to take your mind off things, to get you smiling again. Why don't you come to Marco's Restaurant tonight? My family is throwing a party for my nephew's baptism."

"We can't spare the time," Antonio says. "We will have to spend every moment cutting hair if we hope to stay afloat."

"The baptism is at seven. Nobody will be asking for a haircut at seven."

Antonio exhales.

"Fine," he says.

Emanuele pats him on the back.

"That's better. I will see you there."

73. BAPTISMAL GOWN

At Saint Bernadette Church, Father Elmo pours out the holy water on little Michelangelo's forehead, splashing on his hair. The baby, eyes barely cracked open, stretches his arms and whines. Anna stands to the side of the baptismal font, alone, watching Rosaria and her husband hold their baby, the perfect image of a happy family. They make it look so easy. Anna imagines herself in Rosaria's place, her own baby gently breathing in her arms, a husband to reflect her joyfulness back so she could see it more clearly and know it is real. If only.

After the baptism concludes, they drive to a local Italian restaurant for the reception, where the tables are piled with trays of cannoli and candied lemon. The room packs close with her brothers, sisters, their husbands and wives, various extended families that fill the room with noise. On the dance floor, everyone grips arms and forms a giant ring, spinning along to the tarantella and the Charleston while the tambourines jingle.

Anna works up a sweat as she spins around with her sisters, and she can't help but laugh away her stress.

"Couple's dance! Couple's dance!" the cheer rises at some point, and the ring of bodies morphs into couples.

"Anna, will you watch Michelangelo for me?" Rosaria asks, sending her away to the tables.

Rosaria and her husband take the center of the floor, pressed close and swaying slowly to their heartbeats.

With the confused baby staring straight up at her, Anna walks to the tables to the side of the dance floor and takes a seat. The dance floor fills with every variety of partnerships—boyfriends and girlfriends, fiancés, newlyweds, parents, grandparents. Anna watches them from afar. While Michelangelo gurgles in her lap, she raises the camera to her eye. *Click.*

Anna admires the way that Rosaria only has to tilt her head to send a starry gaze into her husband's eyes, and she has never seen eyes sparkle so much. They had so much joy between them, those two. The last time Anna went dancing, she had felt a loneliness, a reluctance, like she was unusual for not having a husband, but now that feeling is gone. She is just happy to share the moment with her family, even if she's not on the dance floor.

The tables are empty except for a few scurrying children who play games while the adults dance. Wait. Anna spots another table across the room, where a lone man sits, watching the couple's dance.

No.

It can't be.

His normally slicked hair and his neat part are overgrown and shaggy, falling in unkempt strands to his eyes. A wiry beard hangs from his face, masking his mouth, while purple bags hang under his eyes.

While patting the baby, Anna finds herself pacing toward the table. She is afraid she might be wrong, that she is imagining things, that the man is a stranger. She walks closer, squinting to get a good look. He looks up and holds her gaze.

"You're shaggy, Antonio," she finally whispers.

"Anna."

The years fall away when she hears his voice, and once again Anna can feel herself sitting in the barber chair for the first time, asking him for a bob. She feels a lump in her throat, yet her nerves could send her sprinting away to hide from him. She does not know what to say. At that moment, the band starts playing a new song, and right away Anna recognizes the slow crooning of *Let Me Call You Sweetheart*. Her favorite song.

Antonio spots the baby bouncing in her arms, blowing spit bubbles.

"Congratulations on being a godmother," he says. "You must be friends with the parents?"

"I'm Rosaria's sister," Anna points at Rosaria, who is slow dancing with her husband.

"That's your sister?"

"Didn't you know?"

"I've never met any of these people. My business partner Emanuele invited me to the baptism."

They sit and watch the dancers some more.

"I'm sorry about Giuseppina," Anna finally says. "I can't imagine how you must feel."

Antonio gives her a half-hearted smile, and she can only see a portion of his beard lift. The wrinkles around his eyes betray his pain. "She is with her mamma now," he sips some of Father Elmo's contraband wine, and Anna can tell that is all he has the heart to say.

"Do you want to hold the baby?" Anna says. "It might bring you some peace."

Antonio finally nods. Little Michelangelo stares up with wide eyes as Anna hands him off and nestles him in the man's arms. Antonio smiles, rocking the baby and making all sorts of cooing sounds and twisted faces, whatever it takes to spark a reaction, but Michelangelo just squints at the world, gurgling, kicking his little shoes against his baptismal gown. Finally, Michelangelo opens his mouth and pulls back the corners of his lips into a grin, as if he were in on some joke. Anna and Antonio lean together and laugh, and the joy of laughter feels so good to Anna that her cheeks are sore. She cannot remember laughing like this, not since Tunisia.

While they take turns making faces at the baby, Anna sneaks glances at Antonio, just to reacquaint herself with his face. His cheeks are hollow. He is different since she saw him last. Thin. Gaunt. Sad. He is falling apart at the seams, and Anna wants to stitch him back together. She cannot imagine the pain of losing a spouse, not to mention running a barber shop on top of that. Yes, that must have been his barber shop that she saw in Little Italy. The poor man. Anna wants to say so many things, to reach out to him and hear his every thought, to just help him carry on when he has nobody, but she cannot put words to these thoughts—they are too much for one meeting. But, when the reception winds down and guests say their goodbyes, Anna stops him.

"Are you heading out soon?" she asks.

"I'm walking back to the train station. I live over in Manhattan, you see."

"Can I walk with you to the train station?"

Antonio nods. "That would be nice."

74. BROOKLYN BLEEDS BLOOD-ORANGE

Antonio steps onto the sidewalk and pulls on his wool overcoat that flaps in the wind. He watches Anna button her coat and press her cloche hat down over her hair as they walk briskly toward the stairwell of the above-ground train on Fulton Street that will take Antonio back home across the Brooklyn Bridge. The automobiles rumble past and the streets are crowded with bread lines and hungry families. He gives away whatever change he has in his pockets.

Looming over their street stands the silhouette of the Brooklyn Bridge—its two gothic towers and sloping cables stretch long shadows over them.

"My Papà helped lay the foundation for the Brooklyn Bridge, you know," Anna says. "When he first came to America, they gave him a job laying granite slabs beneath the East River. He never spoke a word of English."

"Even so, he'd probably speak it better than me," Antonio laughs. "I've been taking night classes to learn. English is a rough language. It sounds like your nose is plugged and you have a sore throat."

His breath mists in the night air. The brownstone apartments are the same color as the leaves, which rise in billowing waves and press against his shoes as the wind vacuums them here and there. He sneaks glances at Anna while they walk, to study her. At age thirty, laugh lines are beginning to show around her mouth, and creases radiate from her eyes, no doubt from hours of squinting over her sewing.

"How is your work these days?" Antonio asks.

He watches Anna smile, but her smile is strong and sudden, like he has asked the wrong question.

"I used to be a designer at a shop on 5th Avenue," she says, "until the economy crashed."

Antonio raises his eyebrows. "What did you design?"

"Wedding dresses," she smiles wistfully.

"Like you always wanted."

She seems taller to him, perhaps from the pumps she wears. He recalls her years of studying and working. He knows that whatever success she has had was won by her own effort. Her achievement fills Antonio with happiness, and he can't help but compare himself to her and feel intimidated.

A shrill train whistle disrupts Antonio from his thoughts. The train will depart the station soon, and there won't be another headed to Manhattan for the next fifteen minutes. He climbs to the train platform, which is plastered in dead leaves. Anna stops him.

"I thought I would never see you again." She touches his arm. "After we said goodbye in Tunisia I—"

"I suppose the Good Lord had different plans."

The smokestack is spouting to signal the train will pull out soon. The pealing whistle explodes the flocks of pigeons into a fluttering mass. They look at each other for a long moment, quiet, as if each waiting for the other to say something. It is October, so at this time of day the sky over Brooklyn bleeds blood-orange, the tomato sun squashing behind the under-construction skyscrapers, tinting them red.

"Are you getting on?" one of the workers calls from the train.

"It's nice to see you, Anna. So nice," is all Antonio can think to say, and after he boards, he watches her from the windows until the wheels start rolling, and the train lurches toward the Brooklyn Bridge, leaving Anna standing at the platform alone.

75. MEMORIES & DREAMS HOLD HANDS

Back home in Brooklyn, Anna walks straight upstairs to the bedroom that she now shares with her younger siblings. The room is stacked high with cardboard boxes from Anna's cancelled apartment. The more she thinks about Antonio, the more she thinks about the old days in Tunisia, and her thoughts close in on the past like a vulture circling over the Tunisian scrubland.

She unpacks one of the cardboard boxes in her room and lays out old mementos—a maroon shawl decorated in green and gold geometric patterns, a few ceramic bowls painted with turquoise starburst patterns like the leaves of a lotus flower. Finally, Anna finds what she is looking for. She lifts a brown paper parcel from the bottom of the box and lays it on her bed, carefully unwrapping the folds. She unfurls a white gown she had begun years earlier, its panels still held together by pins. The draped veil falls to the floor and trails behind, its white fabric jeweled with beads and embroidered flowers. This is the wedding dress that she never wore. Fradji would have seen her wearing it as she proceeded down the aisle.

Anna debates if she should try reaching out to Antonio and follow up on their meeting. Not in a romantic way because she assumes it is too late for that. Anna just wants to support him, just to help him manage his life. She knows he can be stubborn, that he and Giuseppina had their differences. She knows he could be stuck in the past and too concerned with what his family thinks. But she also knows the Sicilian saying, *nuddu si pigghia si 'un s'assumigghia*, that no one is attracted to someone they do not share something with. They had taught each other many things, and they had laughed together too. Anna cannot shake the thought of visiting his barber shop, just to talk to him.

Please accept what I am about to do, she prays to Giuseppina. *I do not think you would have approved of this during life, but now that you are an angel and know my heart, I believe you will understand. Please accept this, and if you are opposed, at least let me know.*

Anna shivers, and she is not sure if it is the cold wind or the kindred spirits breaching the mortal fabric, but she feels Giuseppina's presence, and a warmth fills her. She knows that memories and dreams hold hands, and a person can be alive in more ways than one.

76. GRAND OPENING

Before the barber shop's grand opening, Antonio pays a publisher to print a stack of promotional flyers, and he pins them on every street corner until he runs out. *Antonio Orlando Barber Shop, Grand Opening,* they flyers say. He tells the teachers and students at his English night school about the grand opening. He and Emanuele even post a pamphlet on the noticeboard at Most Precious Blood Church, and they are soon inundated with people asking for jobs at the barber shop, but no customers. It seems very few people can afford a haircut, and the few who can go to the already established shops.

The final night before the grand opening arrives, Antonio lays awake in bed, thoughts racing, staring at the empty space beside him where Giuseppina would have lain. Finally, his bedsprings creak and he gets up, head throbbing with a sleepless headache. It is still dark. The hour hand of his clock rests on four. He stands in front of the mirror and considers shaving his beard, which has grown too wild to manage. Perhaps slicking his hair back with pomade wouldn't hurt either. But he does not bother with either.

His heart races, and he worries if he will have what it takes to compete with the more established barber shops. He does not feel ready. Something is missing from this moment. As a boy, he never imagined himself opening his own shop, but rather continuing his family's. Even as he matured, he still imagined that he would have more of a family presence with him, people to hold close and share his pride with as he performed his first haircut, maybe even a son to pass down his knowledge to. But in these dim hours before sunrise, there is only Antonio Orlando, a dingy apartment, looming debts, and only a few weeks until his last dollars are gone. Still, he buttons on his white barber's coat and prepares to meet the day.

He leaves his apartment and walks down to the barber shop, pulling out his keys, unlocking the front door. The shop is even more beautiful than Zio Pietro's with its Victrola record player, its music collection, its reclining chairs, its sparkling porcelain sinks. He remembers the first time he cut hair, snipping away at Anna's bangs in the shop in Tunisia. He remembers all the years spent shadowing Zio Pietro and absorbing his every word. As he peruses the shop, he feels a swelling pride in his chest that he has arrived at this moment, imperfect as it may be. If only he had someone to share his pride with.

By the time the sun rises between the skyscrapers, the streets slowly awaken. The occasional trolley grumbles past, and workers commute to work, clutching their coats for warmth. The bell tinkles as Emanuele enters the shop.

"I have a gift to give you," Emanuele says, "before we enter the fray."

He pulls a wide, flat envelope from his coat and hands it to Antonio.

"Thank you, Emanuele."

Antonio breaks the seal and pulls out a cardboard sign. On one side, it says *Come in, we're open!* while on the other side *Sorry, we're closed!*

"The final piece of the puzzle," Emanuele says.

"It's a nice sign," Antonio says. "Let's hope we still have a shop to hang it in come November."

"You are an Orlando," Emanuele says. "You were born to run a barber shop. Just do what you do best—cut hair."

"What if being an Orlando isn't enough?"

"It has to be," Emanuele says. "Now will you do the honors?"

Antonio, with all the ceremony he can, proceeds to the front window, where he props the cardboard sign against the glass so the families outside will be able to read the words *Come in, we're open!*

77. WITH LOVE, GIUSEPPINA

Anna is sitting at her parent's kitchen table, leafing through her old copy of *The Wonderful Wizard of Oz* when the daily mail falls through the slot on the doorway. *Thud*. One of the envelopes hits the ground hard. Curious, Anna finds a yellowed envelope, scuffed with black scrapes, bearing the stamps of America, France, and Tunisia. *Anna DiNicola*, the envelope reads, and in the corner, in looping cursive, the sender. *Giuseppina Orlando.*

Anna gasps. The mess of international postage stamps show that it was lost in Rome, then Paris, then London, circling around Europe before finally reaching America. The envelope is heavy in her palm, and as she raises it to their humming electric lightbulb she can spot a metal object inside.

In a flash, Anna locks herself in her bedroom, diving onto her bed as she carefully slits the paper and unfolds the letter.

Dearest Anna,

I am writing to you from my bed in Tunis. Yes, you may think that I am snug and settled with Antonio in a little house, perhaps announcing we are with our first child. I am sorry to say that I have fallen ill and am once again bedridden with tuberculosis. I have been feeling absolutely horrid, and I imagine you know what it is like to gasp for breath, with your asthma history.

I have had plenty of time to reflect, and I must tell you that I am not well, Anna. I am in a bad way, very bad. I know you will not believe me, you will say that I should not speak of such things and to focus on the positives, but I know that heaven is close. I can feel my mamma's presence with me.

You have been a friend to me in this life, Anna. I would add adopted older sister to that title as well. I remember the times we would go to the hammam with your zia, the times I would stop at your house so you could teach me to sew. Do you remember how we would laugh when Antonio bumbled over my hair at the barber shop on Rue Pierre de Coubertin? You were always so bold, so modern, with you coming from America and all, and you taught me to pursue what I want, Anna.

You will not listen to me if I say I am short on time, but even so I have enclosed a gift for you to wear and think of me, whether I am here or not. I have no sisters, no aunts, no godmother, no daughter, no mamma on this earth. You are the only person I would share this with.

"Oh Giuseppina, you poor thing," Anna sniffles.

She shakes the envelope, and out falls a ring—a platinum ring with an S-swirl and three diamonds. Anna remembers seeing the ring flashing from Giuseppina's finger the very day Antonio proposed to her, catching the Tunisian sun. She remembers seeing the ring glinting off the church candles as Giuseppina paced down the aisle in her wedding dress. She reads more.

This ring belonged to my mamma, Maria Minore. She was the daughter of a fading Duke in Sicily, and when she fell in love with a lowly barber named Pietro Palazzolo, her family disowned her for breaking the noble lineage. She received every manner of death threat, and so she and my Papà moved to Tunisia and opened a barber shop. My mamma took only one memento of her noble lineage with her—this ring. I want you to have it, because I have a feeling I will not be needing it much longer.

Shivering, Anna clutches the ring in her palm.

I have one more thing to say to you. When I am gone— and do not protest this point—you will be Antonio's last true friend. Please be kind to him. Go to Antonio with your heart if you are inclined. Promise me that you will help Antonio to move on and enjoy all the blessings I wish I could have given him.

I will see you again Anna, and until we are together again, I will pray for you.

With Love,
Giuseppina

78. JASMINE FLOWERS

Giuseppina would have celebrated her thirtieth birthday today.

At noon, Antonio takes off his white coat and flips the storefront sign to *closed*. He walks a few blocks to the Church of the Most Precious Blood, crosses himself with holy water, and sits in for the noon Mass. Weekday Masses are not highly attended, so the pews are sparse. Antonio sings the Latin responses and kneels. He listens to the Scalabrini priest raise the Gospel high while the pipe organ vibrates. The bread and wine send shivers down his spine.

After Mass is over and the parishioners file out to the street, he lights a candle for Giuseppina and kneels onto the cushion, thinking of her. Is she happy now? The priests say that in heaven all the saints are reunited, so that must mean Giuseppina is up there with Mary and Joseph and all the other holy people that he learned about in school. Antonio likes the thought of that.

In the empty church, the only sound is the echoed bubbling of the baptismal font, reminding him of baby

Michelangelo's baptism, the baby who bounced in Anna's arms at the reception. He thinks of Anna's black coils of hair, flawless as always.

Antonio frowns. Would Giuseppina be hurt that he is thinking of Anna? Would Giuseppina feel forgotten, like he left her behind in Tunisia, in the white marble mausoleum with the bouquet of jasmine flowers?

He imagines how Anna would feel, perhaps only feeling wanted as a substitute for Giuseppina. But that was not true. Giuseppina could not be replaced, and Anna could never be anyone other than herself.

Antonio reaches into his pocket and pulls out the pewter medallion of the Virgin Mary, which Anna had pressed into his hands at the Tunis pier seventeen years earlier. He had been terrified out of his mind, arriving in a new country by himself, escaping the nightly mafia shootings of Sicily. Right away, Anna had recognized his fear and put him at ease. He thinks of how hardworking she has always been, throwing herself into her work with the Sarfatis, learning French and Arabic, working her way to the rank of a professional wedding dress designer just like she always wanted. He has been rooting for her this whole time, otherwise he would not have kept the medallion this long.

Should he visit her again?

Antonio realizes it would be wrong not to, not after everything they'd been through. He finds himself caught between not wanting to hurt Giuseppina and not wanting to ignore Anna.

Antonio has been kneeling before the candles for a good half hour now, and soon he will have to return to his barber shop. He crosses himself and rises to leave, but as he is walking he notices something in the pews. Someone has left a bouquet of flowers. Curious. He walks closer and picks up the flowers from the pew.

It is a bouquet of jasmine flowers.

He does not have to wonder if Giuseppina is with him because he can feel her in the silence. She is like an embrace wrapped around him, living in his mind, sending her thoughts to him.

"Thank you for the flowers, Giuseppina," he whispers to the silence. "I know what I have to do now."

79. My Whole Life

Go to Antonio with your heart if you are inclined. Promise me that you will help Antonio to move on and enjoy all the blessings I wish I could have given him.

Anna lets the letter feather-float to the floor. She slips Giuseppina's ring on her finger, watching the diamonds catch in the light. On the opposite end of her bedroom, draped on a chair, is Anna's half-finished, never-worn wedding dress. She looks back to Giuseppina's ring, then to the wedding dress, as if Giuseppina's spirit has unspooled an invisible thread between them.

A shiver runs down her spine, and she suddenly knows what she wants to do. Anna goes to the stack of cardboard boxes from her apartment and digs out her dressmaking supplies. She lays out her spools of white thread, her needles, her pin cushions, her scissors. She reassembles the dress form by screwing the wooden posts together and standing it upright, a perfect clone of herself, and she pins the panels of the wedding dress onto the form, unfurling her measuring tape and getting to work.

"Anna, are you coming downstairs for dinner?" a few taps on the door signals Mamma's entry into her bedroom.

Mamma creaks the door open and gasps at the mess of fabric and thread strewn across the floor. Anna cannot reply because she is holding several pins in her lips, and she cannot wave Mamma away because her hands are carefully threading a needle along a pearly-white sleeve.

Anna expects Mamma to protest, but the sight of the glittering wedding dress silences her. She watches Mamma back away on her tiptoes, as if afraid to disturb her work. A few minutes later, Mamma returns with a plate of pasta, setting it on her bedstand, and an unspoken agreement passes between them. Anna will finish this dress, and Mamma will feed her until then.

The shadows grow long in the evening, and by this point Anna has begun embroidering the remaining flowers on the train. Her head aches from the prolonged squinting, but her thoughts are precise. She pins the train to the shoulders, then drapes it several feet across the floor, imagining how the fabric would trail when she processes down the aisle at Saint Bernadette Church. The dress imprints itself in her thoughts, and she can see the final design clearly, revealing itself to her like the Tunisian beaches at low tide.

Mamma brings her a small cup and saucer of espresso, along with some biscotti. "You are almost there, Anna," Mamma says, flicking on the lightbulb, dispelling the shadows. "You know what you have to do."

Soon, Anna's younger siblings—Marietta, Lucia, Concetta—jump into their shared bed, yawning, asking to turn the lights off.

"Anna, you can finish the dress in the morning. Just let us sleep now."

Anna ignores them and continues embroidering, switching the lights on every time her sisters switch them off.

"Mamma!" Concetta cries. "Anna won't let us sleep!"

Mamma shows up in the doorway. "Let Anna finish her work. If she is bothering you, sleep with me and Papà."

Anna's sisters choose the latter, leaving Anna to continue her work. As the moon rises through the window, thoughts of Antonio keep her company. He was the first person she met after stepping off the boat onto the Tunis pier—a little boy sitting on the bench, pale with fright. She remembers the first haircut he gave her, when he was so nervous, he cut off her bangs. She remembers the flamingos ascending toward heaven and their kiss by the mudflat.

By the time the sky pales, when the first feather of dawn breaks over the Coney Island horizon, Anna finally finishes embroidering the veil. She sets down her needle, stretching out her hands. One final touch. She sets the veil atop the dress form, draping it around the lace sleeves, the train, the skirts.

"Good morning, Anna," Mamma steps into her room, rubbing the sleep out of her eyes, setting down a bowl of oatmeal on her bedstand. "I made you breakfast, love."

"I finished my wedding dress, Mamma."

Anna lays down on her bed, and a wave of exhaustion hits her. Her head is foggy after working all night.

"Anna, it's too beautiful," Mamma touches the white satin. "How long did it take you?"

"My whole life ."

80. CAN YOU DO A BOB?

It is closing time. In his teenage years, Antonio would scrub every mirror and even pick away the soap residue with his fingernails to ensure the washbasins were perfectly sparkling. But now he throws the towels and makes a few half-hearted sweeps across the floor. He locks up the door and flips the sign to *closed*. He looks in the mirror and sees his face hopelessly overgrown with a patchy fuzz of beard. Stray hairs corkscrew at every angle.

He collapses into his chair and wishes for sleep to take him, for his head to crash onto a pillow. The ledger book is nearly empty because he has received so few customers, yet the streets are crowded with homeless families, and he is torn between wanting to help them and being unable to help himself. The first biting winds of winter snake through the skyscrapers, and the homeless families huddle under tarps that flap in the cold wind, even as police officers extinguish their campfires and tell them to leave, threatening to arrest them for loitering, threatening to arrest them for eating out of the trash because trash is valuable city property.

At Antonio's workstation, he pins a collection of photographs—himself and Zio Pietro, himself and Giuseppina. If only he still had his hatbox full of his Italian lire, his French francs, his American dollars, a time capsule of his life. He considers giving the coins away to the homeless families that sit outside, wishing them well. But it would never be enough to restore their dignity. He had felt the same way about the poor families of Partinico, caught by the ebbing tides of history.

Tap tap.

A few fingers tap against the glass on the door, and Antonio raises his eyes. He must squint because the sun is low in its smoldering at this time of day, throwing a marinara glare on the glass.

He sees a woman looking back, also shielding her eyes from the dying light.

He knows those curls.

Antonio is walking to the door, unlocking it, letting Anna in.

"What brings you here?" Antonio asks, taking off her coat and hanging it on the wall. "Can I get you a lemon soda? Or something warmer?"

"Lemon soda will do," Anna says, and she takes a seat on the cushioned barber chair, sinking down a thumb deep.

Antonio opens the ice box and pops the cap off the bottle, wondering why Anna is in his shop. Is she in trouble? How did she even find him? He hands her the soda and studies her while she sips at the bottle's lip.

"I see you finally opened your shop, just like you always wanted," she says, peering around, studying the electrical gramophone that crackles Italian opera, the humming electrified ice box, the stack of records from Enrico Caruso. The slat blinds are half-closed on the windows, striping the tiles in alternating rays of blood orange and pearl white.

"My shop might not stay open for long," he says, "not in this economy."

"Your shop is nothing like I imagined," she says. "It's… modern."

"Thank you," Antonio says, and Anna passes him the bottle. He presses his lips to the lemon fizz. The soda is sour and bubbles flutter in his stomach.

A silence hangs between them. There is so much Antonio wants to tell her, too much for comfort. He does not know where to start. He imagines the same worries circle through her head because she is also silent as they trade the bottle back and forth over the hair-strewn floor.

Anna finally looks up at him from under her dark lashes. "Can you do a bob?"

Antonio swallows, and then his grin curls like an orange peel for the first time in months. With every degree of ceremony, he ties the cloth over Anna's shoulders, unties her bun and lets it fall, spritzes the water on her hair with the spray bladder, and starts combing. Her hair has grown down past her shoulders since returning to Brooklyn.

Snip, snip, snip.

Her coiled curls gracefully feather-float to the floor to rest in little nests on the tile, and once again her hair brushes her jaw like it did in Tunisia, in her youth. He studies the three familiar freckles at the nape of her neck, the way her hair-part meanders to the left, her comma eyebrows, and the sights plucks him back seventeen years to the first trimming in Zio Pietro's barber shop. Antonio has spent his entire life searching for the feeling of home, of familiarity. He did not truly find it in Tunisia, nor in America, at first. But perhaps, at last, he is finding it in Anna. Gripping the curling iron, Antonio loops her hair into a single curl that comes to rest on her left cheekbone. Flawless. Beautiful.

"Now it's my turn," she says, dusting off her shoulders, standing up from the chair. "Let me cut your hair for once."

She guides Antonio into the chair, drapes the cloth around his shoulders, and trims the long tufts of beard which have grown wild over the last few months. Antonio has not shaved since Giuseppina went to heaven. He looks at himself in the mirror, at the profound bags under his eyes denoting many late nights spent counting his dwindling savings, the trans-Atlantic crossings, the difficulty of sleeping alone, the loneliness of missing Giuseppina and wanting Anna.

When his beard is finally neatly trimmed, Anna pops open the tin of shaving soap, scrubbing it with the horsehair brush until foaming into a lather. She brushes his face in the white lather and draws the pearl-inlaid walnut razor from its sheath, scraping down his jaw, occasionally stopping to wipe the razor on a cloth.

Antonio watches his beard fall away. A spray of water, a wash, and he views himself in the mirror. His face feels clean for the first time in weeks. He looks ten years younger and feels ten pounds lighter, and the air is fresh against his skin. He draws back his shoulder blades, puffs out his chest, two inches taller.

"It's so curious how a haircut can transform a person," Anna tilts her head, kicking at the combined pile of both their hairs. He shivers as Anna reaches out to feel his recently shaved face, running her palm on his cheek. Her touch is enough to still his thoughts, and he leans into her palm as if finally at rest.

"It will be dark soon," Antonio mutters. "Your parents will be expecting you at home for dinner."

"My family can wait," she says.

"But the day is old. You must be tired."

"I'm more awake than ever."

"I don't want to keep you from your family."

"I'm not leaving you." Her voice cracks.

He notices her eyes are glistening.

"I'm not leaving you," she repeats in a whisper, and he can tell by the inflection of her voice that she is not talking about dinner.

Antonio holds her hand, and their faces grow closer. She loops her arms under his, nestling her feather-soft hair into his neck. He wraps his arms around her, pulling her close, until he can feel the rise and fall of her breaths against his chest. "I have nothing to offer you. My shop has left me in debt. The bank failed and my savings are gone."

"I have no job and live with my parents," Anna says, pulling back to look up at him. "I'd say we're even."

She studies his face like one of her fabrics, and Antonio can tell she is searching for something, some bending of the brow, some parting of the lips. He does not look away.

"I have something to return to you," he says, pulling something from his pocket and closing her hand around it. "For courage."

He watches Anna turn over the pewter medallion of the Virgin Mary, not sure if she remembers it. Finally, a smile breaks over her face.

"Oh, Antonio. Were you keeping it all this time? Through the war and the tuberculosis and the immigration?"

"Not a day goes by without it."

"Why?" she asks, and he can tell they both know the answer, but it is important that he say it.

"Because," he looks down at the medallion, feeling such a truth that it could only have been instilled in him by the Queen of Peace herself, then lifts his eyes to meet hers. "Because you are the only home I have ever known."

Through the window, the sun casts its terminal glimmer over them, turning them both to gold. Antonio bends down to press his mouth to hers. Anna raises her face to his for their second kiss. One. Two. Three. Four. Five. A kiss long enough to guide them home.

AUTHOR NOTES

While this book paints a picture of Anna and Antonio's lives, it does not paint every color. I did not set out to write a biography but a novel, not to inform readers but to transport them. This inevitably led to decision points—what details to keep, what details to omit, and what details to embellish. For example, in the 1920s Antonio made several trips between Tunisia and America about every six months. Instead of encumbering the readers with the tedium of a dozen boat rides across the Atlantic, I streamlined it into one single move. I made many decisions like this during the writing of this book, bringing into focus the emotional journey of the characters, avoiding the maze of small details that accompany them.

For my own family members and for other interested readers wondering how close this book was to reality, I am adding the true-to-history timeline of Antonio and Anna's lives from 1900 to 1930. The following information is accurate to my knowledge.

Antonio's Childhood in Partinico

Antonio Orlando was born February 20th, 1900 in the village of Cinisi outside of Palermo. He was the son of Anna Palazzolo Orlando and Giuseppe Orlando, an accountant. Notable family members included the recently deceased Luigi Orlando, an engineer and shipyard owner in Livorno, and Vittorio Orlando, a politician who would eventually become the Prime Minister. Antonio spent most of his upbringing in Partinico, another mid-sized town near Palermo.

As described in the book, the island of Sicily was languishing in economic and political turmoil since Garibaldi abolished the feudal system in 1860. A drought and famine on top of that led to a power vacuum soon filled by the mafia, also called the Black Hand, who recruited young men into their gangs. When Antonio was eleven his two older brothers Pete and Sam left Sicily to escape recruitment from the Black Hand. They moved to the United States and settled in St. Louis while Antonio remained in Sicily.

Anna's Childhood in Brooklyn

On May 26th, 1903, Anna Maria DiNicola was born in Ciminna, another village near Palermo. She was the fourth of nine children. Her father Michelangelo and her mother Angelina, like many others, were struggling to secure a life in Sicily.

Her father, a six-foot tall stone mason, had moved to Brooklyn several years earlier, where he would work six months at a time building the Brooklyn Bridge, then spend the other half of the year with his family in Sicily.

He might possibly have been one of many "sandhogs," immigrants who worked for $2 a day building the Brooklyn Bridge caissons, digging to bedrock under the East River to lay the foundation, often suffering from decompression sickness.

He did this for about two years until finally saving enough money to move the whole family to Manhattan. Crossing the Atlantic by boat took three weeks, and Anna was only about six months old at the time. Upon arriving in the Manhattan, they initially lived in an apartment above a drug store on the corner of Elizabeth and Houston, but eventually they built their own house in Brooklyn.

Anna spent her early years at this house in Brooklyn with her many siblings. She was the shortest in height of all her siblings and the poorest in health. New York City braved blizzard conditions in the winter and endured hot dusty summers, and in both seasons Anna would fall into coughing fits. Her symptoms appear to be consistent with childhood asthma. The best cure the doctors could recommend was a mild climate and fresh air.

Anna Moves to Tunis

In 1912, nine-year old Anna and her mother Angelina crossed the Atlantic once again, where Anna was dropped off to live in Tunisia with her aunt Rosaria Cuti Ribaudo and her uncle Leonardo Ribaudo. This was the same year the *Titanic* sank, to illustrate the perils in trans-Atlantic travel. Upon arriving in Tunis, Anna found the balmy Mediterranean climate to be a relief for her asthma.

Tunisia was a French protectorate at the time, although the Sicilian immigrants far outnumbered any French immigrants living there. For any lower- or middle-class Sicilians, Tunis was a great place to seek refuge from the poverty and instability of Sicily. Aunt Rose and Uncle Leonardo were among these Sicilian immigrant-farmers. They owned a farm estate outside of Tunis where they raised sheep, chickens, rabbits, and goats. Since Leonardo was aging at around sixty-two, he hired local Tunisian farmhands, a cook, and a seamstress to assist him.

Antonio Moves to Tunis

In 1913, thirteen-year-old Antonio finished his schooling in his hometown of Partinico, Sicily. Just like his brothers before him, he was sent away to avoid recruitment into the Black Hand. Like Anna, his family sent him to Tunis, where he would live with his uncle Pietro Palazzolo on his mother's side. They paid five lire to buy a boat ticket across the Mediterranean and said goodbye. For the rest of his childhood, Antonio would live with his Uncle Pietro and his three cousins on 4 Rue Pierre de Coubertin, where he learned to cut hair in the barber shop.

Uncle Pietro was born in 1877 in Antonio's hometown of Partinico (This is conjecture based on his immigration papers saying he was born in Tartinco, a possible misspelling of Partinico). He married Maria Minore, who according to family tradition was the daughter of a duke and duchess, though this is not confirmed. Tradition has it that in 1904, Maria Minore was disowned by her noble family for marrying a lower-class barber. If this story is true, a possible candidate for the duke and duchess could be Duke Vincenzo Grifeo II and Duchess Rosa

DeFrancesco who owned lots of land near Partinico. However, this is not confirmed. Supposedly because of the falling-out, Maria and Pietro left the country, moving to Tunis in 1904. In Tunis she gave birth to two sons, Pietro and Vincenzo, and in 1908 a daughter Giuseppina. Maria died young in 1911 in Tunis, when Giuseppina was only three years old.

Anna's Teenage Years

From 1912 to 1920, Anna grew into adulthood on the Tunis farm with her Aunt Rose and Uncle Leonardo. Servants dressed her in fine clothes while chefs taught her to prepare couscous, carrots, and lamb. She went to a private school most likely taught by Catholic nuns. Being the fourth in a family of nine children, Anna had never known such attention before. She was practically a princess.

Aunt Rose taught her to use a sewing machine and would often give her life advice about avoiding men— "When you see a pair of pants, look at the floor." Aunt Rose had one child, a daughter named Giovanna who was already grown up and living with her husband.

Anna knew of Antonio during her childhood in Tunis, but they rarely crossed paths and did not speak to each other very much, a big difference from the novel.

Antonio in World War I

Antonio tried emigrating to the United States in 1917 when he was seventeen, but he ran into a complication. After registering for a passport, he was drafted into the Italian army for World War I. His cousin Vittorio was elected Prime Minister of Italy that year, a source of great pride to him. Vittorio wrote a letter recommending him to be a barber to the military officers from 1917-1919. The officers would give him tip money because he sang Italian opera while cutting hair, entertaining them.

In 1919, Antonio felt assured that his cousin Prime Minister Vittorio Orlando was negotiating the terms of victory in the peace conference at Versailles. This was the same year that Benito Mussolini created the Fascist Party on mainland Italy.

After the war, Antonio returned to Tunis and probably moved into an apartment at 68 Rue de Mars. This was in the Bab el Khadra neighborhood, also referred to as Halfouine or the Medina of Tunis. He continued to work as a barber in Tunis for another three years.

Anna's Marriage Proposal

In 1920, an older man proposed to Anna, who was only seventeen at the time. We have no idea who the man was, a major difference from the novel. When Anna's mother back in Brooklyn heard about it, she was furious. Fearing that her daughter would settle down in Tunis and never see her family again, her mother crossed the Atlantic to talk sense into her. Upon arriving in Tunis, her mother was accused of being an Italian spy by the local authorities and arrested until Anna came to vouch for her. Her mother clashed with Aunt Rose, insisting that Anna break up the engagement and return to Brooklyn with her family.

"You have eight other kids in Brooklyn, let me keep this one!" Aunt Rose shouted back.

Ultimately, Anna followed her mother's wishes and broke off the engagement. Supposedly, her fiancé was so distraught that he ended up in the hospital. After spending eight years in Tunis, Anna finally returned to Brooklyn and reunited with her siblings. She would often make her own couscous to remember her time in Tunis. Anna got a job in a Manhattan clothing factory using the sewing machine skills she learned from Aunt Rose.

Antonio Moves to the United States

In 1922, Antonio's cousin Vittorio Orlando completed his term as Prime Minister of Italy. Everyone was very disappointed when they found out who the next Prime Minister was, a fascist Benito Mussolini. Antonio's family advised him to join them in the United States and live with his father and uncles in St. Louis.

When Antonio was trying to enter the United States in 1922, the quota for Italian immigrants was already full. According to family stories, he wrote his cousin the ex-prime minister Vittorio Orlando for help, and Vittorio recommended he go to France to circumvent the quota. So Antonio sailed from Tunis to Marseille, then took a train to Le Havre. He sailed out from Le Havre on a ship called the *Paris*, arriving at Ellis Island in New York Harbor on the evening of Saturday, September 30th, during which time Ellis Island "was closed," based on stories from the family. He waited until the morning of Sunday, October 1st, 1922 to enter Ellis Island to have his immigration papers filed. After that, he took a train to St. Louis to finally reunite with his father and brothers. He worked as a barber in St. Louis from 1922 to 1927, and during this time he frequently traveled between Tunis and the United States to visit Giuseppina, perhaps every six months.

Antonio Marries Giuseppina

In 1926, Uncle Pietro remarried after eighteen years of being a widower. He married Giovanna Messina in Tunis. In the year following his uncle's wedding, Antonio returned to Tunis to finally marry Giuseppina. He was twenty-seven and she was twenty-four. The priest who married them was possibly Father Francois Miquet at Sacred Heart Parish.

Shortly after, the newly married couple moved to the United States. They arrived at New York, then took a train to St. Louis to live with his brother Sam, a shoemaker, his brother Pete, a barber, and his father Giuseppe, an accountant. St. Louis contained an Italian neighborhood called The Hill, but at the time only Northern Italians were permitted to live there, while the Southern Italians lived closer to the Mississippi River. St. Louis was not to their liking—the muggy weather was oppressive, and they felt separated from the rest of their family who settled in New York City.

On Tuesday, May 15th, 1928, Antonio and Giuseppina left St. Louis and moved closer to the bulk of their family in New York City, where Antonio started a barber shop near West 30th Street and 8th Avenue in Manhattan. There, Giuseppina reconnected with Anna, an old acquaintance from Tunis. At this time, Giuseppina gave Anna a three-diamond ring to remember her by. According to family stories, the ring had belonged to Giuseppina's mother Maria Minore who was the daughter of a duke and duchess.

In Brooklyn, Giuseppina's unknown respiratory illness worsened. She possibly had tuberculosis. The doctors gave her the same prescription they gave Anna seventeen years earlier—a mild climate and fresh air. A return to Tunis was in order. Throughout late 1929 and early 1930, Antonio cared for his wife in the place they grew up. In August, Antonio obtained his driver's license and took time to "perfect himself in his work as a barber," according to one family member.

To be clear, Antonio did not know that Giuseppina was dying. He expected that she would stay in Tunis a few months and recover. This is why Antonio returned to New York City to attend to his barber shop.

Giuseppina's condition worsened unexpectedly, and she died in Tunis Sunday June 1st, 1930, at 10AM. She was 26. The family immediately sent a telegraph to Antonio in New York City, but he did not receive it. Next, they sent him a letter notifying him his wife had passed. In the letter, Antonio is addressed as "Nino," which in Italian is a pet name for Antonio. According to the translated letter, *"She suffered, but I cannot tell you how much…she lost three quarts of blood in the last night…she always spoke of you… she received communion and last rites…she died happy…you always took great care of her."*

Antonio and Giuseppina's marriage spanned two years. For most of it Giuseppina was very sick, so they were unable to have children. Antonio supported her and took care of her diligently.

Giuseppina's funeral in Tunis proceeded as follows. Antonio left a large sum of money to pay for a walnut coffin, the most expensive kind. According to Giuseppina's wishes, they hired a first-class funeral carriage with horses and built a white mausoleum big enough for three people marked "Orlando." Her funeral procession took place around 4:00 p.m., starting at 7 Rue de Chateaubriand and proceeding to the cemetery. She may possibly be buried at Belvedere Christian Cemetery in Tunis because there is a high concentration of other Sicilians buried there from the same period, but this is not confirmed.

Anna and Antonio Reunited

In the months following Giuseppina's death, Antonio returned to his barber shop in New York City, where he reconnected with Anna, a close friend of his wife's and an old acquaintance from his childhood in Tunis. Anna and he both loved Giuseppina and mourned together.

On September 7, 1931, Anna and Antonio married. He was 31. She was 28.

Right after the wedding, Antonio purchased a house in Brooklyn for $6,000. He paid for it all up front. He had to borrow $1,000 from his father, but that was enough.

Together, Anna and Antonio enjoyed a long and happy life. They were married 62 years and had four children and fourteen grandchildren

ACKNOWLEDGEMENTS

My first knowledge of Anna and Antonio came from food. Every Easter, my mom would prepare a six-person platter of fluffy garlic couscous soaked in broth and heaping with steaming lamb, carrots, parsnips, potatoes, and zucchini. The herbal aroma of the steam filled the whole house. The dish was Tunisian, my mom would explain, and the recipe came to us from my great grandmother Anna. This always confused me. Anna was Italian, not Tunisian. Why not make spaghetti and meatballs? Why not lasagna, which we ate for every other holiday?

Easter is also the day my mom would tell me stories about Anna, or Nanny, who passed away peacefully in her sleep one Easter morning years ago. I knew Anna was from Sicily, and I vaguely remember stories about a barber shop, a prime minister, a shipyard, and a ring that belonged to a duke. Nevertheless, I had most of the details wrong.

In October 2020 I took a greater interest in my Italian heritage, so I researched the history of the Orlando family and wrote a report that I thought was good at the time.

My nana Anita Josephine Behan took one read and said, "That's a nice story but it's not true." This only made me more curious to discover what I was missing, so I enjoyed endless conversations asking Nana about her parents. I found Anna and Antonio's old possessions—letters, photographs, even a sewing machine. Most emotional of all was the letter written to Antonio in 1930 notifying him of Giuseppina's passing, which we translated from Italian.

In the early 2000s, my nana was lucky enough to visit Antonio's hometown of Partinico in Sicily. During this trip, she re-established contact with the Orlandos who remained in Sicily, particularly my distant relative Francesca Orlando. Without Nana, this book would not have been possible.

I am also grateful to the New York University Summer Publishing Institute, which I attended in 2023. During this time, I met dozens of professionals from major publishing companies, gaining their feedback and professional opinion on my book. While in New York City, I visited many of the places where Anna and Antonio lived, including Antonio's Manhattan barbershop once located on West 30th Street, and Anna's childhood apartment on the corner of Elizabeth Street and East Houston Street.

I also read several books—fiction and nonfiction—to learn more about the Italian American experience. I am grateful to authors like Spencer Di Scala who wrote *Vittorio Orlando: Italy*, Juliet Grames who wrote *The Seven or Eight Deaths of Stella Fortuna*, Rosanna Chiofalo who wrote *Bella Fortuna*, Viola Ardone who wrote *The Children's Train*, and Laurie Fabiano who wrote *Elizabeth Street*.

I am also thankful to the staff at *Italian America*, a magazine by the Order Sons and Daughters of Italy in America (OSDIA), and then-Editor-in-Chief Miles Fisher, who published a short work of fiction I wrote about Italian immigrants. Also, my thanks to *Sixfold*, a literary magazine that published one of my short stories about Italian immigrants. This was the signal of confidence that encouraged me to write a novel-length story about my ancestors.

Through these resources, I widened my understanding of my Italian roots. However, Tunisia was a different story. My family knew very little about Tunisia, save the recipes scrawled in Anna's cookbook. To learn more about life in Tunisia during the 1920s, I read *The Pillar of Salt* by Albert Memmi, an autobiographical novel about a Sephardic Jewish boy in the same period. I was also lucky to meet Sara Maamouri, a Tunisian American documentary filmmaker who I consulted with on the accuracy of the depiction of Tunisia in the novel. Sara also put me in touch with Esme Maamouri, a Tunisian poet with an encyclopedic knowledge of the country's history. Esme helped me to understand the political nuances of the many communities living in Tunisia at the time, and most importantly she helped me understand the hospitality of Tunisia's people. Their country is a jewel on the Mediterranean, and the iconic architecture of the white stucco houses with the turquoise balconies will forever capture my imagination.

I am also grateful to the community of friends who read early drafts of the book and provided their honest feedback—Allison Steinebrey, Angela Jones, Jathan and Heather, Melissa Swan. Thanks to Jordan Mulligan, an editor who provided freelance developmental editing. Thanks to Carolina VonKampen, who also provided developmental editing.

I am thankful for the dedicated professionals at Amphorae Publishing Group who played the most instrumental role in publishing this book: Lisa Miller, Kristy Makansi, and Laura Robinson.

I am also grateful to my family for reading early drafts of the book and providing their feedback—my Aunt Kitty, cousin Liz, godmother Robin, Uncle Rich, Grandparents, Nana and Poppy, Uncle Ronnie, Aunt Angela, Aunt Diane, and countless others.

Last, I am thankful to my siblings and parents who read early drafts and provided their constant encouragement, and to my fiancé Sophia who painstakingly read endless drafts and gave her thoughtful feedback. I love you all!

ABOUT THE AUTHOR

Ryan Byrnes was born in North Dakota on a nuclear missile base during a tornado. His previous historical fiction novel *Royal Beauty Bright* won a gold medal in the 2020 Independent Publisher Book Awards and was a finalist in the 2019 Foreword Reviews INDIE Awards. His short fiction has appeared in *December, Sixfold, Pembroke, Italian America*, and more. He lives in New York City where he attended the NYU Summer Publishing Institute and works as an editor for Apress at Springer Nature.